AT THE FAR WALL was a life-size statue of a man who most likely was Saint Bruce the Warrior Poet. What was kind of neat was that, even though his face was carved wood, his armor was real: a plate-metal helmet (the visor was up, which is how I saw his face), gauntlets, shin protectors, and a surcoat of mail—thousands and thousands of interlocking circles of metal.

"Wow," I said. "Impressive."

When Feordina didn't say anything, I asked, "Uhm, what does this have to do with me and the ring?"

She waggled her finger at the statue, and my heart sank. "I hid the ring in the coat of mail." She smiled apologetically, showing little brown teeth, and I winced, not for the teeth but because I saw what was coming. "I wish I could remember where. But the rightful owner can call it forth."

"How?"

"Why, by reciting poetry, of course."

Of course.

"But it has to be a poem of your own making."

"Oh," I said. How hard could that be?

"Of course," Feordina said, "if Saint Bruce doesn't like your poem, he chops your head off."

Other Books by Vivian Vande Velde

DEADLY PINK

REMEMBERING RAQUEL

ALL HALLOW'S EVE: 13 STORIES

THREE GOOD DEEDS

THE BOOK OF MORDRED

NOW YOU SEE IT . . .

WIZARD AT WORK

BEING DEAD

MAGIC CAN BE MURDER

THE RUMPELSTILTSKIN PROBLEM

THERE'S A DEAD PERSON FOLLOWING MY SISTER AROUND

NEVER TRUST A DEAD MAN

A COMING EVIL

SMART DOG

CURSES, INC., AND OTHER STORIES

TALES FROM THE BROTHERS GRIMM AND THE SISTERS WEIRD

COMPANIONS OF THE NIGHT

DRAGON'S BAIT

USER UNFRIENDLY

A WELL-TIMED ENCHANTMENT

A HIDDEN MAGIC

heir
apparent

heir
apparent

Vivian Vande Velde

sandpiper

Houghton Mifflin Harcourt
Boston   New York

All rights reserved. Published in the United States by Sandpiper, an imprint of
Houghton Mifflin Harcourt Publishing Company. Originally published in hardcover
in the United States by Harcourt Children's Books, an imprint of Houghton Mifflin
Harcourt Publishing Company, 2002.

For information about permission to reproduce selections from this book, write to
Permissions, Houghton Mifflin Harcourt Publishing Company, 215 Park Avenue
South, New York, New York 10003.

SANDPIPER and the SANDPIPER logo are trademarks of Houghton Mifflin
Harcourt Publishing Company.

www.hmhco.com

The text of this book is set in Berling LT Std.

The Library of Congress has cataloged the hardcover edition as follows:
Vande Velde, Vivian.
Heir apparent/by Vivian Vande Velde.
p. cm.
Summary: While playing a total immersion virtual reality game of kings and
intrigue, fourteen-year-old Giannine learns that demonstrators have damaged the
equipment to which she is connected, and she must win the game quickly or be
damaged herself.
[1. Virtual reality—Fiction. 2. Science fiction.] I. Title.
PZ7.V2773He 2002
[Fic]—dc21
2002002441

Manufactured in the United States of America
DOC 20 19 18

4500549659

This book is dedicated with affection for
but no patience with
those who would protect our children through
humorless moralizing and paranoia about fantasy

contents

heir
apparent

GIFT CERTIFICATE

RASMUSSEM
ENTERPRISES

$50.00
FIFTY DOLLARS AND 00 CENTS

A gift to _Giannine Bellisario_

NOT REDEEMABLE FOR CASH

Nigel Rasmussem

721068076

THIS CERTIFICATE MUST BE PRESENTED IN ORDER TO BE REDEEMED.

Valid at any Rasmussem Gaming Center™ Virtual Reality Arcade, Total Immersion Game Rooms, or concession counters. Some restrictions may apply. If total value of certificate is not used at any one time, another certificate or Rasmussem Gaming Center™ tokens may be substituted as reimbursement, at manager's discretion.

RASMUSSEM ENTERPRISES IS NOT RESPONSIBLE FOR REIMBURSEMENT IF THIS CERTIFICATE IS LOST OR STOLEN.

Acceptance of this certificate by Rasmussem Enterprises in no way constitutes nor implies liability for any loss of property that occurs on premises, nor for personal injury incurred. A small minority of those participating in Total Immersion situations may experience such usually short-term effects as but not necessarily limited to light-headedness, decreased appetite, increased heart rate, blurred vision, memory loss, inability to concentrate, and/or loss of motor control.

See disclaimer on back for further details.

CHAPTER ONE

Happy Birthday to Me

It was my fourteenth birthday, and I was arguing with a bus. How pathetic is that?

Even before the bus had started in on me, my mood wasn't exactly the best it's ever been. Birthdays do that to me. This year I didn't even have a good excuse: I had actually received my birthday gift from my father on time, which might have been a sign he was making an effort to be a more considerate and involved dad. Of course, if he was really considerate and involved, he wouldn't have had his secretary call to ask me what kind of gift certificate I wanted for my birthday.

Whatever. Birthday = don't-mess-with-me mood.

So there I was, on my way to cash in my gift certificate, riding on a bus powered by artificial intelligence— emphasis on the *artificial*.

I saw the picketers just as the bus paged me: "Passenger Giannine Bellisario, you asked to disembark at the

Rasmussem Gaming Center, but there is a civil disturbance at your stop. Do you wish to continue to another destination, or would you prefer to be returned to the location at which you boarded?" The voice was kind and polite and only slightly metallic.

I was not polite. I sighed. Loudly. "Are they on strike?" I asked into the speaker embedded in the armrest.

There was a brief pause while the bus's computer brain accessed Central Information. "Rasmussem employees are not on strike," the bus reassured me, at just about the same time that I could make out the picketers' signs. "The demonstration is by members of CPOC."

I sighed even louder. They pronounce it, *C pock*. It stands for Citizens to Protect Our Children. As a fourteen-year-old, I qualify—by society's definition—as a child. I am willing to accept protection from stray meteors, ecoterrorists, and my seven-year-old cousin, Todd. But I don't feel in need of protecting by CPOC, which strongly believes that only G-rated movies should be made and that libraries should stock only nice, uplifting books that promote solid family values—*nice* being defined as nothing supernatural, nothing violent, nothing scary. That about kills my entire reading list. I think there are a couple alphabet books they approve of. Still, as far as I knew, this was the first time they'd ever come after Rasmussem.

I have excellent timing like that.

As the bus passed by the patch of sidewalk the picketers had claimed, I could read their signs: MAGIC = SATANISM and VIOLENCE BEGETS VIOLENCE and INAPPROPRIATE FOR OUR CHILDREN.

4

"Why can't you drop me off?" I asked. "Legally, they aren't allowed to obstruct anyone from going in." I'd learned that in Participation in Government class.

"Rochester Transit Authority is prohibited from letting a minor disembark into a situation that might be hazardous," the bus told me.

A little bit of artificial intelligence can be an annoying thing. "What are they going to do: smack me on the head with a pamphlet?" I asked.

The bus didn't answer and kept on moving. I was not going to win an argument, I could tell.

"Well, then," I said, "let me off at the next stop."

"Not if you intend to return to the Rasmussem Gaming Center stop," the bus responded.

I checked our progress on the real-time electronic route map displayed on the back of the seat in front of me and told the bus, "Of course not. I want to be dropped off at the art museum."

"That is on this vehicle's route and is only one block away," the bus told me. "Estimated time of arrival, thirty seconds."

So much for artificial intelligence. A human bus driver could have guessed that I had not developed a sudden craving for culture. Then again, a human bus driver probably wouldn't have cared, any more than the other passengers did.

The bus stopped in front of the museum. "Have a nice day, Giannine Bellisario," the bus told me.

I smiled and gave a Queen Victoria wave, and muttered under my breath, "Your mother was a toaster oven."

———

AS I APPROACHED the gaming center, I could see the picketers were quiet and orderly; so using my *human* intelligence, I deduced they weren't dangerous. Once I got in front of the building, I sprinted for the doorway. It was beneath a large red-and-gold sign flanked by rearing dragons: RASMUSSEM GAMING CENTER.

At least one of the picketers realized my intent and started quoting some Bible verse at me, complete with *yea*s and *thou*s and *wicked one*s.

I started walking faster, and he started quoting faster, which would have been fine except he was also moving to cut me off. I reached the door and a Rasmussem employee opened it for me, which was better service than they'd ever provided before. He was probably set there to make sure the picketers didn't physically interfere with the customers. Once the door was shut behind me, that blocked out road noise and protester noise alike.

The lobby of a Rasmussem Gaming Center looks pretty much like the lobby of a movie theater. Lots of slick posters advertising the latest games, a concession stand, booths where you can feed in tokens and play some of the older virtual reality arcade-type games. For a Saturday on a nice May afternoon, the place looked dead, though the popcorn machine was going, wafting the enticing smell of fresh popcorn all the way down to the doors where I'd come in.

But I was self-disciplined and resisted. I went up to the reception desk in the waiting area. The total immersion gaming rooms were beyond, where they hook you up to the computer—as an individual or with a group— to experience a role-playing fantasy.

There were a pair of older boys, late high school or maybe even college age, sprawled in the comfy chairs in the waiting area, looking as though they'd been there awhile. They glanced up hopefully when they spotted me, then returned to leafing through their catalogs and poking at each other and trying to look cool for the receptionist, who was tapping her computer keys with the speed, concentration, and fervor of someone who had to be playing Tetris instead of working.

She must have made a game-ending mistake for she scowled and looked up. "Welcome to Rasmussem Gaming Center," she said. She wore a gown that was a medieval style but that shimmered and slowly shifted color, going from pink to lavender to deep purple to blue. I knew that if I watched long enough, it would cycle through the rainbow. There was one of those new genetically engineered dragons on her desk, hamster-sized and unpleasant: It had been trying to tip over the receptionist's nameplate, and when I placed my gift certificate on the desk, the little beast lunged at me. "He's just playing," the receptionist assured me as I snatched my hand back. "It's his way of greeting you."

Sure. I have an uncle who'll tell you the same thing about his rottweiler.

The receptionist looked at the gift certificate. "This will get you half an hour of total immersion game time or forty-five tokens for the arcade games up front. You can play your own module, or you can join other players." She pointed toward the older boys. Her desk dragon dove and nipped at the trailing edge of her sleeve. The tiny chain that tethered him to her pen holder yanked him up short, and he hovered, his leathery wings fluttering. The receptionist ignored him. "They're trying to form up a foursome to play Dragons Doom. Interested?"

I don't like to play role-playing games with people I don't know, and besides, I figured an eighth-grade girl with a seventh-grader's figure probably wasn't exactly what they'd been hoping for, either.

"No, I'll play with computer-generated characters," I said.

The receptionist nodded. I could see her set herself on automatic pilot. "Because the computer directly stimulates your brain, you will feel as though you're actually experiencing the adventure." She must have said this about a million times a day, because she spoke quickly and without inflection, so that if I hadn't known what she was talking about, I wouldn't have known what she was talking about. "Half an hour of game time will take you through the three days of your chosen computer adventure. You will smell the smells, taste the tastes, feel the texture of the clothes you're wearing and the things you touch. You will experience cold if your computer persona is in a situation where he or she would feel cold, just as you will feel hunger and you might feel pain. If your persona is killed off, you will not, of course, feel that pain. You are guaranteed at least thirty minutes of playtime. If you get killed before your thirty minutes have been used up, you will be given another life and the adventure will automatically restart. Once you have started a life, you will be able to continue until you successfully finish or until you are killed, even if your thirty minutes runs out partway through. Any questions?"

I shook my head.

"Want to check out the promos?" She pointed to the alcoves, and her dragon once again lunged and missed.

At the promo station, the computer recognized my handprint and showed the names of the games I'd played the other times I'd been here, as well as the game I'd played when I'd visited my cousins in Baltimore and we'd gone to the Rasmussem Center there. The screen showed the dates I'd played and the scores I'd received. I pressed the button indicating I wanted to view the trailers for games that could be played in half an hour or under.

Alien Conflict I didn't even bother with, nor Dinosaur Safari. I watched the promo for Lost in Time and decided it looked too complicated. It was probably the kind of game where you had to come back four or five times before you got anywhere. Weatherly Manor was a haunted-house game that looked like a possibility, though the computer knew my birth date, which meant I would get the toned-down version for those under sixteen. A Witch's Stew sounded too young even though this list was supposed to be age specific. Sword of Talla looked interesting, and I was thinking I'd probably go with that, when I pressed the button for Heir Apparent.

The voice-over described Heir Apparent as a game of strategy and shifting alliances. "The king has died," the voice said. "Are you next in line for the throne, or next in line to die?" There was a flurry of quick scenes: a castle on a hill, an army assembling, a dragon, someone being pursued through the woods, a wizard tossing powder into the air, and an eagle forming from the powder and lunging—talons outstretched—so that he looked about to come straight out of the screen, and I instinctively jerked back. "Who can you trust?" the voice asked. The screen went dark with an ominous thud like a dungeon door slamming. A child's voice whispered, "Bad choice," and cackling laughter echoed while the name Heir Apparent flashed on the screen, then slowly faded.

I found myself more inclined toward Heir Apparent than Sword of Talla, and knew myself well enough to know why. In the montage of scenes, there had been some really good-looking guys. Probably *not* the smartest way to choose a game. On the other hand, it made no sense to pick a game specifically because it had nobody interesting-looking.

I went back to the receptionist. "Heir Apparent for girls as well as boys?"

The receptionist had been filing her nails while waiting, and now that she paused, the desk dragon leaped and clung on to the emery board, gnawing at the edge. She shook him off. "Yes," she told me, "a female character can inherit the throne and become king if she makes the right decisions."

"Is there only one set of right decisions?" I asked. That could make for a frustrating game, the kind you have to play over and over.

"Heir Apparent," she said, "is like bean soup."

"Excuse me?" I said.

"Playing Heir Apparent," she explained, "is like making bean soup, whereas Dragons Doom is more like making a peanut butter and jelly sandwich."

I had *no* idea what she was talking about.

"With Dragons Doom, all you've got to do is remember you're making a peanut butter and jelly sandwich, and you'll end up with a peanut butter and jelly sandwich. Barring, of course, dropping the bread, peanut-butter-side down, onto the floor."

"Of course," I agreed, just to humor her.

She continued, "But with Heir Apparent, you can approach in any one of several ways, and still end up with bean soup. You can use pinto beans or black beans or navy beans. You could maybe add macaroni, or not, and you'd still end up with bean soup. But there're all sorts of dangers—if you *do* decide to use macaroni but you add it too late, it's undercooked, maybe even crunchy. Add it too early, and it becomes mushy. You can have too much salt, not enough pepper. Tarragon might help, or it might make the whole thing bitter." She leaned forward confidentially. "And that's not even getting into the question of boil or simmer."

Just my luck to get an explanation from someone who didn't know when to give up a bad metaphor. "Not just one set of right decisions?" I interpreted. "Okay, I'll go for it."

Just then her desk dragon pooped on the desk.

I should have taken it as an omen.

CHAPTER TWO

Off to a Fantastic Start (Not!)

Rasmussem Enterprises must have a vice president in charge of bad smells.

It makes you wonder—or at least it makes *me* wonder: What kind of person takes a job where, when you go home every night and your family asks, "How did the day go, dear?" you answer, "Oh, very nice, thank you. Some kid I don't know paid a couple weeks' allowance money to get hooked up to the computer to enjoy a nice fantasy game, and I got to plunk her into a pile of sheep dung"?

I woke up thinking I'd been set down in a barn, which is sort of a Rasmussem specialty, I guess. But I could hear birds chirping, and I could feel grass prickling me through my clothes, and when I opened my eyes, there was blue sky and a warm sun above me. I could hear sheep bleating not too far off.

I sat up and was amazed to find nothing under me except the grass.

Which was when I realized that the stink was coming from me.

My shapeless, scratchy, rough-spun, and many-patched dress of unbleached wool was a far cry from the rainbow-hued gown of the Rasmussem receptionist. The people who work for Rasmussem have a pretty weird sense of humor.

Why do I put myself through this? I wondered. When my dad, who rarely calls except for the week before my birthday and the week before Christmas, had asked—through his secretary—what kind of gift certificate he should send for my birthday present, I could have named a clothes store or an electronics store or a bookstore. But no, I asked for Rasmussem, and I'd crossed a CPOC picket line to get here.

On the other hand, as soon as I stopped sending mental hate messages to Rasmussem, the computer conditioning kicked in. My mind filled with details of memories I'd never had. The effect is like holding two pieces of tracing paper up to the light, one on top of the other: At first all you can see is a jumble, but as you concentrate on one drawing—or on one life, as the case may be—then suddenly you can make it out by ignoring the pieces that don't fit.

So I ignored those parts that were Giannine Bellisario, eighth grader at St. John the Evangelist School. I ignored Rasmussem Enterprises and its overpriced computer that lets you see, hear, feel, taste, and—yes, thank you very much—*smell* a fantasy adventure in quarter-hour segments that seem to last for days.

I let myself become Janine de St. Jehan, sheepherder. Along with the identity came all sorts of snippets of information that I'd have known if I'd been born and raised in the village of St. Jehan.

Most of that information had to do with sheep.

If one of those woolly critters came over here, I could milk it, shear it, cure it of ringworm by an infusion of ringwort, castrate it, or help it in case of a breech birth. Not all at once to the same animal, of course.

"Janine!" a voice called. "Janine, come back to the house."

A dog came bounding up to me, black and white, with floppy ears. Did animals in this world talk? No, my implanted memory told me—well, mostly not. And definitely not in this case. This was merely Dusty, who helped me with the sheepherding. Dusty was old and her energy came in bursts, but you wouldn't guess that from the way she put her front paws on my shoulders and licked my face to greet me after my midmorning nap.

"Hiya, Dusty," I said at the same time I tried to fend her off.

The voice called again: "Janine!" And this time I recognized it as my mother's voice.

That distant, half-buried part of me that was my true self surfaced long enough to bark, *Ha! Fat chance.*

I tried to bury me even deeper. *Play the game,* I told myself. *Did you pay big bucks just to find fault with everything?* My real mother lives in New York because that's where her employer wants her to be, so I only see her one weekend a month during the school year, when she comes and stays with my grandmother and me. That, and for two weeks during the summer, which—apparently—is all she can take of me in her New York apartment, which is, as she says, "cozy for one." I told myself not to be bitter about my mother's attitude toward me. It is, after all, better than my father's: My father demanded a paternity test before the divorce settlement, when I was five. And—excuse me very much—but while five might be too young to catch all the nuances, I didn't need nuances to understand that my father wasn't willing to love me, much less pay child support, unless my mother could prove I was his.

But none of this, I told myself, was true in *this* lifetime, so none of it was important. In *this* lifetime I lived with my mother, named Solita, and my father, Dexter, who was a peat cutter, and my three younger sisters and two younger brothers. And we all loved each other unconditionally.

I stood, despite Dusty's attempts to knock me over. Instinctively my eyes found the right hut out of a cluster of eight—the entirety of the village of St. Jehan in all its glory. All the huts were made of straw and held together with sheep you-can-probably-guess-what. There was my mother, nearly as broad as she was tall, waving to me from the front yard, a swirl of chickens and small children stirring up the dirt around her skirts. "Stay, Dusty," I ordered the dog. "Guard the sheep."

Dusty lay down on the spot I'd vacated, resting her head on her paws. I assumed that if a wolf or thieves came, she would know what to do.

I waved my woolen cap at my mother and started down the hill.

The part of the scene below that didn't fit was the man standing beside my mother. He had an ostrich-feather-plumed hat and was holding the reins of a fine horse that had obviously never pulled a plow. Between the two of them, man and horse, there was enough gold trim to keep the village of St. Jehan fed for a year. I could see he'd been talking with my mother, though he took great care to keep out of the way of chickens and children alike.

"Hello, Mother," I said when I finally reached them. "Hello, sir." It couldn't hurt to be polite, whoever he was.

The man wrinkled his nose. "Is this the lass?" He pulled out a lacy handkerchief and breathed through that. Did I smell *that* bad?

"Yes, sir," my mother said. "Stand straight, Janine, and don't fidget." When my mother in the real world deigns to visit, she has the same sort of advice for me, as does my grandmother. It must be a mother thing.

I stood straight and didn't fidget.

My mother shooed off the children and as many of the chickens as she could. "Janine," she said, "I have something to say to you, which I probably should have told you before. I wish I could delay it until your father gets home from the bog."

The well-dressed man waved his handkerchief at her. "Get on with it, woman."

Just because she was a computer-generated figment of my imagination was no reason for him to be rude.

"Hey," I told him. "That's my mother you're talking to."
If my real mother hung around more, I'd defend her, too.

But, "Wrong," the man said. "That's the whole point."

Quick on my feet as always, I said, "Huh?"

"This woman is not your mother. And the man you
take to be your father is also no relation to you."

It made sense, considering the Heir Apparent scenario
had indicated I was one of several in line for the throne.
But if ever there was someone who obviously delighted
in delivering bad news, this was the man. And meanwhile, "this woman," as he'd called her, looked ready to
cry. She told him, "Sir Deming, you said *I* could break it
to her."

"You took too long."

I shoved him away from her, even though I was a full
head shorter. I was mad enough to tell him, "Look, as far
as I can tell, you're just some well-dressed messenger boy.
You say one more word to my mother, and I'll set the
dogs on you."

Actually, we only had Dusty, and the chances were
she was asleep by now. But "I'll set the dogs on you"
sounds more impressive than "I'll call my dog, and if she
hears me, and if she obeys, she'll make her way down
here and maybe even bite you with whatever teeth she
has left." And it certainly sounds more impressive than
"I'll set the chickens on you."

Deming looked down his nose at me and sneered.

I told him, "I'm assuming you were paid to deliver a
message?"

With his lip still curled, Deming said, "These people
who have raised you are in truth your foster parents. You

17

were delivered to them for your own safekeeping. Your true parents..." He rolled his eyes. "Well, your mother was a servant woman."

I could tell he enjoyed telling me that. "And my father?" I asked, suspecting, because of the nature of the game.

With a sigh, Deming admitted, "King Cynric, God rest his soul."

"'God rest his soul'?" my mother repeated. "The king has died?"

Deming removed his ostrich-feather-plumed hat and bowed his head for a moment of silence. I suspected his sincerity when the first thing he said after that was, "And he chose a very inconvenient time to do it."

My mother fanned herself with her hand.

"I have brothers?" I asked. As an inhabitant of this land, I had heard talk of princes; but as a lowly inhabitant, I wasn't familiar with their names.

"Yes," Deming said.

"For someone who was so eager to talk before," I told him, "you certainly seem tongue-tied now. What are their names, and what are they like?"

"There are three princes," Deming said. "All older than you. Which gives them priority over you for the crown. As does your..."—he gave a patronizing smile—"irregular birth."

He let the smile drop. "Wulfgar is the firstborn," Deming told me. "He was educated away from home and has...certain..." He paused to consider. "Perhaps the word I'm thinking of is *exotic*. He has certain *exotic* ideas."

Something about the way he said it made me suspect that *exotic* wasn't the word he was thinking of at all. "Ideas about what?" I asked.

"Everything," Deming said. Which was no help at all. "The second son is Abas, a young man of incredible physical prowess in the classical sense."

"'Classical sense'? What does *classical sense* mean?"

Deming ignored me. "And lastly Kenric, who displays—as far as *I'm* concerned—altogether too much interest in the magical arts."

I fought off a mental image of someone in a black cape and top hat, pulling coins out of people's ears and sawing lovely assistants in half, for I seriously doubted that was what Deming meant. "What—" I started.

"Perhaps it would be best if you waited to form your own impressions." Deming gave a toothy smile.

My mother asked, "You're bringing her back to court?"

Deming nodded.

"But I thought she was in danger there?"

Deming pursed his lips to indicate it wasn't his idea. "The king commanded it."

I said, "I thought the king was dead."

Deming sighed to let me know what an idiot he found me. "*Before* he died. It was his deathbed wish. Of course, he was quite feverish by then." Deming clearly thought the king hadn't been in his right mind. "When you were born, you were a royal embarrassment. Your servant mother had died during the long and difficult labor, and there were those among King Cynric's advisers

19

who pointed out that there was nothing unusual about a young mother and her firstborn *both* dying under such a circumstance. But the king was a kindhearted man." Deming sniffed—or snorted—into his handkerchief.

I'll bet. It was hard not to picture my *real* father as the king. "So, when he knew he was dying, he had a twinge of conscience?" I finished for Deming. "He decided to see if I was alive after all?"

"Oh, he knew you were alive," Deming assured me. "He sent for you to have you named his heir."

"Oh my!" my mother gasped.

I had assumed that the succession had been left unclear—that I'd have to fight it out with the other three. The other three, who were all older than me and who, presumably, had *two* royal parents. "Why me?" I asked.

Deming stuffed the handkerchief back into his sleeve. "Heaven knows," he said. He wiggled his fingers at me. "Go on," he said, "get on the horse. Time to pull yourself away from the sheep."

I didn't tell him that so far I liked the sheep more than I liked him. I kissed my mother and my brothers and my sisters good-bye.

"You're leaving now?" my mother cried in dismay. "Without saying good-bye to your father? I sent word to him that Sir Deming was here, and he should be coming home from the bog soon."

I was eager to get the game moving. Rasmussem builds in a little extra time, for soaking up the local atmosphere and because they assume people playing a game for the first time will make a fatal mistake or two and have to rely on additional lives—how many depends on how soon they mess up badly enough to get killed. I don't know how many players actually make it through a game in the first sitting, but my grandmother couldn't afford to send me here on a regular basis. That—and remembering the last time I'd said good-bye to a father—had me frantic not to wait around.

"I'll send for you when things get settled," I promised. Even if the game ended before I could, saying it was worth the look on Deming's face.

CHAPTER THREE

Fun and Games with the Family

When Deming and I arrived at the castle, there were pages to blow a trumpet fanfare, and guards who saluted and called me "Highness" without the superior mockery of Deming's tone. In the courtyard, two squires rushed forward to help me dismount. Having never, in the real world, ridden anything livelier than a carousel horse, I'd been pleasantly surprised that my character had memories of riding a horse. Of course, that had been bareback on the plow horse the community of St. Jehan shared, but if I didn't try to analyze and I just let my character's instincts take over, it wasn't too hard to stay on.

A good thing, because I suspected that if I'd fallen, Deming would just have left me, king's wishes or not.

But now servants lifted me off his horse as though I were a delicate lady, and both I and my character enjoyed that.

Deming disappeared into the crowd—probably to

take a bath, if I was to take all his sniffing and whining seriously.

A gray-haired man in a crushed-velvet suit was waiting by the entrance to the castle proper. "Welcome, Princess Janine," he said, bowing. "I am Counselor Rawdon, one of King Cynric's advisers. Allow me to escort you to the Great Hall, where the royal family awaits."

Though his smile looked sincere, I kept in mind what Deming had said about the king's advisers' suggestions at my birth.

I was half expecting that the people at Rasmussem would give me a castle that was a wreck—run-down and rat infested—but it was the one I had seen in the promo. It was like a magnificent old cathedral, except without the incense: polished stone walls and floors, high vaulted ceilings, stained-glass windows.

Rawdon led me down a wide gallery; one wall was made of mirrors, the other was a series of marble arches opening onto a formal garden with fountains and crushed-stone walks. I tried not to gawk like a tourist.

Finally we came to a massive set of carved doors. Two guards in ceremonial dress saluted, then opened the doors, while a third man blew yet another fanfare.

"Her Royal Highness," Rawdon proclaimed, "Princess Janine."

My first impression was that I had just been announced to an empty room, but then I saw that everybody—and everybody was only four people—was clustered around two thrones way down at the other end.

Rawdon whispered, "Good luck," my first hint that he was about to abandon me.

I whipped around to see him bowing his way backward out between the doors. Once he cleared the opening, those two guards swung the doors shut with a massive *thud*.

Leaving me with my back exposed to . . . ? My three half brothers would have been the obvious guess. And the woman I'd glimpsed? One of their wives, perhaps. Or she could be the queen, my dead father's wife, and mother to his sons. I hadn't thought to ask Deming if she was still alive or what her name was, putting me at a definite social disadvantage.

Obviously, I wasn't going to find out anything by standing with my back to them, the closed doors five inches from my nose. Someone tittered, and I had the impression it wasn't the woman.

"Hello," I said, turning to face them. There was a huge leaded-glass window behind them, so that they were little more than dark silhouettes. My footsteps echoed hollowly as I crossed that vast distance all alone, aware of the four sets of eyes watching me, evaluating. Should I have waited to be invited to approach? *No,* I thought. *I'm a princess.*

Or at least half princess.

Princesses do not wait to be summoned.

Do they?

Close up I determined the woman was definitely the queen. For one thing, she was sitting on one of the thrones, and she had a crown. She was also forty or fifty years old, a bit old for any of these guys—even for an arranged marriage. The princes ranged from one who was only a couple years older than me to the other two, who were probably in their early to mid twenties. They were the good-looking guys I'd noticed in the coming attractions.

"Hello," I said again, remembering to stand straight, and trying not to fidget, which was tough, considering I didn't know if I was supposed to bow, seeing as how we were all royalty. "It's a great honor to—"

The queen turned to the prince who stood at her right. That one was Abas, I thought. I suddenly understood what Deming had meant when he'd said Abas was strong in the classical sense. He looked like he'd stepped out of one of those old Hercules movies: huge muscles bulging out of an outfit consisting mostly of leather straps with metal studs. His skin was tan and slick—I wouldn't have looked that healthy with a whole tube of skin bronzer.

"This *girl*," the queen said to Abas, "smells like a goat."

The prince wrinkled his nose. "Yes," he said in a strained voice that sounded as though he was trying not to inhale.

"Ahm," I said, "a sheep, actually."

The queen gave me a look like oh-I-didn't-know-turds-could-talk.

"I've been working tending sheep." *Don't get started,* I warned myself. She didn't want explanations or clarifications—she just wanted to put me in my place. But the

25

silence sat there and sat there, so I babbled on, "I probably smell more like sheep than goats."

One of the other princes snickered. *Wulfgar?* I speculated, *the foreign-educated one?* since he wore a goatee—not
a wispy end-of-the-chin–Colonel Sanders look, but a
sexy one—while all the other men I'd seen so far were
clean shaven. He was looking at me with undisguised
contempt.

The third prince—the youngest, who would be Kenric—fidgeted, using his hand to cover a smile. He was
sitting sideways on the arm of the empty throne, which
might indicate he was trying to insinuate himself into the
kingship. When he saw me looking at him, he flashed his
smile openly, which could have meant that he was
friendly or that he was amused or that he realized I was
too dumb to be serious trouble.

"I think," the queen said, "we should kill her now
and be done with her."

"All right," Abas said agreeably. One of those straps
crisscrossing his chest must have been a harness to hold
his sword on his back, for he reached over his shoulder
and whipped out a blade almost as long as I was tall.

"Wait a minute." I scrambled backward. Lucky for
me, I had outgrown my stinky and patched gown, so that
the edge of the dress came only halfway down past my
knees. Although this clearly showed my bare and dirty
feet, at least I didn't trip as I took a couple hasty steps
backward. "Wait a minute," I repeated, as a grinning
Abas stepped toward me. I had a skinning knife on my
belt, all of about four inches long. Abas's sword was

26

broader than that. All things considered, it was probably best not even to go for it.

"Just don't move," Abas told me in his calm, slow voice. "It'll be faster, and you won't bleed as much."

Was he concerned about hurting me, or about messing the inlaid marble floor?

"But," I said, dodging him, "but..."

"You can't kill her," his brother Kenric pointed out. "She's already been seen by too many people. If you wanted to kill her, you should have done so before."

Well, gee, thanks. I think.

Abas glanced at his mother for confirmation.

"I suppose," she conceded, clearly disappointed.

And only then did he lower his sword.

Wulfgar spoke for the first time. "How about if we start all over again?" He smiled at me in a way that was definitely not friendly nor amused nor even, I suspected, you're-too-dumb-to-count. "You come in, you're introduced, we ascertain exactly what it is that you smell of. Let's start there."

"No," I said, beginning to be ticked off at all this, "how about if we go back to the introduction phase, and *you* introduce yourselves to *me*? Sort of an as-subjects-to-your-new-king kind of thing."

The prince's smile momentarily froze, but then he said, "Certainly. I am Prince Wulfgar, the firstborn. By common tradition, the heir apparent. This bulwark of humanity"—he indicated Mr. Olympia—"is Abas, the second born. And this is Kenric, the youngest." Abas let that sit for a couple seconds. "Excluding yourself, of course." His hand swept in the direction of the queen, who looked miffed to be introduced *after* the others. "Our mother—that is, the mother of the king's *legitimate* children—Queen Andreanna."

The queen sat forward in her throne. "Now," she said, "Janine." Her tone indicated what she thought of that name.

Before I could learn what she was about to say, the room went black, as though someone had turned the lights off.

Except, of course, that medieval castles don't have light switches.

And except that we were in a room with about twenty floor-to-ceiling windows—not even counting the big leaded-glass one behind the thrones, through which, a moment ago, the midmorning sun had been streaming.

"What—" I started, but was drowned out by a crash of thunder that seemed to go off about half an inch from my ear. Simultaneously, jagged lightning streaked past the window behind the royal group.

Usually, Rasmussem is more subtle with its special effects. I could feel my scalp get all tingly from the electricity, which I thought was a great detail, but the storm didn't *look* right. They should have darkened the sky more gradually, and as I glanced around the room, I saw that there were identical bolts of lightning in each of the windows, which was pretty shoddy, like cheaply made animé, where they use the same background in multiple scenes, hoping you won't notice what's going on behind the main characters. Still, I couldn't help but jump. The thunder continued to boom and crackle as though the lightning bolts were striking at the parapets of the castle itself.

"Princess Janine." The queen sounded impatient, and I realized she had repeated my name several times already.

"I'm sorry!" I raised my voice over the thunder. "I didn't hear." I tapped my ear just in case *she* couldn't hear *me*.

In the flickering light of the near-continuous lightning, I saw her look at her sons. They were all watching me warily. Maybe they were worried about how they'd been treating me. Maybe they'd realized they shouldn't have been so open in their hostility. The queen said something I couldn't hear.

"What?" I said. "I can't hear you over the thunder."

Again the royals exchanged a look among themselves. The queen raised her eyebrows; Kenric, sitting on the arm of the throne, stopped swinging his leg and leaned forward; Wulfgar took a step away from me as though nervous; and Abas, still holding his sword, raised it defensively.

And no—I decided as the queen said, *"What* are you talking about?"—no, that wasn't a this-is-someone-we-shouldn't-have-threatened look. That was a maybe-this-is-someone-who's-totally-out-of-her-mind look.

At which point the lightning moved inside the castle.

And not a one of them twitched.

I took a step backward as a jag of lightning lit up the area between the back wall and the royal family.

"Move!" I screamed at them. Obviously, the storm was not natural. But that didn't mean it couldn't fry us all. "It's getting closer! The next one will hit you!"

Weren't the little hairs on *their* arms all standing up and marching around from the charged air? Sure, they wouldn't know the word *ozone,* but couldn't they smell it?

Wulfgar tapped his head in a loose-screw gesture, and the queen rested her face in her hand as though I was a bigger burden than she'd ever anticipated. Abas was obviously waiting for his mother to tell him what to do. Kenric stood and took a hesitant step toward me, the only one to trust my warning even that far.

And then the light came back. No lightning, no vestigial rumbles of dying thunder. The sky was blue and bright outside the window.

"Oh," I said. "Never mind. It went away."

Magic, obviously. But whose, and why? Deming had said Kenric dabbled in magic, but why would he call up a storm only I could sense? If it was to make a fool of me, then why was he the one person to heed my warning and step away from the window?

And judging from his face, *he* was thinking that *I* was the one who had set out to make *him* look foolish in front of his family.

"There was a storm," I said. "In here, in this room. With thunder and lightning, and my skin all goose bumpy from the electricity."

"I never knew you were so gullible, Kenric," Wulfgar smirked. "I'll have to remember that."

That was sure to endear me to Kenric.

"Enough of this nonsense," the queen said. "Janine, I don't know what you think you're doing, but stop it or I may yet change my mind about having you killed. For the time being, my husband—in the derangement of his dying—named you his successor. Let's see how long you can keep the job. And your head. Come, Abas." She swept out of the hall with a rustle of stiff skirts, which nearly toppled me as she brushed past.

Hercules Jr. followed, putting his sword back into its harness with a glance at my neck as though evaluating for future reference how hard he'd have to swing for a decapitation. Kenric glowered as he passed, and Wulfgar grinned before he followed—which didn't look quite as friendly as his brother's glower.

Ouch. Not a very good first impression on my family.

And what was that awful smell?

Oh yeah. That was me.

CHAPTER FOUR

A Heavenly Visitor

The point of Heir Apparent is to make good decisions, choose capable and trustworthy friends and advisers, and survive long enough to be crowned as king two days from now, game time.

Judging from what I'd seen of my family, none of them would fit very snugly into the trustworthy-friends-and-advisers category.

Maybe my first decision should be to have the guards throw all four of them into the dungeon. But, seeing as the only other people I'd met here at the castle—not counting stable boys, doorkeepers, and trumpeters—were Deming and Rawdon, it didn't seem a good plan to throw four-sixths of the people I knew into prison.

I had to find an ally—and *fast*. As I ran after my family like a puppy that doesn't want to get left behind, I considered.

The queen had every reason to hate me, as her husband's illegitimate child. Also, she had the welfare of her three offspring to advance if she could not gain the throne for herself.

Abas seemed to be the queen's favorite—after herself, of course—but he obviously wasn't going to make any move that his mother hadn't previously approved.

That left Wulfgar and Kenric, both clearly trouble-makers.

I based my decision on something totally frivolous: Kenric was dressed all in black. That might have been a heavy-handed hint on Rasmussem's part that he was the villain, or it might have meant that—with his dark hair and light eyes—he knew he looked good in black. On the other hand, it might mean that he was in mourning. If so, he was the only one. I didn't know anything about King Cynric, whether he'd been a just king or a loving husband or a kind father. But so far nobody had said a word about the poor guy being dead except in how it re-lated to the succession to the throne.

"Kenric!" I called. I don't know what I'd have done if he'd ignored me, but he waited for me to catch up as the others moved on without us.

Still, he didn't look happy. He had no reason to trust me any more than I trusted him.

We were standing by one of the gates leading outside, with sunlight and the chirping of birds and a soft breeze that carried the scent of lavender, as though nature wanted to rub in the idea that I'd imagined or made up the storm.

"Are there wizards that live nearby?" I asked.

From his expression, it was a dumb question. From his expression, everybody knew. Kenric crossed his arms over his chest. "Xenos and Uldemar."

"Well," I said, "apparently one of them magically created a storm that I and only I could see."

"Uh-huh," he said. "Why?"

"I don't know," I admitted. "Maybe to make me look like a crazy person."

"Uh-huh," Kenric said again. "That you did." But he looked more amused than angry now, which I suppose was a step in the right direction.

Before I could ask if *he* could think of any reason one of the wizards might have called up the storm, there was a commotion in the courtyard. Two guards in chain mail were dragging along a boy who couldn't have been any older than nine or ten. The boy was crying and trying to squirm away, and the guards were not being gentle about holding firm. "Prince Kenric," one of the men called out, "and, uh, Princess Justine..."

"Janine," I corrected.

The man shrugged, like *What's the big deal? Didn't I get it mostly right?* He was looking at Kenric as the person in charge, not me, and no doubt considered himself extremely gracious for even acknowledging me. "We caught this boy poaching. He killed a deer. The usual punishment?"

Kenric opened his mouth to answer, then turned to me. "I don't know. Janine?" His voice and manner dripped with innocence. "What do you think, the usual?"

One thing I was certain of: He wasn't asking for advice; he was testing. "What's the usual?" I asked, ignoring the answer the Rasmussem program was prodding forward from my subconscious.

"First-time offense for poaching small game might be branding or to have his hand cut off," Kenric told me. "For deer, it's the death penalty."

"No," the boy whimpered. "I didn't do nothing. I found 'im dead already. I was dressing 'im down so's the meat wouldn't go to waste, but I didn't kill 'im."

Kenric was watching me appraisingly.

I said, "The boy says he didn't do it."

"Of course he does," Kenric said.

I looked at the boy, all ragged clothes and tear-streaked, with his bones showing under his dirty skin. "Did you see him kill the deer?" I asked the guards.

"No," said the one who was doing all the talking, "but look at his hands." They were bloody to the elbows.

"He already admitted to dressing down the carcass," I said. "Did you see him kill the deer?"

For an awful moment, I thought one of them was going to say yes. But then both guards shook their heads.

"Then let the boy go." My first command as the would-be king.

The guards looked to Kenric, unwilling to take my word for it. Kenric spread his hands out, indicating it was my decision. The guards let go of the boy and saluted smartly. Perhaps too smartly. Like when you jump out of your seat and shout, "Good morning, sir!" to the teacher you hate the most.

I didn't know what to do next, so for a moment I did

nothing. Kenric turned and walked away, back into the castle. I suspected I was probably supposed to say or do something to make him stay, but the game's time limit for my trying to figure what that should be must have run out. The guards, too, left to do whatever guards here did when they weren't terrorizing nine-year-old boys. Probably another missed opportunity.

"Are you all right?" I asked the kid.

He was watching me through the fringe of hair that hung down in his eyes, looking like a headlight-startled rabbit. He was so dirty, I couldn't tell if the guards had beaten him.

"Are you all right?" I repeated, tipping his face up by the chin.

He kicked me, hard, on the shin, and ran off.

"Ungrateful wretch," I muttered as he ran over the open drawbridge, vaulted over a short fence, and took off through the meadow beyond.

I turned to go back into the castle, when suddenly there was a brilliant shaft of light from the sky. Clouds billowed up out of nowhere, then rolled back; harp music sounded, an angelic choir sang a note of infinitely sad sweetness, and a white-robed figure descended on a golden beam.

"Giannine Bellisario," the white-robed figure said in a voice like the voice of God from the videos they show in religion class.

Outside of the fact that I was too stunned to speak, he was calling me by the wrong name. Here, I was Janine de St. Jehan.

And this sure didn't sound like any Rasmussem program I'd ever heard of.

"Giannine Bellisario," the white-robed figure repeated.

The closer he got, the more I could see he wasn't God after all, which was a relief no matter how you look at it. For one thing, his white robe turned out to be a lab coat, and for another, he was wearing glasses. I felt fairly certain God wouldn't go around wearing glasses.

The figure came to rest with his Reebok'd feet about six inches from the ground, so that—even though he couldn't be much taller than me—I had to tip my head back to look him in the face. "Giannine," he said, "this is Nigel Rasmussem. Don't panic."

I'd been surprised and confused but doing fine until he said that.

"There has been a slight emergency. Nothing to worry about."

I began to hyperventilate.

"People from the Society to Prevent Cruelty to Children...What?" Somebody I couldn't see or hear must have corrected Mr. Rasmussem. He waved the interruption away. Which was good. He was already speaking infuriatingly slowly, like someone who doesn't trust the mental capacity of his audience.

"What do you mean, 'emergency'—" I started, but he talked over my question.

"People from the Society to Protect Our Children," he said, still getting it wrong, "have broken into the building. They have damaged our equipment. Don't worry. There is no physical danger to your body. The intruders have been removed by the police."

"What do you mean, 'no *physical*'—"

But again he kept on talking.

He can't hear me, I realized. He probably couldn't see me. I shut up and listened, since I wouldn't be able to ask him to repeat.

"We are working to regain control," Mr. Rasmussem was saying, which wasn't comforting at all, especially from someone who had ink stains on his lab coat where he'd forgotten to use his pocket protector. "There are fail-safe measures to keep external stimuli, like power failures or surges, from affecting your mental state. But while these safeguards are in effect, you will find it difficult to exit the Heir Apparent program."

I was stuck here?

"The only route," Mr. Rasmussem said, "is to successfully complete the game. Unsuccessful solutions will loop you back to the start of the program."

I can do that, I thought. What he was telling me was that I was getting free extra tries. I began to breathe normally again.

"Unfortunately," Mr. Rasmussem said, and my breath caught again, "this is the last time we will be able to communicate with you. And, unfortunately, I cannot tell you the solution to the game since there is no one, single, right path. There are an infinite number of permutations, depending on which characters you take into your confidence, how you react to the problems with which you will be presented, and what policies you set for your government."

Mr. Rasmussem might have been counting on this going over my head, but I could figure it out: If there were an infinite number of possible right ways that could get me out of here, there had to be an infinite number of wrong ways that would set me back on that hill in St. Jehan.

"Don't panic," Mr. Rasmussem said again. Their readouts on my heart rate and blood pressure must have been going wild. "All you have to do is play the game as well as you can as quickly as you can."

And while that was still sinking in, while I was mentally repeating *quickly?* Mr. Rasmussem said, "Wait!"

Wait? That seemed all I could do. But he wasn't talking to me.

He was beginning to float upward again. The heavenly choir started humming. The clouds took on a pink hue. Mr. Rasmussem was again talking to someone else, arguing. "No, this is foolish. She needs to know the urgency." He turned back to me, speaking in a rush now, so that I suddenly suspected his earlier comments had been scripted. "What I said before isn't entirely accurate. I don't want to frighten you—you should be fine. But there is no time to waste. The prolonged direct stimulation to your brain is dangerous. The longest game we have is supposed to be over in an hour, and our equipment would normally be safe for up to five times that exposure. But with the damage these people have inflicted, your safety zone is much, much less. We don't know how long you have, but the longer you're in the game, the more you risk fatal overload."

Overload? What was he saying? And *fatal overload?*

Now it was my turn to cry, "Wait!" to him. But even if he could have heard me, it was obvious that there was nothing he could do about remaining.

"Advice," Mr. Rasmussem called down at me as the clouds foamed about him. "Kenric and Sister Mary Ursula don't work well together."

Who in the world was Sister Mary Ursula?

Mr. Rasmussem's voice was fading despite the fact that he was obviously shouting. "And next time, don't forget the ring."

"What ring?" I shouted back up to him. All I could see, far above, were the bottoms of his sneakers.

"And whatever you do, don't..."

But, naturally, I couldn't make that out.

BACKGROUND: The Rochester, New York,
facility has been compromised by
unauthorized persons who have forced
entry and damaged equipment *while it
was in use*.

See attached file for damage assessment
and equipment specifics.

The intruders have been removed and
arrested by local authorities. Security
believes them to be politically
motivated local individuals working
spontaneously in an isolated incident
rather than organized terrorists, BUT
TIGHTEN SECURITY IN ALL GAMING CENTERS
NONETHELESS.

See attached file for background on
CPOC political lobby group.

At the time of the raid on the
facility, 2 gamers were in the VR
arcade and were not harmed, one group
of 4 TI gamers had just gone under and
were successfully retrieved by the
premises technologist, but a lone player
was already fully in total immersion

41

and the technologist believes serious bodily harm would result from disconnecting this gamer before successful completion of the game.

Access code #703-592-B-3 to monitor subject's vital signs.

Note: Gamer is a 14-year-old minor believed to have limited gaming experience.

Using the residual power in the grids, contact was made with the gamer to apprise her of the situation, though on the advice of Lisa in psychology, the risk was downplayed so as not to cause nonfunctional anxiety. Once that power drained, contact was obstructed and cannot be reestablished.

CURRENT SITUATION: We do not know exactly how much time we have and we need all possible input from all available technologists with all possible speed. We require estimates, advice for repairing the equipment in minimal time, contingency plans to disconnect the gamer in case of systems failure before game completion.

Legal is working to make sure we are covered, but I DO NOT want R.E. to be the first VR company with a fatality.

CHAPTER FIVE

Simple Math

What kind of cheesy outfit was Rasmussem that crazies could walk in and endanger innocent kids? A picture flitted through my brain of the Rasmussem Gaming Center receptionist—the last defense between immobilized semiconscious kids and crazed CPOC members taking out their frustrations on Rasmussem's equipment. She'd probably been too wrapped up in her nails or in a game of Free Cell to notice the intruders. And what about those idiots at CPOC? Wasn't their whole purpose to protect kids? Did I not count because they considered me some sort of evil deviant for having come in here?

You're wasting time, I told myself.

I tried to work it out in my head: Rasmussem's engineers said I *should* have had five hours for the supposed safety zone. Since Heir Apparent took only half an hour to play, that should have given me ten tries. . . . Except those CPOC demonstrators had caused enough damage that however much time I had, it was less than that. And time before . . . what? What did "overload" mean?

Stop it, I told myself. *Panicking is not going to help. Think calmly; plan things out.*

Would my brain literally fry, getting so hot that I would feel fevered, or like I was stranded in a desert, or like I was being cooked alive?

Don't be melodramatic, I told myself.

It would probably be more like an electrical shock. Or an epileptic convulsion.

Would I—immersed in the game—feel it? Would I know it was happening?

I tried to drag myself away from that line of thinking. Lots of drastically wrong things could be happening inside a person's body without that person even knowing. It wouldn't necessarily hurt.

On the other hand, I knew that the Rasmussem technology sometimes made it so that a sick person who didn't even know she was sick would—while playing the game—feel sick. The gaming-as-diagnostic-tool scenario.

Not that I felt sick yet.

Did I?

I felt all clammy and my stomach was in a knot and my throat was tight and my chest hurt, but that was probably from the tension. Probably. I touched my forehead and didn't think I had a fever. Or at least not yet.

At the most, I would have had ten tries, feeling like thirty days, which would have been a long time to feel sick. But Mr. Rasmussem said I had less time than that— "much, much less," I remembered him stressing. What was much, much less time than thirty days—half of that? A quarter?

Did I, in fact, have only one try?

No. He'd said, "Next time..." So, at least one more try. I hoped.

There is a possibility, I told myself firmly, *that you will make it. You need to play smart and maximize your chances.*

Nigel Rasmussem had talked about infinite possibilities of ways to play Heir Apparent correctly.

I might stumble on one. In...whatever time I had left.

If I played carefully.

I was so preoccupied, I wasn't aware of anyone approaching until someone grabbed me from behind—which I guess was a pretty good indication I wasn't playing carefully enough. Someone spun me around, and I saw that I was facing a group of about twenty of the castle guards.

Something about them was spooky. I mean, in theory, weren't they there to guard me, the officially named heir apparent of this realm? Surely it wasn't proper guard etiquette to come up behind the person who's scheduled to be crowned as your king, to lay hands on her and spin her around. And several of them had swords or knives drawn.

I glanced around. Maybe something had happened, I thought. Maybe they were here to rescue me from some danger?

Right.

"She's too weak to be a proper king," said the guard who'd spun me around, the guard I'd ordered to release the boy accused of poaching. "She'll be the death of all of us."

And with that he stuck a knife into me.

It didn't hurt. I felt fizzy, like an ice cube in a glass of ginger ale, all covered with carbonated bubbles. My knees gave out from under me, and my eyes grew heavy. When I opened them again, I was on the hill above the cluster of huts that was the village of St. Jehan, and my mother was calling, "Janine! Janine, come back to the house."

So much for playing smart.

CHAPTER SIX

"Do Not Pass Go; Do Not Collect $200"

O*K*, I thought, *that brings me down to ... what?* Whatever I'd had before minus half a day.

Never mind, I told myself. *Just play smarter this time.* Nigel Rasmussem had given me two hints: *And next time,* he'd said, *don't forget the ring.* OK, I'd be on the lookout for a ring. And, *Kenric and Sister Mary Ursula don't work well together.* I'd be on the lookout for Sister Mary Ursula. I would concentrate on being a good heir apparent so that I would win the game, and I wouldn't distract myself by keeping a running calculation on how much time I might or might not have left.

Just as last time—until I did something different, *everything* would be just as last time—Dusty, my dog, leaped on me and began licking my face. "Down, Dusty!" I ordered. "Stay. Guard the sheep."

Dusty lay down and either guarded the sheep or went to sleep.

I ran down the hill. "Hello, Mother," I said. I glanced at her hands. No rings. Of course not, she was a simple peasant woman, and peasants don't wear jewelry.

I asked, "Who's this?" Even though I knew Sir Deming's name and business, my character wouldn't.

Sir Deming was just as rude as last time. Waving his handkerchief as though to dissipate the smell I brought with me, he asked, "Is this the lass?"

Who cared what he said? I saw he was wearing a ring. *Aha!*

"My, what a nice ring," I said, talking over my mother, who was telling me to stand straight and not fidget.

Deming looked as though he suspected I was a ring thief as well as a sheepherder, and he crossed his arms over his chest, tucking his fingers under his arms.

In games, certain events are keyed to certain actions. It was probably too early for me to actually get the ring.

I listened, antsy with impatience, while I was told, once again, that I had been living with foster parents; I learned, once again, about the death of King Cynric, my father.

When Deming said that the dying king had sent for me, I eyed his hand and asked, "Did he send some token?"

"He sent me," Deming said in his snooty, snotty manner.

OK, maybe it was still too early.

I didn't bother asking about my half brothers or the queen—we could discuss them on the ride to the castle, without taking any extra time.

Once again my foster mother wept when I left, saying

that my foster father would be heartbroken to miss saying good-bye to me. (*Yeah, yeah.* In my experience—in two worlds now—fathers were just big sentimental softies.) If I had felt rushed the first time, now I knew myself to be in a race. No time to waste on characters who were there just for the scene-setting.

This time as we rode away on Deming's horse, I asked Deming all sorts of questions about my new family, to show I was interested. Deming, of course, was *not* interested.

"Who's Sister Mary Ursula?" I asked.

Again Deming gave me a suspicious look. "Interfering old busybody," he said. "Has she been in clandestine contact with your family?"

Oops. I realized I shouldn't give away that I knew things I shouldn't know yet.

"No," I said.

"Then where have you heard her name?"

"I can't remember," I said.

Deming snorted.

I still didn't like him, and he still didn't like me.

As we approached the castle, I once again tried for the ring. "I can't help but notice the interesting design on your ring," I told him. "What do you call that?"

"I call it," he said, "the letter *D*."

D was his initial—not mine; not King Cynric's. Maybe this was the wrong ring after all.

When we got to the castle, I traded in Sir Deming for Counselor Rawdon, who was not wearing a ring. OK, so it had to be one of the royal family. That made more sense, anyway.

Queen Andreanna and her three sons, Wulfgar, Abas, and Kenric, were just as charming as last time, lounging about the thrones in the Great Hall, looking down their noses at me.

"Hello," I said. Last time I had approached timidly and hesitantly, wanting to make friends. I was determined not to make that mistake twice. Going for brisk, confident, and assertive this time, I said, "May I offer my condolences—"

"This *girl*," the queen said to Abas, "smells like a goat."

Back to that again. I wouldn't let myself get caught up in that argument.

"Excuse me," I said in a tone that would have gotten me a lecture from my grandmother, "I believe the king died and named me his heir. That makes you my subjects. Obviously, you're so overcome by grief at the death of your old king that you're forgetting yourself. I will forgive you this once, but from now on you are to show me proper respect."

"*'Proper respect'?*" the queen snapped. "Abas, show her the respect she's due."

Luckily for me, sarcasm was a bit beyond Abas's mental grasp. He began to bow. This gave me time to take a quick step back.

"Kill her," Queen Andreanna clarified for her son.

I remembered Kenric's reasoning from last time. "Too many people have seen me already," I said.

Abas had unsheathed his sword and wasn't even slowing down.

I ducked behind a pillar.

"Everyone would know who killed me," I called back to the queen. No use trying to reason with Abas. If the queen didn't call him off, my attempts at logic certainly wouldn't.

For such a big guy, Abas was incredibly quick and agile. He jabbed with the sword, left and right of the protective column, and sooner or later I was going to move too slowly, or he was going to correctly anticipate my next dodge.

I said, "You'll be in trouble for killing the appointed heir." That sounded feeble, even to me.

Abas's sword caught on the trailing edge of my dress that swirled a second slower than I did. With his free hand, he caught hold of my hair and dragged me from behind the column.

"She's probably right," Wulfgar drawled.

"Probably," the queen agreed equably.

Her voice was the last thing I heard.

CHAPTER SEVEN

Shuffle and Deal Again

Janine!" my foster mother's voice called. "Janine, come back to the house."

I couldn't believe it. I'd wasted another half day. What was the matter with me? Surely, the programmers at Rasmussem didn't intend for their game to be so complicated that a reasonably intelligent fourteen-year-old couldn't get beyond the first hours of a three-day game.

Was my brain overloading already? Was the damage the CPOC saboteurs had inflicted making me stupid?

All in all, I preferred to believe that I just wasn't playing this game as well as Rasmussem's average teenage gamer.

"OK, OK," I told Dusty as she once more licked my face. "Sit. Stay. Guard."

At the foot of the hill, I again rushed my mother and Sir Deming through the introductions. Did Rasmussem *have* to start me at the very beginning every single time?

Deming told me the king had named me his heir. I acted surprised. My foster mother wept that I had to leave. I told her to give my love to my foster father. I spared a thought for my real-life father, who'd given me the Rasmussem gift certificate. *Gee, Dad,* I thought, *you shouldn't have.*

When I was introduced to Counselor Rawdon, I interrupted him when he said he'd take me to meet my family.

"And what are they like?" I asked, though I knew well enough. "Are they to be trusted?"

"'Trusted,' Princess Janine?" Rawdon repeated.

"Do they present a danger to me?"

"Well..." Rawdon said, and I was sure he was going to give an evasive answer. But he said, "Probably."

OK, I liked that honesty. "Should I take steps?" I asked.

"Assuredly," he told me.

For a counselor, he wasn't very forthcoming with counsel.

"Would, for example—just in theory here—would it be a good idea to have my family confined?"

"It *might,*" Rawdon agreed. "On the other hand, you *are* new here. An unknown element. The soldiers who would have jumped to your late father's orders might not be so quick to respond to you." He smiled and added, "In theory."

"I understand," I said. No royal beheadings on the first morning.

I sighed, suspecting that I wasn't imaginative enough

to figure out half of what needed to be figured out. I was already in a rut: hill, Deming, Rawdon, family, death by various unpleasant means. I said, "Perhaps I should dress more suitably before I meet my royal kin. So I don't offend them."

"Certainly," Rawdon told me.

After I was scrubbed and coiffed—that was the word Lady Cynthia, my newly appointed lady-in-waiting used, *coiffed*—and perfumed, I was given a beautiful gown of burgundy-colored velvet.

I almost did feel like a princess as Lady Cynthia brought me to the Great Hall.

The guards blew their fanfare, opened the doors for me to walk in, closed the doors after me.

And nobody was there.

Oops.

Apparently my royal kin didn't like to be kept waiting—even more than they didn't like me smelling of sheep. Who could have guessed?

I went out the way I had gone that first time with Kenric. No sign of the royal family in the courtyard, although one of the guards was raking the dirt. I started to go over, then realized what he was doing: covering up blood. With a sinking feeling, I remembered the peasant boy accused of poaching. Apparently by taking the time to bathe, I'd missed the opportunity to keep the guards from chopping his head off.

It was just a game, but I didn't like the turn it had taken.

"Guard!" I called the man over to me so that I wouldn't have to go any nearer.

"Princess Justine," he said.

I didn't correct him. "Where's the queen?" I asked.

"I believe she and Prince Wulfgar are in the topiary maze."

Maze. I sighed. "I don't suppose you know the way through?"

He looked surprised that I would ask such a thing. "It would be more fun if you figured it out on your own."

"Show me," I ordered.

The hedges were boxwood, which is a smell that always makes me think of cat pee. The bushes were full, so that I couldn't see through them at all, and they were about seven feet high, which is about two feet taller than me. I was just thinking that I should have been paying closer attention to the turns, when we found ourselves in the center, an open area with a pair of stone benches, and sitting there—drinking tea—was Queen Andreanna. But the guard was mistaken: With her was her youngest son, Kenric, not Wulfgar.

"Ah," Andreanna said, "the sheep princess. I thought I smelled something bad."

"I *did* take a bath," I said.

"A bath," the queen said, "no matter how long, is not sufficient to wash off the stink of a bad birth." She waved her hand at the guard, so that her ring caught a glint of the sun. "You," she ordered him, "go."

"I'm sorry I kept you waiting," I said. "I tried to make myself presentable before appearing before you. I know this is a difficult time for you—"

"Oh, hush, you tiresome thing!" the queen commanded. "Kenric, can't you do something about her?"

"What exactly?" he asked.

"Well, I was thinking you could kill her."

Apparently there was no pleasing the woman.

"She *has* been seen here," Kenric pointed out.

"Maybe she'll have an accident," Andreanna said wistfully.

"Maybe," Kenric agreed.

"Listen," I said, "obviously you're upset by the king's decision to name me—"

"Go away," the queen ordered me. "You may speak to us at supper." She gave a dismissive wave, fluttering her fingers.

Maybe, I thought, *I was playing too cautiously.* This time I caught her hand. "My, what a lovely ring."

Kenric grabbed my wrist even as the queen demanded, "Unhand me immediately."

"Sorry," I said. I let go; Kenric did not, and his grip was beginning to hurt. "I was just wondering if that ring was meant for me."

"It's my wedding ring, you stupid twit of a sheep girl."

"Sorry," I repeated. How could it not be the right ring? Mr. Rasmussem needed a good shaking. "Sorry."

"Just leave."

Kenric finally let go of my wrist.

"Could one of you—" I started.

The queen gave a snort of impatience.

All right, all right. I'd make my own way out of the maze.

Except I *really* should have paid more attention to the turns when I'd been with the guard.

I was sure three right turns, then a left, would bring me to a Y-shaped intersection I remembered, but it didn't. Maybe three left turns, then a right? I tried backing up but realized I'd bypassed one turn, yet when I went back, I lost track of which way I'd been facing: I thought I should be at a T intersection, but found myself in the middle of an X—and by then I had no idea where I was.

OK, I thought. *There is a strategy to mazes.* In most mazes, if you consistently choose one direction, you eventually find your way—maybe not the quickest way, but *a* way. So, I told myself, I would choose left.

The sun was hot on my velvet gown, and the smell of boxwood was making me cranky and itchy.

Come on, I told myself. Surely I should be out of the maze by now, or back in the center.

And then I heard a sound behind me, a single footfall. Andreanna? Kenric?... Except I had the momentary impression of an animal. I'm not sure why. Maybe it was the growl.

I didn't have a chance to turn around. Something struck me hard on the back, knocking me face first to the ground. I cried out at the pain in my palms and knees—and at the back of my neck. I felt fizzy bubbles all over my skin. "No!" I screamed. Then I heard my foster mother call, "Janine! Janine, come back to the house."

I pounded my fists on the ground. "I hate this! Hate this! Hate this!" I screamed.

Dusty licked my face to show me that she loved me.

CHAPTER EIGHT

Hey, Loser, Start Over Again (Again)

I was going to die. I was *never* going to get past the first step of the game, and I was going to die. And this was going to be the rest of my life—this hill, and the trip with Sir Deming, and fatally ticking somebody off moments after arriving at the castle, and experiencing a death that, while not painful, was fizzy and disorienting—I would relive that whole boring, frustrating routine for whatever was left of my life.

I'll be READY to die by then, I told myself.

But I knew that wasn't true. I didn't want to die now, and I wouldn't want to die in the few hours I had left, either. Boring was one thing. Feeling like a dissolving Alka Seltzer was another thing. But the prospect of really dying was something else entirely.

Well, then, I told myself, *DO something.* I got out from under Dusty, who was still trying to lick my face to let me know how glad she was to see me. If I had any time to spare, I might have tried just staying here, refusing to go to the castle, where I would be surrounded by surly retainers, murderous family, and treacherous guards. *No, I could tell Deming, I'm not interested. Go away. Let somebody else be king. I'll just stay here with the dog and the sheep.*

But I doubted the Rasmussem program would allow this. It would probably have the sheep get rabies and attack me. Or have Dusty lick me to death.

I forgot to tell Dusty to tend the sheep, but apparently she didn't need me to tell her her job. She was obviously a smart dog. She could probably make better choices in this game than I had. I started down the hill, and she stayed behind.

All right, I thought, *I was supposed to already have gotten the ring by the time Mr. Rasmussem came to me, after the family conference.* It had to be the lack of the ring that was causing me to bomb out so quickly. When I thought about it, Rasmussem was doing me a favor: It would be worse to let me keep on playing for three days, get to the end of the game, then fail because of something I had overlooked in the first minutes of the first day. This was like—in the old games—not being able to make it to the next level.

OK, I thought. It probably wasn't a member of the royal family who had the ring, since my three half brothers didn't appear to have any rings and the queen had only a wedding band. I doubted I was supposed to bully a widow out of her wedding band. Besides, the person who had been the friendliest and most helpful—Rawdon—didn't know anything about a ring. Still, who else had I met before Mr. Rasmussem's appearance?

I mentally retraced my steps.

And could have smacked myself on the forehead when I got to the boy accused of poaching. Of course, a normal peasant boy wouldn't have a valuable ring. But a boy who was willing to break the law by poaching might also be a thief, and there was no telling what kind of goodies a thief may have accumulated.

Exasperated that it had taken me so long to reason this out, I ran the rest of the way down the hill. I sailed through the preliminaries with my mother and Sir Deming: The king is dead? Gee, that's too bad. I've been named his heir? Well, how nice. Hang around long enough to say good-bye to Dad? I don't think so.

Deming and I once again rode to the castle in sullen silence. When I spoke to my family, it was humbly and quietly, with no attempt to defend myself against their rudeness. The queen once again ordered Abas to kill me, and Kenric once again came to my defense, in his own sentimental way, by advising against killing me now that I had made a public appearance at the castle.

This was the exact point at which—during the first game—the strange storm only I could see had moved inside the Great Hall. I now knew that the storm was the physical manifestation of the CPOC demonstrators damaging the Rasmussem Gaming Center, setting the equipment to which my brain was linked to "deep fry."

I got to hear what the thunder had previously prevented my hearing.

"Now," Queen Andreanna said, wearing the same pained-and-disgusted-but-still-trying-to-carry-on expression that might flicker across your face if you realized you'd just publicly sat on a plate of Jell-O, "Princess Janine. Obviously, you are neither trained for nor suited to life in the political arena. Between the barbarian hordes waiting at our northern border for the first sign of weakness, and the peasant uprisings in the east, now is not the time for an inexperienced sheepherder to play at being king. For your own safety, as well as that of the country, it would be best if you left the rulership of this kingdom to those who understand its intricacies. My suggestion is that we send you to one of the manor houses in the country. You can bring your foster family with you, if you wish. There will be servants under your command, guards to protect you, luxury to surround you."

I said, "And I won't need to worry my pretty little head about all that nasty politics and complicated decision making and stuff."

The queen smiled tightly, as though looking at me gave her a headache.

"That's a very kind offer," I told her. "But King Cynric named me his heir apparent, and I don't intend to shirk my duty."

"There are those who would eat you up," the queen warned.

Pass the barbecue sauce—I knew that already. "Thank you for your concern," I said.

She swept to her feet. "It's your funeral."

Unfortunately, I knew she meant that literally.

Her three sons made to follow her out of the room. Since Nigel Rasmussem had seemed to warn me away from Kenric, I switched to a different prince. "Wulfgar, may I walk with you?"

Wulfgar bowed. Remembering that Deming had said

Wulfgar had been raised abroad, I tried to believe his courtesy was foreign manners, but I suspected he was just being ironic.

The queen didn't react well to my talking to her oldest son. "Wulfgar," she snapped, just as she might have to any lowly subject, "I need to speak with you in the topiary maze."

Wulfgar grinned, obviously relishing being the prize in a power play between the queen and the heir apparent. "In a few moments, Mother," he said.

Even I could see that was the wrong answer. She linked arms with Abas and Kenric, as though afraid I would try to steal them away, too, and walked out of the Great Hall in a huff.

"So, Wulfgar..." I said as we trailed them. Slowly. So they couldn't listen in. (Make alliances, the Heir Apparent directive said. I realized I had no idea how to go about doing that. Talk sweetly. Make nice. That was what my mother did, in her New York job.)

Wulfgar didn't help. He waited for me to say something.

"I think we need to call together the old king's advisers," I said, proud of myself for remembering to say "we," for including him, which his mother seemed not inclined to do. "We should have a counsel, decide what direction the kingdom needs to take."

"All right," Wulfgar said.

"I was thinking your advice might be helpful."

He seemed to like that thought. "All right," he said again. Just as I was fearing he was no help at all, he said,

"That would be Sir Deming, Counselor Rawdon, and Sister Mary Ursula."

Finally! "Oh," I said, "Sister Mary Ursula—what's she like?"

"She's a fusty old meddler," Wulfgar said, which surprised me—since Mr. Rasmussem had said *Kenric* didn't work well with her. "Why do you ask about her in particular?"

Was I ever going to learn not to give away too much? "No special reason," I assured him. "It's just, I've already met Deming and Rawdon."

That answer seemed to satisfy him. He said, "You should also meet with those in the kingdom who know magic."

"That sounds like a fine idea." In my eagerness to please him, to flatter him, to make sure he liked me, I suspected I was sounding like an overly enthusiastic kindergarten teacher. "Who would they be?"

"Orielle," Wulfgar said, which was a new name to me. "And Xenos and Uldemar," whose names Kenric had mentioned.

"Anything I should know about any of them?"

Wulfgar paused to consider. "Orielle is better-looking than Xenos and Uldemar."

"OK," I said. If I were a fifteen-year-old boy, that might impress me.

By then we had entered the courtyard. And we were once again just in time to see the armored guards dragging along the boy accused of poaching—the boy I was convinced had the ring I needed.

"Prince Wulfgar and Princess Justine," one of the guards called out to us.

"Princess *Janine*," Wulfgar corrected, and he rocketed up in my estimation.

"Sorry, sir," the guard said, apologizing to the person who was important rather than to the one he had actually slighted.

"What's all this?" I asked, though I already knew. I had been thinking I wasn't going to be too sympathetic to the boy—remembering how he had kicked me. I needed to rescue him because I needed what I'd deduced he had—but he looked so young and scared, I couldn't help myself.

Still looking at Wulfgar, the guard said, "We caught this boy poaching. He killed a deer. The usual punishment?"

"Yes," Wulfgar said.

"No," I said.

Wulfgar gave me an annoyed look.

The boy whimpered, "No. I didn't do nothing. I found 'im dead already. I was dressing 'im down so's the meat wouldn't go to waste, but I didn't kill 'im."

Wulfgar gave *him* an annoyed look, too.

I said to the guards, "Let the boy go."

The guard who was doing all the talking protested, "Punishment for poaching is death."

"You didn't actually see him poaching, did you?" I asked.

Looking sulky about it, the guards shook their heads.

Wulfgar leaned in to me and hissed, "You asked for my advice. So heed me now: This is not wise."

Impatiently I gestured for him to back away from me.

"There have been uprisings among the peasants. Now is not the time to be *soft* with them." He practically spat the word *soft*, as though to get the taste of it out of his mouth.

"On the contrary," I said. "Perhaps the whole problem is that you have been too harsh with them." I realized as soon as I said it that I shouldn't have said "you." I meant "the old regime," but it came out sounding as though I was criticizing Wulfgar himself.

Wulfgar spun on his heel and left. The guards saluted and left.

Well, that hadn't gone particularly well. And I'd have to figure out some way to protect myself from the guards who would be spreading the word that I was weak and unfit to rule. In the meantime, I grabbed hold of the kid by the shoulder of his grimy tunic so he couldn't run away and spoil everything. "It looks," I told him, "as though you owe me a favor."

"Yeah?" he asked, sounding not at all grateful to me for antagonizing both Wulfgar and the guards on his behalf. "You looking for a payment? You need to be bribed into mercy? I coulda guessed your fine talk was all a act. You're worse'n the rest of 'em."

"It wasn't," I protested. "I'm not." *Worse than let's-just-kill-her Queen Andreanna?* "I only meant..." Well, to be honest I only meant: *If you've got a ring, hand it over.* But obviously I couldn't say so. "Sorry," I finished lamely.

"If you wanna get paid," the kid said, "you gotta talk to my father—I got nothing."

"I don't want to get paid," I insisted. "Is your father near here?"

"Somebody's sure to have told him I got brought in. He's probably in the woods nearby."

I noticed that the two guards I'd humiliated by taking the boy's side were talking to another pair of guards, and all four of them were glancing over in my direction with looks that reminded me that they'd already killed me once today.

"Look," I said, getting a whole new picture of what making alliances could mean. "I'm new here. The royal family hates me, the guards distrust me, and from what I can see, things here have obviously been run badly for a long time. I think it's time for a change. I want to talk to your father, to some of the regular people in this kingdom." Peasant unrest, did the queen say? Maybe I could start my own revolution.

The kid looked at me for at least five seconds before he remembered to close his mouth. Then he grinned. "All right," he said. "Follow me."

He led me over the drawbridge and through a meadow and into the forest. Once we were among the trees, he put his hand to his mouth and gave a whistle that sounded like a birdcall. I didn't know woodland birds enough to know if someone answered.

I heard a rustling and a thud, and I felt a dull pressure in my back. It shouldn't have been enough to knock me over, but I fell to my knees and then fell forward again, onto my face. Looking over my shoulder, I could see an arrow sticking out of my back, and that was when I realized that I felt all fizzy. I wanted to tell the boy that he could keep the damn ring. But by then he was jumping over a fallen log and running to embrace a big man who had to be his father; and a couple other woodsy-looking guys were coming out from between the trees, some of them carrying bows, and I was just so tired I had to rest my head on my arms and let the fizziness take over.

CHAPTER NINE

Stop Me If You Think
You've Heard This One Before

When I woke up to hear my mother calling me, I cracked. OK, the ring wasn't with the royal family or with the poachers, it *had* to be the one Deming had. I went tearing down the hill, Dusty barking her encouragement to me.

As my foster mother said, "Hello, Janine. Stand straight now, dear—" I launched myself at Sir Deming. We hit the ground hard, scattering chickens and younger siblings alike. I had his arm pinned and tried to unwedge the ring from his fat little finger. But with the element of surprise having run its course, he squirmed out from beneath skinny little me.

My mother was fluttering worse than the chickens, crying, "Janine! Janine, what are you thinking?"

I bit Deming's hand, and I would gladly have gnawed off his finger if he hadn't pulled out a knife and stuck it between my ribs.

"Oh, Janine!" Mother cried. "How am I ever going to explain this to your father?"

As the fizziness bubbled over me, the last thing I saw was her wringing her hands helplessly.

"There is no ring," I observed, trying for defiant, but recognizing that my voice was only a faint mumble. This was all just an evil plot thought up by Nigel Rasmussem to torment me in my last hours.

"Of course I have no ring," my mother told me as my vision blacked out. "It's your father who took the ring."

CHAPTER TEN

Family History

I'd been sabotaging myself. I blamed Rasmussem, of course: In this day of fractured families, what made them think the average gamer would be willing to hang around just for a parental good-bye?

The next time I went down the hill, I spoke politely to my foster mother and to Sir Deming. Then, when my mother said, "Aren't you going to stay long enough to say good-bye to your father?" I drove thoughts of paternity suits and cheap birthday-and-Christmas gift certificates from my mind.

"Why, of course, how could I leave without saying good-bye to my father?" I said.

"Oh, for goodness' sakes!" Deming snapped. "We haven't the time!"

"Sure we do," I told him.

He continued to grumble and complain, but from what I'd seen in playing this game so far, there was absolutely nothing I could do or say to make the man act pleasantly.

My father didn't take long to arrive. He came running over the hill that my computer subconscious identified as the direction of the bog. "Janine!" he cried, sweeping me up into a great bear hug that took me totally by surprise. He was such a big guy, I found my face pressed into his chest. Considering that he had come straight from cutting peat in the bog, this was not the best position in the world in which to be. I held my breath, trusting that he would let go before I suffocated.

I could hear my little foster siblings chanting for his attention, "Father! Father!"

"Hush now," my mother said. "Run along. Your father, your sister, and I must speak with this man."

Then—still pressed against my father's chest, I could both hear and feel the rumble of his voice—my father asked, "She's been told, then?"

"Yes." Deming sighed impatiently.

My father held me out at arm's length to look me over, and I was amazed to see that his eyes glistened with tears. "I was hoping we'd have more time," he said.

He was going to miss me? My father was saying he was going to miss me?

Though he was just a stupid computer simulation, I felt my throat tighten. "I'll come back," I promised. "Or, better yet, I'll send for you."

He forced a smile. "We'll come," he assured me. Then he glanced in Sir Deming's direction before he said to me, "Janine..."

He hesitated, and Deming said, "Get on with it, man. Shake her hand, wish her luck, repeat after me: 'It's been nice knowing you; good-bye.'"

I sincerely hoped that at some time during the progress of the game, I would be called upon to kill Deming. Surely *one* of the infinite variations Mr. Rasmussem had talked about could accommodate that. "Could we have some privacy here?" I asked.

Yet again Deming sighed, but he strode several long steps away.

"Janine," my father said, "when you first came to us, you were less than a week old—just a tiny little bundle, wrapped in a blanket."

My mother nodded mutely, dabbing her eyes.

I glanced at my father's rough and dirty hands and saw no ring, but why would a peat cutter have a ring?

He continued, "The midwife who brought you said that you were the daughter of the king and of a servant woman who had died in childbirth."

From off to the side, Deming complained, "She's been told all this."

"Go *farther* away," I ordered him.

He took a few more steps, and I wiggled my fingers at him to keep going, until he was practically at our neighbors' pigpen.

In a lowered voice, Father continued. "When your birth mother died, and she didn't have any relatives to send you to, your uncle Mayer, who was the king's gardener, suggested to the king that we might take you in. The king knew that at court your life would be in danger because the queen was obviously not pleased by the idea of your competing with her own children."

"And the king favored you," my mother said, "because he'd loved your mother so, and because the queen brought up her sons to love only her, not him."

That explained some things.

Father glanced at Deming, who was facing the other direction and was a good thirty yards away. Still, Father lowered his voice to a whisper. "So the midwife brought you here, but she also brought something else."

"Yes?" I prompted.

He nodded. "A ring."

"Really?" I said. "Imagine that."

"It's a magic ring," Mother told me.

Now, that was interesting. I'd been assuming it was just a keepsake to prove I was the king's choice. "What kind of magic does it do?" I asked.

Father said, "The midwife didn't say. She just said it was something your mother had asked with her dying breath to be given to you if you were ever summoned to court."

When that seemed to be the end of his story, I said, "Which I just have been."

"Which you just have been," he agreed.

"So . . . where's the ring?"

"The midwife has it. I decided it would be safer with her, just in case the queen knew of its existence and tried to get it from us. I didn't even tell Solita here."

OK. That made sense. Sort of. "Where's the midwife?"

"She has become a hermit," Father said, "in service at the Shrine of Saint Bruce the Warrior Poet."

I'd heard of it, but no memory stronger than name recognition surfaced.

"So I need to go to the shrine," I said.

"If you want the ring," Father agreed.

After what felt like a dozen false starts because I *didn't* have it?

"Be safe," he told me.

"Be good," my mother told me.

I kissed them both. I kissed my brothers and sisters. This time I really felt as though I were leaving my true family behind. I was tempted to go back up the hill and kiss Dusty, but I was sure Deming would ride off without me if I tried.

"Are you *finally* quite through?" Deming asked.

Father stepped to within a nose length of him and said, "She's your new king, little man. Treat her respectfully."

For some reason—maybe because Father was about a foot taller and about two feet wider—Deming bobbed his head and stammered, "Yes, of course. I meant: Does it please you to go now, Highness?"

My father winked at me as Deming lifted me onto the horse before he mounted in front of me, the first time he hadn't left me to scramble on by myself.

"Good-bye, good-bye," my family and I called out. I kept looking back and blowing kisses until I could no longer see them.

Maybe the people at Rasmussem need to develop a new game called something like Happy Family, where there's no gathering treasure or fighting hostile warriors or solving puzzles, just nice people who speak kindly to you and don't make you feel like one of those Christmas trees you see by the curb on December 26. I bet other people, besides me, would be interested.

Maybe.

OK, probably not.

When we got to the crossroads beyond the boundary of St. Jehan, I told Deming, "We need to go to the Shrine of Saint Bruce the Warrior Poet."

"Why?" he demanded, his newfound respect strained.

"Because I'm your new king and I command it," I told him.

Deming sighed but turned down a different road from the one we had taken in all the previous games. "I don't even like poetry," he complained.

It was the first thing he'd said that I could relate to.

THE ROAD led into the woods, where Deming chose a path that more or less followed a stream. He insisted that, though not a lover of poetry, he knew the way. I wondered if we were going to meet the bow-happy relatives of the poacher boy, which got me to wondering what would happen to him, since I wasn't going straight to the castle. But if I was supposed to play a part in that, his capture by the guards must be triggered by my arrival at the castle.

It wasn't a long ride before we reached what looked like an about-to-fall-down lean-to of twigs and hide that sagged against a hill.

"There she is," Deming said, stopping the horse half a city-block length away. "Feordina the Knitter. I'm not going any closer."

Feordina the Knitter? I squinted my eyes in the direction he was looking, at what I had supposed was a heap of forest debris piled by the wind into a corner formed by the lean-to and the hill. I became aware that the pile of debris had looked up and was watching us.

"Wait for me," I told Deming, dismounting.

"Yeah, yeah," he said. He, too, got off the horse and led it to the stream to drink.

I approached the lean-to. "Good day to you," I said.

The reason the person—Feordina—looked like a compost heap was that her clothes seemed to be made entirely of vegetation. She had a basket by her feet that was filled with dandelions, and that was what she was knitting with. I mean, she had knitting needles made of smooth sticks, but she was using dandelion stems as yarn. Dandelion stems not being very long, every few stitches she'd reach down into the basket for a new dandelion, lop off the top with her thumb, then add this new stem to the garment she was knitting. And I knew it was a garment she was making because she seemed to be wearing last season's model, over a fashionable chemise of what I was guessing to be moss and lichen, with accent points of leaves and a hint of heather. She had a two-foot-wide mushroom cap on her head.

"Hold on," she told me, "I'm counting knits and purls."

I waited while she got to the end of the row.

"So"—she didn't set her project down, but she looked up at me through her bushy eyebrows, which themselves almost looked knitted—"who are you and why are you here?"

"I'm Janine," I told her.

She looked at me blankly.

"Janine de St. Jehan." Still no reaction. "You were midwife at my birth. In the king's castle. Where my mother died. You brought me to my foster parents, Solita and Dexter the peat cutter." She *was* the right woman, wasn't she?

"You don't look like the Janine I remember," she said.

"Well"—I was beginning to get worried—"it *has* been fourteen years."

"Hmmm," she said noncommittally.

"My parents—my foster parents—said that they left a ring with you that my mother wanted me to have."

"We'll see," Feordina said. She carefully set her knitting down in the basket and stood, creaking and snapping. I couldn't tell if that was her bones, or something she was wearing. She was even shorter than me, probably only four feet tall. "Well, come in, then."

She motioned me to follow her into the lean-to, which hardly looked big enough for two. But it turned out to be only an entryway, protecting a huge crack in the side of the hill. There were burning torches set into nooks and crannies in the cave surface, so I had no trouble seeing.

The cave must have been formed by an offshoot of the stream we'd been following, for it was quite damp, which made me sneeze. The cave was roundish and about as big as, say, your average one-stall-and-a-sink public bathroom, which it also kind of smelled like. At the far wall was a life-size statue of a man who most likely was Saint Bruce the Warrior Poet. What was kind of neat was that, even though his face was carved wood, his armor was real: a plate-metal helmet (the visor was up, which was how I saw his face), gauntlets, shin protectors, and a surcoat of mail—thousands and thousands of interlocking circles of metal.

"Wow," I said. "Impressive."

When Feordina didn't say anything, I asked, "Uhm, what does this have to do with me and the ring?"

She waggled her finger at the statue, and my heart sank. "I hid the ring in the coat of mail." She smiled apologetically, showing little brown teeth, and I winced, not for the teeth but because I saw what was coming. "I wish I could remember where."

I ran my fingers over the metal, but nothing came loose. "Any hints?" I asked. "Arms? Shoulders? Back?"

She just shook her head. "But the rightful owner—and according to you, that's you—can call it forth."

"How?"

"Why, by reciting poetry, of course."

Of course.

I asked, "You mean like"—I paused to remember—"'Listen, my children and you shall hear / Of the midnight ride of Paul Revere'?"

"Cute," she said, "though a bit short."

"No, that wasn't the whole thing." I started panicking because I didn't *know* the whole thing. I'd just said all I remembered. Did I know any poem in its entirety?

No matter, for she said, "But it has to be a poem of your own making."

"Oh," I said. How hard could that be?

"Of course," Feordina said, "if Saint Bruce doesn't like your poem, he chops your head off."

CHAPTER ELEVEN

A Poem
Can Be a Home
to Those Who Roam
(Or, Like, Whatever)

If Saint Bruce didn't like my poetry, he got to chop my head off? That was even stiffer than my teacher Mrs. Kascima, who isn't satisfied with the quality of her quizzes unless half the class fails.

"I don't know," I said, though a moment before, I'd been convinced this ring was my only chance to succeed in the game—or at least to succeed in *starting* the game.

Feordina folded her arms across her chest and sighed. "That's all right; don't worry about me," she said in a tone that was just the slightest bit insincere. "Take your time; think it over." As though I couldn't hear, she muttered, presumably to Saint Bruce, "Like she's got a choice in the matter." She smiled brightly at me, then a moment later heaved another sigh.

"What, exactly, does this ring do?" I asked.

"I'm not going to answer that question at this point," she said, "not until I know it's really you."

Well, it wasn't like getting killed would be a new experience for me. "All right," I said. "Any rules I should know about?"

"Nope," Feordina said. "Just so long as it's your own poem." She considered before adding, "And Saint Bruce was very well-read, and was known for his incredible memory."

Which sounded like she was saying I looked like a cheater. I was offended but suspected it wasn't worthwhile defending myself to her.

"And he chops people's heads off," I asked for clarification, "if he suspects the poem is somebody else's . . . ?" I drifted off, hoping that was the extent of it.

"Or if the poem stinks," Feordina finished for me. "You wouldn't believe the number of people who come in here with stinky poems. What a mess. Speaking of which, I should probably get the mop and bucket out now. Well, never mind, we'll see." She gave me that bright smile again. "Did I forget to mention there's a time limit?"

"You most certainly did." Could things get any worse? Silly question: Things can *always* get worse. "You mean there's a limit to how long the poem can be?"

"I mean there's a limit to how long you can wait between entering the shrine and starting—*and ending*—the poem. Bruce doesn't like a lot of dithering, you know."

Before I had time to throttle her, she added: "I'd say your time's probably . . . oh, about half gone."

Which didn't give me enough time to throttle her *and* think up a poem. "Any particular subject or type of poem he prefers?"

I figured she'd say he wanted a *rondel* or a *sonnet* or some other kind of poem I could name but not remember how to structure; I also feared that he might be especially fond of deep, meaningful, symbolic poetry. But she just shook her head. And glanced warily at that sword the statue held aloft, as though revising her estimate of how much time I had left.

Did I detect a smear of red along its length, or was that just the light from the torches?

All right. What, exactly did I have to lose? I announced: "An Ode to Saint Bruce." He had to like a poem praising him—didn't he?

No reaction.

OK.

Except, of course, that my mind was blank.

OK...

It made no sense to just stand there without trying while my time ran out. I started:

"A warrior poet named Bruce..."

My mind ran through a series of words rhyming with "Bruce," none of which seemed particularly apt.

"...wrote odes to his horse and his goose."

I fully expected the sword to come down then, but it didn't. I cleared my throat. OK, that took care of the "poet" part, what about the "warrior"?

"He won honor and prizes..."

Prizes? What was I thinking of, *prizes?*

"...'gainst foes of various sizes..."

'Gainst was poetical, even if the line itself was forced. And now what about the "saint" part?

Knowing it sounded like the pathetic begging it was, I finished:

"...and protected young poets from abuse."

Feordina winced and ducked.

I closed my eyes and braced myself for the blow from the sword.

No pain. No fizziness. No maternal call of, "Janine! Janine, come back to the house."

Maybe I was still alive. I peeked to check.

The statue just stood there, like a good statue should.

Stood/good/should: Now the rhyming was coming to me.

Feordina lowered her arms from protecting her head and gave a snort of disbelief. "He must be in a good mood," she proclaimed. "Lucky you: He's accepted your poem."

I couldn't fault Feordina for being surprised. I was amazed myself. "Now what?" I asked.

"Now you ask for what you want," Feordina said, "and if it's within Saint Bruce's power, he'll grant it."

I closed the mouth I had opened to ask for the ring. "If it's within his power," I repeated.

She nodded. "'If it's within his power.'"

"What does that mean?" I asked.

"It means: If he can do it." Feordina rolled her eyes despite her polite smile.

Oh, well, thank you very much for clarifying that particularly challenging question. Though I had come to get the ring, suddenly I wondered if the ring was my best option. "What sorts of wishes does he grant?" I asked. "And what sort doesn't he grant?"

"Well," she said, "I've never known him to turn down a request for facility at rhyming or meter, which I do have to point out are areas in which you seem to be particularly weak."

"Ahh," I said, suspecting that she wouldn't recognize sarcasm, "very useful to peasant girls who need to take on the royal court."

"Hmmm," she said as though maybe she *did* know sarcasm when she heard it. "Of course, Saint Bruce does tend to get cranky with greedy people who are granted one wish then ask for more."

"Cranky," I said. "As in..." I glanced at the upraised sword.

"Hmmm," Feordina agreed.

"So what do you suggest?" I asked.

She sighed audibly. "You came here looking for something in particular. Is your attention span so short that you've forgotten?"

"I came looking for my mother's ring," I said.

Feordina leaned close as though she was about to whisper something to me, but instead she shouted: *"Well, then, ask for it!"*

"I wish for my mother's ring," I said.

There was a slight *ping* as something metallic fell—I couldn't see from where on the statue—and hit the floor of the cave. I caught the glint of metal as the ring rolled to bounce off my right big toe.

"Oy!" Feordina smacked her palm against her forehead. "Was that so difficult?"

I picked up the ring. It was a pewter band with a design I recognized from the medieval paraphernalia catalogs as a Celtic knot. "Thank you," I said to Saint Bruce. All right, he was a statue, but what could politeness hurt? I asked Feordina, "Now do you believe I'm Janine de St. Jehan?"

Feordina sighed. Feordina was great at sighing. "I suppose."

"Then can you tell me about this ring?"

"If you give it to someone," Feordina said, "that person will do your bidding."

"You mean...like..."—I shrugged—"...what?"

"I mean, like, your father put the ring on your mother's finger, and—even though she knew better— she was compelled to love him."

"Eww!" I said. "You mean she didn't want to, and had to because of the ring?" The king, who had never been high in my estimation, took an express elevator into the subbasement. "She shouldn't have accepted the ring," I proclaimed.

Feordina looked close to smacking her palm against *my* forehead, but she refrained. "You don't listen too well," she said. "You really should learn to listen. *Compelled.* Did you not hear me say *compelled,* or don't you know what the word means?"

"You said," I reminded her, "that once my father put the ring on my mother's finger, she was compelled to love him—and, yes, I know that *compelled* means she had to, whether she wanted to or not. You never said she was *compelled* to accept the ring."

She put her hands on her hips and stood on her toes to stick her face up into mine. "Well, I should think that was obvious."

I raised my voice to match hers. "Well, then, OK." But getting her mad wasn't going to help. Making an effort to sound pleasant, I said, "OK, thank you."

"Don't you take *that tone* with me," Feordina snapped,

which made me wonder if her character might not be based on my grandmother, who can discern *a tone* at fifty paces.

"Sorry," I said meekly. "But, no, really, thank you. That is valuable information. You're saying that when I give the ring to someone, that person *has* to accept it, and then he or she *has* to do whatever I command."

Feordina nodded. "You can give the ring only once, and that person will do all your bidding, or die trying, for as long as he or she lives, never able to remove the ring, no matter what you bid, even if it's to jump off a castle battlement. Which—not that you asked, but I'll give my opinion, anyway—would be a wasteful thing for you to ask for, because even if your person dies within moments of getting the ring, you can't take it back. Well, you can, but it won't work for you again."

Seeing what looked like a flaw in her reasoning, I asked, "What if I bid the person to take the ring off?"

"What are you, a fledgling lawyer?" Feordina asked. "Can't be done."

"Just wondering."

She shook her head. "I really hate lawyers," she said. She turned to complain to the statue of Saint Bruce. "Who would have ever guessed that my little Janine would grow up to be a lawyer?" She waved me away. "Go on, go on," she said. "I have a sweater to finish knitting before the nights start getting chilly. Don't you have a kingdom to inherit or something?"

```
SUBJ:    URGENT RESPONSE NEEDED--Repair
         Team
DATE:    5/25  03:50:13 P.M. US eastern
         daylight time
FROM:    Nigel Rasmussem
         <nrasmussem@rasmussem.com>
TO:      dept. heads distribution list
```

The patch suggested by the Palo Alto
group didn't work.

The gamer has only now broken through
level 1 for the first time. We are
concerned over her lack of progress,
which makes it seem unlikely that she
will finish the game in the short time
she has left.

Note that we're already seeing
degeneration of the bios, even earlier
than forecast. We do have medical
personnel present.

Options needed immediately for
stabilization. Please respond ASAP.

CHAPTER TWELVE

One

So, tying the ring to the laces of my bodice, I said good-bye to Feordina the Knitter and the statue of Saint Bruce the Warrior Poet, and I woke up Sir Deming, who'd fallen asleep on the stream bank, though he claimed he was just thinking with his eyes closed.

"Are you quite ready yet?" he asked as he helped me mount the horse. "Maybe we can go visit the seashore next, or perhaps you'd like to tour the great cathedrals of the midland provinces? I mean, it isn't as though there's any sort of rush or anything, with the old king dead and the new king not yet crowned."

What had he done—awakened on the wrong side of the stream?

"The new king," I said, "doesn't appreciate sarcasm."

I could give him the ring and order him to like me— or at least to be civil to me and protect me from others' rudeness—but I suspected that would be a frivolous waste.

Once we had been riding for a long silent while, he asked, "What did you ask for, back at the shrine?"

I'd had plenty of time to consider what I might answer should he ask that question—something clever, I'd calculated, and believable, and at the same time implying that I was not someone to be taken lightly or messed with: a deception he might pass on to the royal family so that they would have a healthy fear of me. But the best I'd come up with was, "That's for me to know."

Deming shrugged and didn't say anything else the whole ride to the castle.

SIR DEMING ONCE again handed me over to Counselor Rawdon, and I once again decided to forgo the bath and change of clothes. After all, if this kingdom included people dressed like Feordina, whose fashion sense began and stopped at forest edibles, the royal family would just have to accept my sheepherder's garb.

Ah, my royal kin. What can I say? After a short interval of aristocratic abuse, punctuated by my polite little apologies (I'm sorry I smell, I'm sorry I was born, I'm sorry the king liked me better than he liked you), the audience was once again over.

"Wulfgar," I said to my eldest half brother, "may I please have a word with you?"

Queen Andreanna went off in a huff, sweeping Abas and Kenric away with her.

"I'm guessing," I told Wulfgar, "that I'm going to be needing a lot of help."

"Yeah," he agreed.

"I'm thinking it can't have been easy for you as the firstborn son, with a domineering mother and two brothers who, I suspect, have always been ready to betray you to advance their own causes."

Wulfgar didn't have to say anything—I could tell I was right by his expression.

"There's nothing I can do about our father passing you over to name me heir." It'd be a lot easier to just give him the ring and *force* him to help me than it would be to *convince* him, but I had to try it this way first, in case I needed the ring during the rest of the game. I said, "Fathers…" I tried to get rid of the mental image of me with my ear pressed to the wall, hearing my own father demand, "How can I even be sure she's mine?" "Fathers," I said, "can be a disappointment."

"'Disappointment,'" Wulfgar snorted.

"You don't have to be abandoned to be abandoned," I told him, and at that he looked thoughtful, and then nodded. I repeated, "There's nothing I can do about our father's decision. But I suspect you would have had competition for the throne even if I had never been born, even if King Cynric had officially named you his heir."

"Oh, I can imagine," Wulfgar agreed.

"If we work together," I said, "that's the power divided between two rather than among four."

Wulfgar looked at me appraisingly, then nodded. "All right," he said.

By then we had walked out into the courtyard, and I saw that same old pair of guards dragging the poacher boy toward us. Though he and his kin had murdered me once already, I couldn't stand by and let the guards execute him for being hungry. That was no way to start my kingship. Still, I remembered that Wulfgar hadn't reacted well to leniency. "What we need to do," I said hurriedly, "is call together a council: the old king's advisers, plus those in the kingdom who know magic. I'll leave *who* to you. And *when*. You make the arrangements. I'll handle this."

Wulfgar noted the approaching guards. He obviously dismissed the oncoming situation as within my abilities and turned to go back indoors.

One of the guards called out, "Prince Wulfgar!"

Wulfgar gave a vague wave and continued walking away.

I stepped into the path of the guard. "May *I* help you?" I asked. "I'm Princess Janine." I smiled sweetly.

The guard bobbed his head in what may have been a bow. "Princess Janine, this boy has been caught poaching deer. We were about to deliver the usual punishment."

"Indeed?" I said, trying to sound regal.

"I didn't do nothing," the boy sniveled. "I found 'im dead already. I was dressing 'im down so's the meat wouldn't go bad, but—"

"You didn't kill him, right?" I turned to the guards. "Were there witnesses to the actual killing?"

The two men shuffled their feet. "No," they admitted, and I was sure I saw disappointment on their faces.

"Then let the boy go," I said. "Prince Wulfgar and I discussed this." Well, only if you counted my saying, "I'll handle this," as discussion, but I remembered how the guards had killed me once before because they perceived me as weak. I couldn't very well give the magic ring to the entire barracks to make them love and respect me.

The guards saluted smartly and released the boy.

"I will not be so lenient again," I said, which was for everybody's benefit.

As though afraid I might change my mind, the boy dashed away—across the courtyard, over the drawbridge, and into the woods.

The guards walked away, shaking their heads and muttering—which didn't look promising.

Surely, I thought, *I'm not supposed to let them kill the boy—that couldn't be the right track to take?*

I was so busy watching the guards, I wasn't aware of anyone approaching until someone laid a hand on my arm. For once I lucked out, for it was a gentle touch, and when I looked up, I saw an old woman. She was about four-and-a-half-feet tall by four-and-a-half-feet wide, and she was dressed in a simple brown gown decorated with feathers and bits of seashell and smooth, polished stones of various colors. *I wonder if she's related to Feordina?* I asked myself. Or was this just the kingdom of the fashion impaired?

The old woman said, "Blessed is the way of the One."

"The one what?" I asked.

"All is One," she answered cryptically.

So I retaliated with a smart-mouthed, "And one is all."

But the old woman didn't take my comment as sarcastic. "That is very profound," she told me, and—while I checked her expression to see if *she* was being sarcastic—she added, "I guessed you might be One."

I was going to ask, "One what?" but I suspected we'd start going in circles again. So instead I asked, "Are you Sister Mary Ursula?" because I wondered if maybe we were talking about religion.

Her face lit up. "Yes," she said, obviously unduly impressed by my perceptiveness, when it was really just a case of having gotten a hint from Nigel Rasmussem. "You are truly One with the world, aren't you? I surmised that, by how you treated that boy. You recognized his Oneness. Many would not have."

"Ah, well," I said vaguely. I took it she was complimenting me, but beyond that I was kind of lost.

"You are the answer to my prayers," she told me. Which is the kind of thing I'd always fantasized someone would say to me—I'd just never pictured that someone as a seventy-year-old nun.

"Uhm..." I said.

"Let us give thanks for our Oneness," Sister Mary Ursula said. She clasped my hands, closed her eyes, and hummed nasally. "I feel the world in my bones," she said. "The wind is in my veins; the spirit of the otter is in my liver."

"Are you..." I started. "I mean, you're not..." She opened her eyes and looked at me quizzically. "I'm guessing you aren't a Roman Catholic nun," I said. I go to Catholic school, so I would know.

Like an actress momentarily stepping out of character, she put one hand on her hip and said in a chirpy little voice totally unlike her normal hazy tone, "Definitely not, because—of course—our intent is not to offend anyone," which was probably a Rasmussem programmer's idea of humor. Sister Mary Ursula resumed her slightly foggy manner. "I am," she said, "of the Sisterhood of One."

"That's a regular order here?" I asked.

"No," she said. "I'm the only one. We are *all* the only one."

Of course. How silly of me.

She said, "I'm afraid King Cynric and his family have not always been quite so One as they might have been."

"Well..." I said. I wasn't sure what to answer, but that made no difference, for Sister Mary Ursula had only paused to take a breath.

"But you are obviously someone who takes Oneness seriously. You're a true treasure, like rain on a plain of drought, or like a peach without a pit." Sister Mary Ursula patted my hand. "You and I are going to get along wonderfully well, I can tell. Together we shall unite this kingdom into Oneness with the universe."

Since she obviously wasn't going to give me a chance to get a word in edgewise, I just smiled at her.

But apparently she was through. "Come, come," she said, starting for the castle, moving at a slow waddle. "If the sun is singing in your marrow, tell it to whisper to the acorns instead. We have work before us."

Not knowing what else to do, I followed her.

In the castle we ran into Wulfgar, who was walking with Counselor Rawdon.

"Yes," Rawdon was saying, "if we send a rider to contact Uldemar, he can use his scrying glass to tell the others, and that will certainly save time with trying to track them all down."

"Oooo," Sister Mary Ursula interrupted, "scrying." She shook her head disapprovingly. As far as I could tell, she was totally oblivious to the annoyed looks she was getting from both men. "Not a good thing. Not a good thing at all. Disrupts the cosmic harmonies. Throws off the balance of One—it's like a fat woman trying to stand on one foot. No, not a good idea at all." She placed her fingertips to her temples and hummed, then shuddered as though she'd had a sudden chill. "Good thing we met you in time to stop you."

"You are not," Wulfgar said, "stopping us." To me he explained, "If you want Orielle and Xenos to attend your meeting, having Uldemar use his scrying glass is the most efficient way to reach them."

This made sense to me, but "Oooo," Sister Mary Ursula said as though Wulfgar had said the one thing she dreaded more than hearing that scrying was about to take place. "Wizard, witch, necromancer. They are *so* strayed from One, you might just as well count them as Other. No, no, no, no—not a good way to start your good work, Princess Janine, definitely not."

No magic? Was that what she was saying: There should be no magic? "Surely that can't be right," I said, remembering the promos I'd seen, which included a wizard and a dragon. Were they only in the dead ends? No magic? What kind of fantasy role-playing game had no magic?

But Sister Mary Ursula was shaking her head. "Of course I'm right," she said. "Right and truth are One with pinochle and rye bread."

Rawdon shook his head.

Wulfgar said, "Princess Janine, haven't you listened to enough of this woman's rantings?"

As though Wulfgar wasn't standing only about two feet farther away from her than I was, Sister Mary Ursula whispered loudly, "He's not to be trusted. He was raised by Others, you know." To Wulfgar and Rawdon she said, "Princess Janine and I dance to the same rhythms of the cosmos. She has chosen me to be her counselor, and we are now as two bodies sharing one mind."

That was a scary thought.

And, anyway, *had* I chosen her? All I'd done was pardon the poacher boy, an action she happened to approve. Did that make her my official choice of counselor?

"Princess Janine," Rawdon said, "are you really planning to dismiss me?"

"I never said anything about dismissing..." I started.

But Wulfgar, who'd been looking from me to Sister Mary Ursula, crossed his arms over his chest and demanded of me, "*What* is she talking about?"

Sister Mary Ursula answered for me, and I realized I was getting pretty tired of that. She said, "The princess showed Oneness with a poor peasant boy."

Wulfgar homed in on what she must be talking about. "The poacher?" he asked. "You let the poacher off? Is that what she's saying? Didn't you hear my mother warn you about the peasant unrest?"

"Yes," I said before Sister Mary Ursula could tell me what I thought about this. "I thought the unrest could be due to the severity of the laws over minor matters."

"'Minor matters'?" Wulfgar snarled at me. "The laws of the land are a minor matter?"

How could every conversation get so far beyond me? I said, "Well, this particular one is."

We glowered at each other, until Sister Mary Ursula finally said, "See? One mind."

"You're welcome to each other," Wulfgar said, and he stormed off down the hall.

Rawdon threw his hands up in the air in frustration. "Princess—" he started.

Sister Mary Ursula put her fingers to her temples and said, "No, no, no Rawdon."

And Rawdon, too, left in a huff.

"Can't I have two counselors?" I called after him.

He didn't answer. And Sister Mary Ursula told me, "One. One sun. One underlying song to the universe. One best way to prepare eggplant. One counselor. We must sit down and discuss all that needs to be changed. I am a much better person than Rawdon."

"Counselor Rawdon." I raised my voice and I was pretty sure he could hear me. "I haven't said no, about those magic-users coming. I just"—I sighed and finished lamely—"need to talk to my counselor about it first."

And of course he didn't answer that, either.

CHAPTER THIRTEEN

Disarming the Troops

"Now," Sister Mary Ursula said, "the first thing you must do is cleanse yourself."

How kind of her to notice. "Yeah," I said, checking out the skirt of my dress, "I *am* pretty disgusting."

She sighed. Loudly. "Physical appearance is not what is important."

Yeah, right. Tell that to any girl who hasn't bothered to put on a presentable shirt or fix her hair because she's only running into the grocery store to get a quart of milk for her grandmother, and who does she see tending the 7-ITEMS-OR-LESS cash register but the guy of her dreams, except she can't even say hi—much less try to develop a meaningful relationship—since she looks like the poster child for the terminally geeky.

But Sister Mary Ursula came from a different world from me. I suspected Sister Mary Ursula came from a different world from the other people in *this* world, too, but

I didn't say so. She told me, "You need to cleanse your soul—make it One with the world."

"How do I do that?" I asked.

"Solitude. Fasting. Meditation. Skinny-dipping in the moonlight."

"I think I'll wait until my second week as king for that," I said, willing to risk that I was skipping something I was supposed to do.

Sister Mary Ursula didn't argue. "All ways lead to the One," she said, "though some ways get you there faster."

"Speaking of getting places," I said, "what I want are people to deliver messages for me. Who would I talk to about that?"

"You could talk to me," Sister Mary Ursula said. "But in all honesty, I don't know much about it. Probably the one you need to speak to is Penrod, captain of the guard."

"Fine," I said. "Thank you. I'll see you later."

"Don't you want to discuss the meaning of life?" Sister Mary Ursula took a few steps after me.

But she stopped following when I said, "In a little bit." She was obviously a dead end. I had chosen the wrong counselor, that was all there was to it. There was no way the game was supposed to be played with me spending my first afternoon here cleansing my soul and listening to Sister Mary Ursula philosophize about life. Or, at least, I didn't think so.

I was sure the ceiling would come crashing down on me at any moment now. Or maybe there would be an earthquake or a tidal wave, something to kill me off and set me down at the beginning again. But in the meanwhile, there was no reason I couldn't try to find out information that would be useful for my next try.

I went back out into the courtyard. No guards this time; if they weren't terrorizing the local citizenry, they were probably huddled somewhere conspiring to kill me. I stopped a servant woman who was carrying a basket of laundry. "Any idea where I would find Captain Penrod?" I asked her.

"He might be in the guardhouse." She pointed to one of the doorways.

Luckily, the door was wide open, because I didn't know if—as a princess-about-to-be-appointed-king—I was supposed to knock. I mean, obviously I outranked them, but I didn't want to walk in on a group of guys who might be in the process of getting dressed or undressed, or who might be sitting around scratching or belching and farting or doing whatever it is guys do when there aren't any civilized folk around. But with the door already open, I rapped my knuckles against the doorframe, called, "Hello!" and walked in.

There were about a half-dozen guards, who were neither walking around naked nor conspiring against me—at least not obviously so. Apparently this wasn't where they slept but just where they hung around. A pair of them were seated at a table, playing a game my subconscious identified as knucklebones. Most of the others were clustered around them, and I gathered, from the snatch of conversation I caught before they saw me and stopped, that they were betting on the outcome of the game. One man was napping on a cot in the corner, and another was making some sort of adjustment to his sword belt. All of the men, except the napper, jumped to attention when they saw me. Not guiltily, I thought, just wary.

"Captain Penrod?" I said.

"Yeah?" The man who answered was the one who had been fiddling with his belt. He was also the guard I'd talked to several times this morning—the one who had arrested the poacher. The one who had killed me two or three games back.

I decided not to hold that against him. "I need to invite the magic-users of the realm to a meeting," I said.

"Done," the man said.

Did he mean, "I will do your bidding so quickly, you might as well consider it done already"? Because he certainly wasn't moving, quickly or otherwise.

"'Done'?" I repeated.

"Prince Wulfgar already gave that order."

"Oh," I said, because—excuse me, but—the way Prince Wulfgar and I had left things, Sister Mary Ursula was my adviser, and she had advised me to steer clear of magic, and he had no reason to believe I wouldn't take her recommendation. Sure, that was what I had decided. But *after* he left. I had certainly not told him to go ahead and give the order.

Some of this—not the details but the surprise and annoyance—must have shown on my face. Captain Penrod gave an unpleasant smile and said, "You and Prince Wulfgar need to consult more to get your stories straight."

I took that as indication the captain had found out I'd misled him regarding the poacher. I didn't like the way

101

the other men had moved in closer—even the guy who earlier had been lying down. I braced myself, but so far their weapons were still sheathed.

"You're right," I told Penrod, told all of them. "As I'm starting my rule, I'm sure to make many mistakes. But I want you to know: You and your men are very important to me. I realize you perform some of the hardest, most dangerous, most thankless jobs in the realm." I had no idea what their duties were, but doesn't everybody feel that describes their jobs? I figured it couldn't hurt for me to be sympathetic.

They *did* seem to—well, not mellow or relax, but maybe loosen a bit at my words.

"I want all of you to feel free to come to me with any of your concerns. And I want you to go ahead and give me advice if you think anything in the way this kingdom is being run is wrong."

Well, that was a mistake.

They started complaining to me about everything from my being too soft on the peasants to the fact that they weren't paid enough and weren't paid regularly, and the food was pretty generally lousy, and they really didn't like the way the queen had a tendency to hit on the younger men.

"Wow," I said the instant there was a pause, "I'm going to look into all of those things. First..." I was going to apologize for undermining their authority with the poacher boy; but on second thought, they might take that as permission to enact harsher measures on the nearest peasants. Besides, I didn't think a king should start her reign by apologizing. "First," I said, "the money owed you."

That certainly seemed the right choice for getting their attention. They all spoke at once, their words tumbling over one another, but I gathered that they'd been shorted their salaries several times over the past months.

"Who's in charge of paying you?" I asked.

"Counselor Rawdon," they all said, seven voices speaking as one.

Rawdon, of course, had walked off in a huff. Had he simply left my presence or had he left the castle? "I will get to the bottom of this," I promised. "Who can take me to Counselor Rawdon's room, or..." I still didn't have a clear idea what I was supposed to be doing in this game. "Or, well, to all the places I need to go?"

They all looked ready to volunteer, which was a distinct improvement to their earlier mood. But it was Penrod who said, "I will accompany you, Highness."

"Good. Thank you." I nodded to the other men. "At ease," I said, which was about all the military-speak I knew.

Penrod and I walked back out into the courtyard. "Any idea how soon before the magic-users will be here?" I asked.

"Uldemar is the only one with a regular house in a town, and that's about a half-day's ride from here. The messenger Prince Wulfgar sent should be there by late afternoon. Uldemar has wizardly ways to contact the others. Depending on where they are and if they can come immediately, I should think they'd be here sometime between noon tomorrow and..." He trailed off, indicating no upper limit for how long it could take.

Ouch. OK, so I guessed I wasn't supposed to wait on them.

Then my new top priority was to get the guards happy with me so they wouldn't kill me again. "What—" I started. But I heard a sound, that stomach-churning *whoosh* of an arrow that I recognized from my death a couple times back, when the woodsmen had fired their arrows at me.

What did I do now? I thought things had been going...maybe not *well* but sort of OK. Hadn't they? Had the guardsmen been only pretending to accept my proposals?

Except that I hadn't felt an arrow slam into me, and I didn't feel any fizziness.

I looked back to the doorway of the guardroom, but there was no bowman there. Could I have imagined that sound? I turned to Captain Penrod, and he wasn't where I had left him.

He was, in fact, on the ground at my feet, an arrow through his heart.

There was a supply wagon parked in front of a servants' entrance, and a man jumped out from behind it. He was a huge, hairy guy, and it was hard to tell where his hairiness ended and his tunic—which my subconscious identified as elk hide—began. On his head was one of those horned helmets worn by cartoon Vikings and fat ladies in German operas.

Before I could get out much more than a squeak, he

clapped a massive hand over my mouth. I kicked, squirmed, and tried to bite—but didn't get much reaction.

Still, my pathetic scream must have gotten someone's attention, for one of the guards came to the guardroom door.

A second man, who could have been my attacker's twin, edged out from behind the wagon and let loose an arrow that struck the guard in the throat.

I was still trying to jab my attacker where it hurts—which apparently is a lot easier in the movies than in real life—as he dragged me backward toward the wagon. There were two bowmen behind the wagon, who covered our retreat, as well as others, I now saw, on top of the wall that separated the courtyard from the surrounding woods. At just about the same time I became aware that the placement of the wagon had hidden a rope ladder the attackers had used to get into the castle compound, I also became aware that it wasn't my attacker's hand that smelled so bad, but the cloth he held in his hand over my nose and mouth.

Whatever he'd soaked the cloth in made my knees wobble and give out, and he flung me over his shoulder as he grabbed hold of the rope. The ground spun, and I lost consciousness.

CHAPTER FOURTEEN

Are We Having Fun Yet?

I woke up when someone threw a bucket of cold water on me. Even in my groggy state, I was beginning to figure this was the only bath I was likely to get in this particular lifetime.

Speaking of baths, two big hairy guys who looked as though they'd never *heard* the word—and who may or may not have been some of the ones I'd seen in the castle courtyard—were standing over me, one with an empty-though-still-dripping bucket in hand. This guy said something to me—a whole string of words I couldn't understand.

"I don't speak your language," I said.

The second man switched to whatever language English passed for in this world. "Where do it be?" he demanded. Despite his appearance, his accent was pleasant and musical—sort of Jamaican but not.

I was smart enough not to check to see if the ring I'd tied to my bodice laces was still there.

"Where do *what* be?" I asked.

"Do na play the dumb one," commanded the other guy, his accent thicker. "The crown, to be certain."

That was a surprise. I had no idea who these guys were or why they were looking for the crown, but I couldn't see any reason not to be honest. "I haven't been officially named king yet," I explained. "Not for a couple more days. I don't know where they're keeping the crown in the meantime."

The two guys exchanged a look that struck me as a can-this-girl-be-real? look.

"What?" I asked.

They talked over me as though I weren't there. "Mayhap she be playin' the dumb one?" the one with the bucket said. "Or mayhap she really be as stupid as she seems?"

I resented that, even though I was lying in a puddle of new-made mud, obviously these guys' prisoner. And there were a bunch of other guys, looking just like these two. A *whole* bunch. Like hundreds, I guessed, seeing their tents, their campfires. I was in some sort of enemy camp.

Bucketless stroked his bushy beard speculatively. "It might be that no one has been telling her yet," he said, but he didn't sound as though he really believed it.

"Nobody has told me much of anything," I agreed.

"You be the new king," said the bucket guy. "How can they be na tellin' you what you be needin' to know to rule?"

"Well," I admitted, "I do suspect some of them are trying to get around that me-being-the-new-king thing."

The guy who spoke better English gave a short, sharp

laugh, and this time I guessed he believed me. "I would bet," he said. Then he asked, "Do anybody be telling you about King Grimbold?"

I shook my head. "Who's he?"

He grinned, his white teeth flashing. "Me."

A king. Another one. Oh boy. "You're not a contender for the throne of..."—implanted memory floated to my mind's surface, and my kingdom gained a name—"Shelby, are you?"

Grimbold snorted. "I be having my own kingdom, thank you—when Shelban kings be not sabotaging us." He could see I wasn't following this. "In the north," he added, which wouldn't have meant anything to me except for what Queen Andreanna had said about us being threatened by a barbarian army in the north.

I didn't ask if he was a barbarian, which sounded a bit rude to me. Maybe it would and maybe it wouldn't to a barbarian, but I decided not to chance it. I asked, "King Cynric took your crown, is that what you're saying? He took away the actual crown?"

"He be *stole* it away," the other man interrupted. "From Grimbold's father, King Tobrecan."

"I don't know anything about that," I said. "I was raised away from court."

Grimbold gave that barklike laugh of his. "Like Wulfgar."

This was not news to me, but for the first time I wondered if Wulfgar and I had more in common than I had suspected. That he had been educated away from home was the first thing Deming had said about him—but had it been to protect him from court intrigue? Had Cynric seen that Queen Andreanna had enough ambitions for herself that she posed a danger to their son when he was too young to defend himself? I saw there were a lot more questions I should have asked at court.

The barbarian with the bucket said, "But now that King Tobrecan is bein' dead and Grimbold is bein' our new king, and now that Cynric is bein' dead, it is bein' time to reclaim the crown that been fashioned by Xenos for Brecc the Slayer, our firstest chieftain."

"Xenos," I said, recognizing the name. "There's a magician today by that same name."

Again the men exchanged a long-suffering look.

They couldn't be talking about the same man, could they? How long ago had this Brecc ruled, and how old would that make Xenos? But, then again, we were talking about a magician.

"She *do* be as stupid as she looks," the guy with the bucket said.

"I be liking her," Grimbold argued. "She does na know nothing, but I na be going to hold that against her."

"So what do that be meanin'?" the other man asked.

"We shall be letting her live," Grimbold said.

That was a relief.

Grimbold said, "We shall be demanding the crown as ransom for her."

The other gave a dismissive snort. "What makes you be thinkin' they be payin' a ransom for her, useless thing that she be?"

I couldn't help but mentally agree. They were going to ask my family to trade something—presumably of value—for me? This opened up a whole new batch of possibilities for public humiliation.

Grimbold stroked his beard pensively as though his companion had presented a new thought. "We can always be killing her later," he said.

Which I guess showed he wasn't all *that* emotionally attached to me.

"Set a guard on her," Grimbold ordered, "and send a envoy to the castle to be demanding the returning of my crown in exchange for the life of their new king."

I couldn't even use my ring on Grimbold. If I said, "Here, take this ring," and he put it on, and then started doing everything I said, then surely this other guy would catch on that something was wrong.

Nor could I use it on my guard: Grimbold had given his orders. There were too many men in this camp who would question why those orders were being ignored if I got this guy to release me.

The barbarian guard got a length of chain and some shackles—not promising an easy escape at all—then he brought me to a tree in the midst of their campground, and he fastened me there, by my left ankle. All in all, they were being more considerate than I had reason to expect from enemy barbarians. The shackle wasn't tight, and the chain was long enough that I could sit, stand, lie down, or walk around the tree—choosing shade or sunlight as I pleased. But I still felt like a leashed dog.

From the position of the sun, I guessed that it was mid-afternoon. The last meal my stomach remembered was a breakfast of hard bread and salted fish back in St. Jehan—a menu the real me had to keep from dwelling on or I would have gagged. I felt hungry, and these guys would have already had their midday meal and wouldn't be thinking about supper for another several hours.

A guard was posted to watch me. He was given the key to the shackles, which I found reason enough to try to strike up a friendship. It was hard to tell if he didn't speak English, or if he simply didn't want to talk.

There were some women in the camp, and one of them brought me a cup of water.

"Thank you," I said. "Any chance of any leftovers from lunch?"

She looked at me quizzically and said something that sounded like, *"Doe naado?"*

"Food?" I said. I pantomimed eating, but she shook her head. I thought she meant she didn't understand rather than that I couldn't have any, but there was no way to know for sure. My guard certainly didn't offer any commentary.

There were even a few kids. Some of them seemed curious, some seemed to be playing a game of dare—approaching, then running away. When I didn't chase after them, a few got bolder and took up a new game of throw-clumps-of-dirt-at-the-prisoner. My guard napped obliviously in the shade of his own tree.

I didn't even know if my royal family was planning to rescue me. Should I be patiently waiting for them to come swooping in, or was I supposed to be working on some plan of my own?

Of course, it would help if I had even the beginnings

of a plan of my own to get me started in the right direction.

Knowing how difficult it is to judge the passing of time when you're bored, I think I waited about an hour and a half, maybe two. The sun *did* lower a bit in the sky.

This can't be right, I told myself. If anyone was going to rescue me, it was probably going to have to be me.

My opportunity came when a new guard took over.

"Do you speak the language of Shelby?" I asked.

"No," the man answered, revealing himself to be not quite rocket-scientist caliber.

I untied the magic ring from the lacing of my bodice. "Take this ring," I commanded.

Sure enough, he understood me well enough that the magic of the ring compelled him to come forward and take it from my outstretched hand. He slipped it onto one of his own fingers, and I figured that had to be another of the ring's magical properties—that it would fit anyone—either that or my mother had had very fat fingers.

"I want you to like me," I told the guard.

"Oh, I do," the man assured me so warmly I feared we were veering into a direction I certainly didn't want to go.

"I want you to like me as your best buddy," I clarified. "I want you to only want good things for me. I want you to want me safe and happy."

"'Safe,'" he repeated, nodding his head energetically. "'Happy.'"

"I want you to release me," I said, "and to get me out of this camp."

He came forward and tried to tear the chain in half with his bare hands.

It looked as though I would have to do the thinking for both of us.

I said, "Take the time to release me without attracting attention."

The guard paused to consider, then took out the key he'd been given when he'd relieved the other guy. He unlocked my shackles.

I stood. "Put your hand on my shoulder. Act as if Grimbold has ordered you to bring me to him, except lead me out of the camp instead. If anyone asks, tell them you're acting under Grimbold's orders. Do you understand?"

"Yes," he told me. "Buddy."

We were fine for about ten paces. Then King Grimbold came around the corner of a tent, and we found ourselves face-to-face.

"What do you be doing?" Grimbold demanded.

And my guard, compelled to do my bidding, answered, "Grimbold's orders."

"I be ordering no such thing!" Grimbold protested. "Bring her back and secure her once more."

My guard tried to stiff-arm Grimbold out of his way.

"Stop," Grimbold ordered.

"Uhm . . ." I said. What in the world was the way out of this?

My guard waited one second to see what I would bid, then he once again tried to shove past his king.

Grimbold stopped the man the only way he could.

He whipped out his sword and stabbed my escort in the chest.

Well, that was too bad, but I wasn't going to let it slow me down. I made a break for the trees.

Grimbold yelled something in his own language, and barbarians came pouring out of the tents. What felt like about seventeen of them tackled me and jumped on top of me before I'd made it more than a tenth of the way I had to.

They took their time about getting off me, too. Now I know what a football feels like.

My captors dragged my bruised body back to where Grimbold knelt beside the dead guard. Though he spoke in Shelban for my benefit, he addressed his men. "I be having to kill Isen because she be having some sort of power over him. I be thinking this may be the source of her power." He held up the ring to show them.

"No," I assured him.

"Give me her finger," he commanded his men.

With this crowd I was lucky none of them was stupid enough to chop one off and hand it to him. I struggled, because he didn't know that all he had to do was order me to take it, but I knew it was a losing battle. The ring slipped snugly over my finger.

"Now tell me true," he said, "do you have to be doing what I say to you?"

Because he phrased it as a command, I had to answer, and I had to answer truthfully even though I tried to deny it. "Yes," I said. The best I could do was to mumble, my hands over my mouth.

For once everybody caught on quickly. One of my captors pulled my hands behind my back.

Grimbold said, "Tell me true. Do you be knowing the whereabouts of my crown?"

"No," I told him.

Obviously, he would be worried that the ring only worked once. "Stand on one leg," he commanded.

I balanced on one leg.

"Sing a song," he commanded.

Maybe it was because I was standing on one leg ready to tip over, but the first song that came to me was "I'm a Little Teapot."

Those who understood Shelban gleefully translated the stupid little ditty for those who didn't.

With great hilarity, the barbarian horde shouted out suggestions to Grimbold, just in case he couldn't think of enough humiliating things to have me do. Dance, spin, spit—they loved that I couldn't stop any act unless specifically ordered to stop, even if I was simultaneously feeling compelled to complete another action. You try spinning, singing, and spitting at the same time—all balanced on one leg.

Luckily, though Rasmussem has nothing against killing off a paying customer, they won't allow sexual harassment, so that was one thing I didn't need to worry about.

"Pretend you be a chicken," Grimbold said.

My singing changed to clucking, and I couldn't help myself—I began flapping my arms.

Barbarian humor.

I was saved from new indignities when the messenger they'd sent to the castle returned. He spoke in his native language, which I didn't have to understand—I could tell by everyone's sour expressions that Grimbold's offer had been refused.

Now what? Would they kill me?

Maybe, maybe not—Grimbold obviously needed time to consider.

"Go back to the tree," he ordered.

Of course, as soon as I tried walking using only one leg, I immediately tipped over.

"You may be walking on both feetses," Grimbold told me.

I walked back to the tree, still clucking, scratching at the ground with my toes.

Even so, Grimbold didn't trust me and had me once again shackled.

Enough with the chicken routine, I thought at him, but apparently he figured his camp needed the entertainment. I suppose I was lucky he rescinded the commands to sing and spit.

If time had passed slowly for me as a prisoner, it passed even more slowly for me as a chicken. The sun set, the smells of cooking carried to me, and still I couldn't stop clucking and scratching at the earth. Thank goodness I found no worms. I *did* try to lay an egg, though.

After those in the camp had eaten, and after it got dark, they finally became bored with me. They returned to their campfires and tents, leaving me with only one guard. I tucked my head under one arm and tried to sleep.

I was awakened when Grimbold himself came to take

the guard's place. "What will I be doing with you?" he asked. He leaned against the tree all the guards seemed to favor, which was out of my range in case I decided to try to peck him to death. "You truly be a useless thing—useless to me, useless to your own peoples. Maybe I be selling you into slavery to one of the nomad tribes. Or maybe I be selling you to the orcs, which have a tasting for human flesh."

I sure hoped the Rasmussem program would send me back to the start of the game before anyone began roasting me on a spit. I tried to tell him that I was sure I could be useful: I was willing to side with him and turn on my royal family. My pleading came out as frantic clucking.

Grimbold started laughing. "I wonder," he said, "when the orcs be cooking you, if you be tasting like human or like chicken."

He was still having a good time with that thought when he gave an odd sound, something like choking but more bubbly. He pitched forward onto the ground, a dark stain spreading beneath him.

A man stepped out from behind the tree—a man I recognized as one of those to whom I'd been talking in the castle guardroom. He was holding a knife in his hand, and I realized he'd just cut Grimbold's throat. It would have been a nice rescue, except for the fact that—with the death of the person whose orders I was compelled to obey—I was destined to spend the rest of this lifetime as a chicken.

"Don't worry, Princess Janine," my rescuer whispered so as not to alert any of the barbarians. "The royal family was willing to leave you here, but we were not."

"Cluck, cluck, cluck," I said: *You stupid idiot, you have lousy timing.*

The man looked startled but nonetheless used his sword to try to pry open a link of my chain. "There are others of us in the woods," he assured me, "so don't worry about the barbarians pursuing."

It wasn't my chief worry.

"Cluck, cluck, cluck," I said: *Look over here, you nitwit,* and I pecked at the dead Grimbold's belt, where the key to my shackle was.

The guard was leaning over Grimbold when a darkness detached itself from the shadows and launched itself at him.

"Cwak!" I squawked: *Wolf!* But the man didn't turn in time, and in an instant my would-be rescuer was dead.

I kept on squawking and flapping my arms, but nobody came; apparently the barbarians had had enough chicken antics for the day.

So it isn't to be orcs eating me after all, I thought as the wolf rounded on me.

But then the wolf did a strange thing; it grew longer, and taller, and less hairy. Then it stood on two legs.

In fact, it turned into Wulfgar, clothes and all.

Wulfgar wasn't raised at the castle, people had kept telling me. No kidding. It was the old cliché, only literally true: He'd been raised by wolves.

But so what if he was a shape-shifting wolf? I was willing not to hold that against him if he'd come to rescue me from becoming orc soup du jour.

But I didn't like the look in his eyes as he picked up

the dead guard's knife and approached me. "Poor Princess Janine," he said with a feral grin. "A shame her gallant band of rescuers didn't arrive in time to keep the barbarians from slitting her throat."

I felt the fizziness start even before the knife touched my skin.

SUBJ: URGENT--Parts
DATE: 5/25   03:58:46 P.M. US eastern
        daylight time
FROM: Nigel Rasmussem
        <nrasmussem@rasmussem.com>
TO: dept. heads distribution list

The suggestion from London looked
good, but the parts are not available
locally and need to be obtained from
Pittsburgh. We have chartered a flight,
but it is very doubtful this will
arrive in time.

We are helpless and dependent on
the gamer herself, which is not a
comfortable position to be in.

There must be something we can do. Keep
thinking. Situation critical.

CHAPTER FIFTEEN

Bright Sword, Dim Brother

Well, I thought as I pulled myself out from under Dusty on the hill that overlooked St. Jehan, *how many more stupid mistakes can I make before my time runs out? I guess that explains what killed me that time in the topiary maze.* People had said the queen was there with Wulfgar, but when I'd seen Kenric, I'd assumed they had gotten the wrong son. Right son, just not human at the moment, thank you very much.

What was going on at the Rasmussem Gaming Center? Were they making any headway in overriding the damaged systems so that they could pull me out? Nigel Rasmussem hadn't sounded as though he thought that was likely. I figured if there had been any real possibility of help from their end, Mr. Rasmussem would have played that up to keep me from panicking.

My optimism didn't improve when I found myself once more standing in front of the statue of Saint Bruce the Warrior Poet, realizing I couldn't remember the poem I'd made up for him.

"An Ode to Saint Bruce," I said, which was *all* that I remembered.

Feordina yawned, loudly, while she waited for me to start.

You'd think someone who's created a poem would be able to remember it.

You'd think.

I recited, "Saint Bruce was a warrior poet..."

That wasn't right.

Too late, I remembered that my former first line had ended with *Bruce,* which rhymed nicely with *loose, juice, puce*—all sorts of possibilities. What did *poet* rhyme with?

"He lived in a cave, don't you know it?"

Was that a little whimper I heard from Feordina?

"He wrote sonnets and verses..."

Hmmm.

"...but never said curses..."

As the moment stretched on and on, I saw Feordina avert her gaze from the sword that hung over me. She began to edge her way toward the cave entrance. No doubt red blood makes a mess of green clothing.

Anything is better than nothing. All in a rush, as though that would·prevent Saint Bruce from hearing the way-too-many beats in the line, I finished, "He'll give you one chance—please don't blow it."

I was aware of Feordina hurling herself to the floor, out of the way of both sword and blood splatter.

I was sure the sword wavered in Bruce's hand.

But it didn't come down.

Sounding astonished, Feordina said, "He must be in a good mood. Lucky you; he's accepted your poem."

Saint Bruce, I decided, might have been a mighty warrior, but he couldn't have been much of a poet.

So once again Sir Deming and I were off to the castle, with the ring once more tied to my bodice laces. As we rode I tried to decide what I should do once we got there. *Wulfgar:* Obviously I shouldn't trust a man who had wolf instincts and who had already killed me twice. Who knew what might make him lose his temper with me and cause him to bite off my head—literally? Queen Andreanna kept rebuffing all my attempts to be nice to her, so that left Kenric and Abas. I had chosen Kenric once before, and Mr. Rasmussem had warned me away. "Kenric and Sister Mary Ursula don't work well together," he'd said. That was fine with me; Sister Mary Ursula and *I* didn't work well together. I'd been planning on asking Rawdon to be my counselor, anyway.

Except...

Except, Mr. Rasmussem had given me that warning before I ever met Sister Mary Ursula. Did that mean I was *supposed* to work with her?

But she doesn't like magic, I reminded myself.

Maybe I was supposed to ask her to be my adviser, and then I wasn't supposed to follow her advice.

Mr. Rasmussem could have saved us both a lot of aggravation by talking faster and more clearly, I thought. "Talk to your father before you leave St. Jehan," he could have said. "Choose Abas and Sister Mary Ursula, and..."

And whatever.

However many more chances I had left, I suspected I was going to need every one of them.

In the Great Hall, I called, "Abas!" as Queen Andreanna—yet again—started to walk out in a huff after our family reunion.

"What?" the middle-brother prince demanded, sounding like a petulant second grader, for all that he looked like the "after" picture in an advertisement for expensive home-exercise equipment.

"Nice sword work," I said, "back there while you were menacing me."

"Oh." He sounded both surprised and pleased. *Pleased* won out. "I *am* quite good," he admitted.

His mother didn't wait for him, and his brothers were definitely trying to make it out of the room before bursting into laughter.

Abas whipped his sword out of its sheath and moved its edge to within an inch of my nose.

Now what?

But he didn't slit my throat or give me instant rhinoplasty; he said, "Toledo steel."

And because he sounded proud and cheery, I gathered this was a good thing, and said, "How nice."

He began talking about the wonderfulness of Spanish-crafted swords, and gave me the entire history of the manufacture of blades, making my eyelids grow heavy with terms and phrases like "heat tempered" and "alloy" and "strong but not brittle."

All the while, I kept him moving toward the courtyard, wondering if I'd make it in time to rescue the poacher from the guards, or if I'd collapse in a bored stupor first.

The poacher and I lucked out.

"Prince Abas," the guard I now knew was named Penrod called out, "and, uh, Princess Justine..."

"Janine," I told him.

Captain Penrod shrugged and told Abas, "We caught this boy poaching. He killed a deer. The usual punishment?"

I waited to hear Abas's reaction, just as—that first time—Kenric had waited to hear mine.

"Certainly," Abas said. Then, as the boy was just starting to explain how he'd found the deer dead, Abas eagerly offered, "Shall I?" Once more he brought his sword forth with that metal-on-metal whisper-hiss that gives goose bumps to any sensible person.

"No," I told Abas.

I motioned for the second guard, who'd forced the boy to his knees, to let him up again.

Abas frowned in concentration. "'No'?" he repeated, as though unfamiliar with the word.

"My new reign is starting," I announced to one and all. "This is a time to review the old laws and to reconsider the old punishments."

Abas pouted. "No more beheadings?"

I didn't want to turn him against me, since this was obviously a tradition he cherished. "Not for now, anyway. My first days should be a time of clemency, of people starting anew, with nothing from the past held against them. This might be a way to settle the peasant unrest."

"'Clemency'?" Abas repeated, obviously downhearted. "You mean, no more public hangings?"

"Princess—" Penrod said.

"No," I told Abas.

"Princess," Penrod repeated, "a friendly warning here: The peasants need a firm hand or they will run wild and take advantage."

"'Hand,'" Abas echoed. "Can I at least chop off his hand?"

"No," I told him. To Penrod, I said, "I understand what you're saying. But we will try it this way. If that doesn't work, we can always return to the more severe punishments later."

Reluctantly, Penrod released the boy.

Even as the boy ran away, Abas was asking, "But we can still use the rack and thumbscrews?"

"No," I said.

"*Later* might be too late," Penrod warned.

"That's why I need you to keep an eye on things. For instance"—I was remembering how Grimbold and his barbarians had swarmed into the castle courtyard—"please post more guards on the walls to make sure intruders can't get in."

"Hot coals?" Abas asked.

"*No.*" I turned back to Penrod. "It's not just the peasants I want to make happy. More important is keeping the goodwill of you and your men." I didn't add, *So you don't come up behind me and knife me.* "We will have regularly scheduled meetings where you will be free to give me your opinions. All the men." I smiled at the other guard to show I included him, not just the officers. "How *are* things in my army?" I asked.

"Well..." The guard shuffled his feet.

"Do you get paid enough?"

The two exchanged a does-she-really-want-to-know? look.

In the silence, Abas asked, "Fingernail extractor?"

"No."

The two guards told how Counselor Rawdon, who was in charge of giving them their pay, had lately shorted them.

"I will look into that," I promised. "Meanwhile, please see to it that the castle defenses are fortified immediately."

Both men saluted smartly before leaving.

They might still think me weak, but I doubted they'd kill me while I was promising them money.

Abas poked my arm to get my attention. "Stocks?" he asked. "Dunking in the millpond?"

I was tempted to say, "Only for you," but luckily I didn't have time. I had spotted Sister Mary Ursula, who was standing by the well and had evidently heard much of our conversation.

"Blessed is the way of the One," she said.

Abas gave a groan of dismay. "Oh, not her!"

That was a surprise. So apparently *nobody* got along well with her. Well, come to think of it, that wasn't surprising at all. But it made me wonder what, exactly, Mr. Rasmussem was warning me against when he said that she didn't work well with Kenric.

I figured I needed to be polite but firm. "Hello," I said. "I wish I had more time to talk to you, but I don't."

Sister Mary Ursula couldn't be put off *that* easily. "I guessed you might be One," she said.

"One," I said vaguely, "two..." I was going to say, "What's the difference?" But the pairing of *one* and *two* like that brought to mind something else. "One, two, buckle my shoe," I told her. She wasn't the only one who could be obscure.

"Hmmm," she said. "I surmised you were truly One with the world by how you treated that boy. You recognized his Oneness. Many would not have." She glanced at Abas.

Abas scratched his head and yawned.

"I *did* recognize his Oneness," I said, "and, you know, I'd like to talk to you about your becoming my adviser"—could she *really* be the one the Rasmussem program wanted me to favor?—"but I also need to talk to Sir Deming and Counselor Rawdon. I'd like to meet with the three of you together."

"Rawdon," she said, shaking her head.

Because she looked skeptical, I added, "Four of us—*one* meeting."

"One," she echoed, smiling.

"I'm on my way to see Counselor Rawdon right now." Friendly as the guards seemed at my promise to investigate their salary dispute, the way to really get on their good side was to actually hand over the money due them. I suspected that then they'd be willing to forgive me a lot. So, Rawdon first. I asked Sister Mary Ursula, "Could you please find Sir Deming and invite him to the Great Hall?"

"I am One with your wishes," Sister Mary Ursula said. She bowed, at the same time pinching the bridge of her nose with her thumb and forefinger and making a nasal humming noise.

I didn't know if she expected me to do likewise, but I only said, "Thank you."

Though Abas was looking bored, I wanted to keep him near me in case those barbarians made it past Captain Penrod's increased castle defenses. "So," I said, "Toledo-made swords are the best. But, it takes a master swordsman to use one well..."

Abas flexed his biceps.

"Amazing," I told him. "Tell me about yourself as we walk to Rawdon's quarters, all right?"

Abas didn't need to be asked twice.

Luckily, I found that all I needed to contribute to the conversation was a rapt expression and an occasional "Impressive!" or "My! That's interesting." I didn't have to really listen to a word of his explanations about his workout schedule or his past triumphs.

When we got to Rawdon's room, he wasn't there.

"Excuse me." I interrupted Abas in the middle of recounting how he'd saved the king of a neighboring land, who'd been gored by a charging wild boar. Abas had broken off the beast's tusks with his bare hands, then strangled it—which sounded pretty gross to me.

A servant woman was on her knees in the hall, scrubbing the floor. I asked her, "Have you seen Counselor Rawdon?"

"No, my lady. Sorry."

Abas didn't need me to invite him to resume his story—frothy sweat on the animal's hide, and hot stinking breath, and all.

The servant looked as though she wasn't quite finished with what she'd been saying, so I put my hand on Abas's arm to get him to stop.

He didn't take the hint, and I had to say, "Excuse me," again.

The woman told me, "He was in his room earlier, Princess. But he's not there now. I know because I'd just washed the floor in front of his door; and when he left, I had to clean that part again because he left footprints in the wetness; but luckily, he came this way, and I didn't have to redo the whole hall."

She was only two doors down from Rawdon's room, which couldn't have taken her more than five minutes.

Abas started talking again as we walked to the end of the hall. There I saw steps leading both up and down.

"What's upstairs?" I interrupted Abas.

"Defense battlements. Servants' quarters," by which I took him to mean *minor servants* since Rawdon's room was on the second level, along with the family's apartments. Abas didn't miss a beat and resumed talking about the boar.

I led the way back downstairs and flagged down a servant woman who was going from room to room providing fresh flowers for the vases. She said she had not seen Rawdon.

I poked my head into the Great Hall. Sir Deming was sitting on one of the petitioners' benches that lined the walls. He was definitely drooping, his elbows on his knees, his head resting in his hands while Sister Mary Ursula, sitting next to him, told him, "...and if you acknowledge the cow's Oneness with you, and then ask her politely, she *will* give forth sweeter milk. It's the same with turnips—"

"*There* you are," Deming said, sounding—for this once—happy to see me.

"Sorry," I said. "Not quite ready yet. We haven't been able to find Rawdon."

"I'd be glad to help you look," Deming volunteered. "Maybe Abas..." He glanced from the still-chattering prince to the still-chattering nun, obviously thinking to pair them off.

"Sorry." I backed out, closing the doors. In case of barbarian attack, Abas would be a good man to have by my side. If he *noticed* we were under attack, that is. I couldn't be sure he'd stop bragging about his physical prowess long enough to notice much of anything.

A door opened and a pair of male servants came out, carrying a platter with an entire roast pig, complete with apple. It must be time for the midday meal that I had missed the last time I was here. I realized that the hunger I'd felt in the barbarians' camp had evaporated once the game restarted and set me back down in the morning. But now, as this new day progressed, my stomach was once again rumbling—not that I found a dead porker with fruit in its mouth appetizing.

"Excuse me," I said to the men, "but have either of you seen Rawdon?"

"Not since he stopped by the kitchen asking for field rations," one said.

"'Field rations?'" I repeated. "You mean, like, to take when you're going on a trip?"

The man nodded.

That was odd. Sister Mary Ursula hadn't insulted him in this round of the game, so he had no reason to leave. "Did he say where he was going?"

Both men shook their heads.

I moved out of their way and told Abas, "Let's check with the captain of the guard to see if Rawdon has left yet."

Still talking, Abas followed me outside. While I hadn't been paying attention, he'd shifted to tournaments he had fought in, and the proper technique for splitting a lance, which, apparently, was a desirable thing.

I glanced at the wagon that was still parked by the supply door, even though I assumed the increased guards I'd ordered had prevented any barbarians from sneaking in. I was just turning my eyes away, when I noticed a shadow that moved beneath the wagon.

"Abas, look out!" I shouted. "Behind the wagon!"

There was the hiss of an arrow.

But no *thunk!* of impact.

Abas had caught the arrow midflight.

So maybe there was something to be said for brawn, even unaccompanied by brain.

With a bellow, Abas went tearing behind the wagon before the archer had a chance to notch another arrow.

Hiding didn't seem a kingly thing to do; I might survive the attack, but such obvious cowardice wouldn't win any loyalty from my people. So, fighting my instincts, I ran toward the wagon also, yelling all the while, "Intruder alert! Intruder alert!" which sounded more science fiction than fantasy, but there was no time to worry about vocabulary, and I needed more guards immediately, because I knew from last time that there were three barbarians in the courtyard—and three against one wasn't fair odds, even if the one was used to fighting off wild boar with his bare hands.

On the far side of the wagon, I saw Abas was doing quite well without me. Since he didn't have a bow, he'd simply used his caught arrow as a dagger; it was sticking out of the chest of one of the barbarians, now dead. Abas had kicked the other archer in the face, and while that man rolled on the ground, Abas was engaged in a sword fight with the third man—the man I recognized as King Grimbold.

"Wait—" I started to tell Abas, but in that moment, his sword swept off Grimbold's head.

Was that an *oops!* or not?

Abas turned to the surviving, though injured, man.

"Abas," I said, "put your sword away. He's obviously not going anywhere. I need to ask him a couple questions."

Grumpily, Abas put his sword back in its scabbard.

I was aware of members of the castle guard on the wall, firing arrows over the side into the surrounding woods.

"Four down," Penrod reported to me. "The rest have

escaped into the forest. Do you want us to pursue them, or concentrate on our defenses here?"

Just what I needed—another decision. I didn't yet know if we needed to attack the barbarian camp, but in any case I didn't want to send the majority of my men chasing after a small raiding party, leaving us defenseless; nor did I want a small party of my men stumbling into the barbarian encampment.

"Send two dozen men after them—with clear instructions not to pursue farther than..."—I had to estimate what was a good distance—"...five miles. If they haven't caught the barbarians by then, have them come back."

While Penrod selected which men of the group should go, I turned my attention to the wounded barbarian. He was sitting up now, his back supported by the castle wall, his hands over his bruised and bleeding mouth. No doubt he was missing several teeth from Abas's kick. His voice was slurred because of his injuries, which didn't help his accent. "You be done killing our king," he moaned. "You be done killing King Grimbold."

I knew that already, but everybody else turned to look at the headless corpse.

"You're one of the northern barbarians, aren't you?" I asked.

The man nodded.

"That's one," Abas said.

Of course there was only one barbarian left; we could all see that. Or was Sister Mary Ursula beginning to wear off on him? Ignoring Abas's irrelevant remark, I asked the barbarian, "Why did you come?"

134

"To be kidnapping you, as the new king," he said. "To be forcing you to be handing on the crown of King Brecc the Slayer."

Of course, I knew all this from last time. But I had to ask or I wouldn't be able to explain to anybody *how* I knew. Before I could ask about the location of his camp and the number of people in it—which was what I really wanted to know—Abas announced, "And that's two."

"What—" I started to ask Abas, when he picked up the wagon and brought the back end down on the barbarian's head, like smushing a bug.

For a few seconds, I couldn't even get my mouth to work.

"What?" Abas demanded, seeing my amazed, angry face. "You said not to use my sword."

"I said I wanted to question him."

"You said you wanted to ask him 'a couple of questions.' A *couple* is two." He shook his head as though unused to dealing with such stupidity. "Everybody knows that," he said. "A couple. Two. Same thing. Didn't your foster parents teach you how to count?"

While I was left speechless, he scratched his belly and said, "That roast pig sure looked good to me. Anybody else ready to eat?"

And with that he went back into the castle, the guards following.

CHAPTER SIXTEEN

Lunch

In a moment only Captain Penrod and I remained.

Penrod knelt in the dust at my feet. He took out his sword and handed it up to me on outstretched palms. "Obviously, I didn't post enough guards, Princess Janine. You could have been killed, and it would have been my fault."

Was he officially resigning his post, or did he expect me to punish him by chopping off his head?

I told him, "Take the sword back. We"—I was getting better at remembering that royal *we*—"simply need to be more vigilant from now on. Come on, apparently it's time to eat." I wasn't going to miss lunch again.

Penrod *did* accept the sword back, then started with me toward the Great Hall.

"Speaking of being vigilant," I said, "did your guards see Counselor Rawdon leave?"

Penrod nodded. "He frequently goes to visit his aged mother in the country."

"Very commendable," I said. "But you'd think he could skip it on the day the new king arrives."

"I gather he's her sole support," Penrod said, "and she's the sole support of several grandchildren from Rawdon's two brothers and three sisters, who all died. He brings great bundles of food for them, but seemingly it's never enough. This morning his packhorse was exceptionally laden."

"Sounds like the family has had incredibly bad luck," I said. I got distracted by the thought that I knew all about grandmothers raising kids, but at least my parents were still both alive. "Any idea when he'll be back?"

"He's said she lives in the town of Fairfield, which is two hours' ride off to the west. Usually when he goes, he spends the majority of the day with her."

We arrived at the Hall, where lunch had already started. The two thrones had been pushed against the farthest wall, right to the leaded-glass window. Dozens of long tables had been brought in, at which people sat, evidently divided by rank. The royal family was at one table at the far end of the room, near the thrones, away from the drafts from the doors and from the bustle of servants toting platters of food and refilling people's cups. I couldn't help but notice that they'd started without me and that they'd left no room for me.

Sir Deming and Sister Mary Ursula sat with a group that had to be the queen's ladies-in-waiting, for I recognized Lady Cynthia from a couple games back. Sister Mary Ursula was still talking to Deming, even though he'd arranged to sit two people down from her. Those servants who weren't serving the food were at one cluster of tables, and then there were lots of other tables for the guards, although there were many empty places for those who were away, busy manning the walls or pursuing barbarians. Dogs roamed among the tables, snapping up fallen scraps of food (which would have outraged my grandmother, who believes dogs belong outside, guarding the house or helping the blind).

Penrod hesitated, not knowing whether I was finished with him and if he should go sit with his men.

I couldn't start making decisions if the adviser I was most inclined to speak with wasn't here. I asked Penrod, "Do you think we could send one of your men to fetch Rawdon?"

Penrod immediately tapped one of his men on the shoulder. "Go to Fairfield," he ordered. "The princess commands Rawdon's presence."

The guard stood, shoving a half loaf of bread under his arm and as much food as he could fit into his mouth. I told him, "Be sure to tell Counselor Rawdon he'll be welcome to return to his family in a few more days." Rawdon would be of little use to me if he was ticked off at having his family outing cut short. "Be polite," I called after the man, then remembered to add, "please."

It suddenly occurred to me that for this particular game, the magic-users had not been summoned. "And Captain," I said to Penrod, "please send a message to ..." Was it Xenos or Uldemar who had the scrying glass? "I'd like to call to the castle those who know magic."

"Orielle, Uldemar, and Xenos," Penrod said. He smacked another of his men on the arm.

"Thank you," I said. "In all haste, please."

Finally I went to the head table.

They were all sitting on benches along one side of the table: Queen Andreanna, Wulfgar, Abas, and Kenric. The queen was making fun of someone I didn't know, an abbot who apparently was very hard of hearing—in fact, practically deaf. Andreanna was imitating this poor guy, saying, "'What did you say? *What?* Oh, you said you couldn't have been the one to murder the blacksmith because you had *no reason* to do it? I thought you said you had *a Norwegian* do it.'"

Very politically incorrect.

The princes were all so engrossed in this merriment that by sheerest coincidence not a one of them noticed me standing there with no place to sit.

They were spread out—four on a bench that looked long enough for six or seven. Their butts weren't *that* big. If they'd all moved over just a bit, there'd have been room for me.

The Hall still buzzed with conversation, but I knew everyone was waiting to see how I would react. Would I be intimidated and slink off to another table? Would I meekly request my family to make space for me? Would I make a scene and *demand* that they make space for me?

I crooked my finger at one of the servants. The noise level was so high, I had to put my mouth to his ear to make sure I was heard. "Get me the king's throne," I ordered.

The servant was aghast. "Surely not for eating in?" Was he worried I'd dribble gravy on the velvet cushion?

He glanced around and pointed out a spare bench, a short one, made for three skinny butts, or two regular-size ones, or one royal one.

Yeah, I thought, *and do what? Set up a TV tray?* "The throne," I repeated.

The conversation abruptly stopped when the servant, with the help of another man, picked up the throne.

Staggering under its weight, they carried it toward where the royal family sat, then saw that—unless the royals moved their bench (and why would they, when they hadn't budged yet?)—there was no room.

I pointed to my feet, to indicate, *Right here.*

The servants came around to where I was, and placed the throne dead center on that side of the table.

I sat down and looked into the startled faces of my family. "There." I smiled brightly and settled my skirt as though it was a voluminous gown, like the queen's. "Isn't this nice?"

And it was, except that the roast pig had been placed before them, so I was looking at his curlicued rear end, not the world's best view.

A servant came rushing up with a bowl of rose-petaled water and a towel, to wash and dry my hands. Other servants provided a dish heaped with slabs of roast pork and luscious fresh fruits, and a cup of mead (which is a sweet beer or wine or something, disgusting in my point of view, and I'm amazed Rasmussem gets away with serving alcohol—even virtual alcohol—to minors).

Kenric leaned forward and told me, "You're sitting on the serving side of the table."

"No," I said firmly, "all of you are."

He considered that for a moment, then gave his extraordinary smile that had caught my notice during the promos.

Wulfgar glared; I was beneath the queen's notice, so she angled herself on the bench to face Wulfgar and began talking to him about the quality of the peaches; and Abas decided I needed an instant replay of his battle against the three barbarians in the courtyard.

I was pleased to note that Wulfgar didn't tear into his meat as a beast would but ate with the same degree of table manners as everybody else. *Those* manners were about equal to what you'd see in an elementary school cafeteria. I could live with that.

"You *were* fantastic," I assured Abas when he paused to take a breath. "One of them mentioned something about a crown—the crown of Brecc." I looked at each of them in turn and was able to tell nothing. "Any of you know anything about that?"

Kenric said, "Father won a crown from one of the barbarian kings."

"Won how? You mean he killed him? Or overcame him in battle? Or he won it in a poker game?" My subconscious tried to warn me the people of this time would not play poker; the phrase *a game of dice* bubbled up.

But the Rasmussem programs are sophisticated enough to ignore most anachronistic phrases and references, otherwise the game would constantly be delayed by the characters saying things like, "*OK?* I do not understand this *OK* of which you speak." Kenric blinked.

Perhaps *his* subconscious—if he had one—told him poker must be some peasant gambling game he'd never heard of before. Or perhaps he just chose to ignore one of the many inane things I'd said. He said, "He won it in a tournament."

Abas interrupted. "I wasn't old enough to participate in that particular tournament except in the capacity of a page helping the squires help the knights get into their armor, but I remember it well. Two years later was my first—"

"In a moment, Abas," I said. "So your father won the tournament, winning the loser's horse and equipment."

"Yes," both Abas and Kenric said. But Abas was inclined to add a blow-by-blow account of the event.

I went ahead and talked right over him. "But if your father won the crown fairly, why do the barbarians feel they have a right to demand it back?"

"Because they *are* barbarians," Abas said.

Which I would have accepted, but Kenric's lips twitched and he chose that moment to lift his cup to his mouth.

"What?" I demanded.

Kenric answered with a question of his own. "Who said anything about winning it fairly?"

"Kenric!" his mother snapped. "That's no way to talk about your father."

From the look he gave her, I gathered he wasn't used to hearing her defend King Cynric's good name.

"Well," Abas admitted, "there *were* certain questions..."

"He cheated," I said. "You're saying he won the

142

crown by cheating. So now the barbarians want the crown back and—in fact—they probably have every right to it."

Kenric shrugged, indicating his indifference to moral nuances.

Abas spoke slowly so I would understand. "No, he won the event, so he won the crown."

Wulfgar was gnawing, with alarming energy, every last bit of meat off a bone, but at least he had the bone raised to his mouth, rather than sinking his face into the pig carcass.

Queen Andreanna was making one of the dogs stand on its hind legs and beg for a strip of meat.

"So where is this crown?" I asked.

"I don't know," Kenric said.

Abas shook his head to indicate he didn't, either.

"Wulfgar?"

"Dunno."

"Your Highness?"

She gave me a blank look. "I'm sorry, what? Were you saying something? I wasn't listening."

Though I'd already seen she had been, I explained, "The crown your late husband won from the barbarian king at the tournament several years back, whatever happened to it?"

"I'm sure I have no idea," she told me.

I summoned one of the servants. "Could you please get that bench"—I indicated the one I had been offered earlier—"and bring it here, then invite Sir Deming and Sister Mary Ursula to join us."

"On the serving side of the table?" the servant asked.

"On *this* side of the table," I corrected him.

When the two advisers had sat down, I explained about the crown and asked if they knew where it was.

"Perhaps in the king's treasure room?" Sister Mary Ursula suggested.

Deming shook his head. "He gave it to the dragon."

"What dragon?" I asked.

Deming sniffed at my ignorance. "The one that was ravaging the southern provinces eight years ago, burning fields, scattering livestock, devastating manor houses, demanding maiden sacrifices."

The faintest hint of imposed memory tickled at the edges of my brain. I'd only been six, and the southern provinces were nearly a week's journey from the safety of St. Jehan, but I had heard people talking.

I said, "Excuse me, I don't understand. This dragon was eating cows, horses, and maidens, and then King Cynric bought him off by giving him a crown that had been won at an iffy tournament?"

Deming rolled his eyes, and the queen gave him a sympathetic look like, *I know, I know.* Deming said, "Dragons like gold."

"And a crown," Sister Mary Ursula added, "that would make the dragon feel as One with all the other kings."

OK. I guessed it made sense. "Do we know where this dragon lives?" I asked.

"No," "Nope," "Haven't a clue," they all told me.

"Any idea how we can find out?"

"No," "Nope," "Haven't a clue," they all repeated.

But then Deming speculated, "Maybe one of the magic-users knows something or could find out."

Waiting for the magic-users again. Estimated time of arrival: tomorrow, if I remembered correctly from last time. And I did. I was working on a deadline—never mind the awful pun.

"Oooo, magic," Sister Mary Ursula said. "Nasty stuff. Best to keep away from it."

"As much as possible," I assured her, just to keep her happy.

Deming sighed. "If," he said, sounding as though each moment of speaking politely was an effort, "*if* you're determined to return the crown of the barbarian king, may I point out to you that the king is, in fact, currently separated from his head, thanks to our prince Abas—and I would consider this a serious drawback to the enjoyment of wearing a crown."

"Good point," I said. "We'll send a messenger to the barbarian camp, apologizing for the unfortunate death of their king, which happened by mischance since he did not openly declare himself but led a raiding party into the castle courtyard. As a sign of our goodwill, we will forgive this raid and return the crown to King Grimbold's successor."

Deming pursed his thin lips. "Do you think they'd accept *an apology* for the killing of their brand-new king?"

Andreanna was looking directly at me as she answered, "*I* would. Accidents happen."

I could imagine. I forced a smile at her. To Deming, I said, "It's the best we can do. See to the sending of a messenger. Now, what about the unrest among the peasants?"

"Our laws are too harsh," Sister Mary Ursula said.

"Too lenient," Deming countered.

"I liked the death penalty," Abas said, "before you abolished it. Can we bring it back now?"

We never really came to a conclusion. I felt I didn't know enough to ask the right questions, and nobody volunteered much of interest.

The servants were cleaning up the remains of the meal, and we were the only ones still sitting. The guards I'd sent in pursuit of the barbarian raiding party returned, having lost the trail in the woods. Another set of guards were sent to find the barbarian camp to offer official regrets for Grimbold's death. Meanwhile, I needed to wait for Rawdon's return to make a decision about the peasants, and I needed to wait for the magic-users to do anything about tracking down the dragon who had Brecc the Slayer's crown.

"Well," I said, looking at my filthy sheepherder's dress, "maybe now is the time for me to clean up."

"Oooo," Sister Mary Ursula said, "I have an extra dress you could use."

Since she looked as though she wore Feordina the Knitter's hand-me-downs, I said, "Maybe something from one of the ladies-in-waiting would be more appropriate."

"I can arrange that," she told me.

She showed me to one of the second-floor rooms, but it wasn't Lady Cynthia's. This lady's name was Bliss. One glance told me that if Bliss shopped at the mall, she would need clothes whose size included at least a couple of Xs.

"Oh, this is such an honor!" Bliss giggled, so pleased, her feet practically fluttered off the ground. "Thank you, thank you, thank you for choosing me."

"Well . . ." I started.

"I have *so many* clothes," she told me, "because"—she leaned forward to whisper as though we shared a secret—"I do have a bit of a weight problem."

OK, I thought. *This might work.*

But as she flung dresses out of her clothes chest onto her bed, I saw that her size varied from big to very big.

"Isn't this a pretty red?" she asked.

"It is," I agreed. I couldn't ask for Lady Cynthia by name because I had never been introduced to her in this lifetime. And I hated to ask for just any other lady, because Bliss was *so* enthusiastic.

Did Rasmussem want me to be nice to her and make her my friend for a particular reason? Or were they only intent on making me look like a fool?

Still, I couldn't look any worse than I did now.

So I chose the red velvet dress, and—after I finally got my bath, and with a lot of tucks and gathers and a belt—eventually got the dress around me. I had just fastened the magic ring around my neck with a length of ribbon when someone knocked at Lady Bliss's door.

"Captain of the guard," Penrod announced from the hallway, "looking for Princess Janine."

Bliss opened the door for him. "And doesn't she look exquisite?" she asked.

I think *clean* was really the best we could say in all honesty, but Penrod didn't have time to quibble. "Bad news, Highness," he announced.

"Regarding the messengers dispatched to try to make peace with the barbarian camp?" I asked, though it seemed too soon for them to have had any result yet.

Penrod shook his head. "Regarding Counselor Rawdon."

Now what?

"The man I sent to Fairfield just returned. He said there is no one in Fairfield answering the description of Penrod's mother."

"But you're sure it was Fairfield that Rawdon said he was going to?" I asked.

"Positive," Penrod said.

I tried to work this out. "Rawdon said Fairfield, and he carried bundles of food for his family . . ." It suddenly struck me that when I'd asked the servants carrying the pig if they'd seen Rawdon, one of them had said something about Rawdon getting field rations for his trip.

Surely field rations weren't carried in great bundles?

"How long has Rawdon been bringing supplies to his mother?" I asked.

"About three months."

"And how long has it been since you've been having trouble getting paid?"

Slowly, Penrod said, "About three months."

I was beginning to get a sick feeling in the pit of my stomach. "Did I hear somebody say something about the king having a treasure room?" I asked.

Penrod took me there, a locked chamber off the king's own bedroom. Guards had to kick in the door because Rawdon had the key. It was an enormous room, bigger even than the king's bedchamber.

And, of course, the room was totally empty.

CHAPTER SEVENTEEN

Treasure Hunt

The next door we broke down was the one to Rawdon's room. I hoped to find some nice clues indicating where he'd be likely to head now that he'd made off with all the loot from my treasury. But we found nothing—no handy map where X marked the spot, no travel brochures from sunny Aruba, no abandoned diary with the crucial page ripped out (but that a clever detective could read by studying the impressions on the page beneath). Rawdon had left behind the rugs on the floors, the tapestries on the walls, and all the furniture; but his clothes were gone and there were no personal items or papers—nothing to show this wasn't simply a spare guest room.

"Any thoughts?" I asked Penrod.

He gestured his men out of the room, then closed the door for privacy. In a low voice he told me, "The news is spreading already—there's no way to contain it."

It took a moment for his meaning to sink in. The guards had not been properly paid for the last couple months, and even now those who knew about the theft were telling the others that the new king had no money left with which to pay them.

"What are the men likely to do?"

"Leave," Penrod said, "most of them. They'll try to find employment elsewhere."

Sure, there was that nice barbarian camp in the vicinity that could probably use some new recruits, being down a few men since morning.

And even if my guards didn't join the barbarians, how long could the castle stand without anyone to defend it?

"I'll stay," Penrod assured me, "of course." It was nice to have him feeling indebted to me. He continued, "I'll try to convince the men to give you a day or two. I'll tell them you're tracking Rawdon down, that it's just a matter of time before you recover the treasury."

"You need to practice saying it with a straight face, or no one will believe you," I warned him. "Where do you think I should start looking?"

Of course it wasn't that easy.

"I don't know, Princess."

Obviously that was part of the fun of the game, figuring that out.

"Maybe I should start in Fairfield," I said. "You said Rawdon always headed off in that direction. Just because the people there never heard of Rawdon's mother, that doesn't mean they didn't see *him*. And wherever Rawdon was taking those bundles of money, it was within a day's journey of here. I'll take men with me, and wagons to carry the money should we recover it." Talk about optimism.

"Do you want me to accompany you or to stay here?" Penrod asked.

He was the only friendly one I'd met—besides Lady Bliss. Well, and Rawdon had been friendly, but now I saw that didn't count. Still, Penrod was more useful here. "Stay," I advised. "Try to talk the men into remaining here. Explain that if they leave now, they've already worked the majority of the month without pay. The worst that can happen if they stay is a couple more days of work without pay. On the other hand, if things work out, they'll get paid when we get back. Bonuses for anyone who stays."

"I'll assign loyal men to accompany you and to guard the treasure on its way back." This time he managed to keep his skepticism from showing on his face.

My good friend, my carefully chosen ally, Abas, refused to come with me, saying if I was just leaving now, I'd be away half the night, and he'd miss his weight-lifting exercises for the evening. But he promised if I *did* get back in time, he'd let me watch.

As for my advisers, Sir Deming told me to ask my officially chosen adviser, and Sister Mary Ursula was going to be busy with her soul-cleansing skinny-dipping-in-the-moonlight routine. As my official adviser, she advised me to join her.

So off I headed to Fairfield.

I rode ahead with five men, leaving the rest of the

squadron to accompany the slower-moving wagons. Guessing I'd need all the time I could get to find Rawdon's stash, I hadn't even bothered to switch out of Bliss's extravagant dress and into more sensible clothes.

Fairfield was much bigger than St. Jehan, which was no surprise: Some of my friends at St. John the Evangelist School have *families* that are bigger than St. Jehan. But Fairfield had a few hundred people, which doesn't sound like much until you begin to think about questioning every one of them.

We arrived at dusk, and our first stop was a tavern. The red dress got a few whistles from having worked its way down so that it revealed more than I wanted revealed, but nobody remembered seeing anyone fitting Rawdon's description.

We stopped at Fairfield's three other taverns. Some of the people had been around that afternoon when my messenger had been looking for Rawdon's mother. They remembered the messenger but not Rawdon. "Isn't there anyone in Fairfield," I asked the tavern keeper at the last place, "who's a bit of a busybody, who sits around watching people, and always likes a bit of gossip?"

"Information costs," the tavern keeper said, "and you and your group haven't spent a penny here yet."

"I'm the new king," I said. "I'm the one who'll be setting your taxes next year—are you sure you want to talk to me about paying for things?"

He directed me to his mother-in-law, who thought she'd seen a man who might have been Rawdon, but she couldn't be sure when or where. She suggested I talk to a friend of hers—a guy who couldn't help but said he got a lot of his news from the goose girl. The goose girl's mother complained that it was past her daughter's bedtime, but she got the child up when one of my men—the only one of us with any cash at all—loaned me a copper penny to pay her if the information was good.

Wiping sleep from her eyes, the eight-year-old assured me that she had seen Rawdon.

"When was the last time?" I asked, suspecting the mother might have coached her so that they could keep the penny.

"Today," she said. "He was carrying big bundles of something or other, bigger than he usually does."

Which was exactly how I had described him to her. But then she added, "He was looking even more fidgety than usual."

Fidgety. How else would a man who'd just made off with a king's treasury look? Except I hadn't said *who* Rawdon was or why we were searching for him. Still, it could have been clever reasoning on the girl's part. Seeing that we were pursuing someone, she might guess that that someone had been worried about pursuit.

"How do you mean, 'fidgety'?" I asked.

"Looking over his shoulder to see if anybody was watching," the girl said. "Pretending to be just sitting there in the shade, eating his bread and cheese, until no one was looking."

"Except you," I guessed.

She snorted. "Grown-ups don't even *see* children unless we're bothering them."

Well, that was certainly something I'd experienced.

"And then?" I asked. "Once he thought no one was looking?"

"He went into the old church."

Church? A man who was making off with the entire assets of a kingdom?

"What church?" I hadn't seen any church in Fairfield.

"The one the barbarians burned down during the time of my grandmother's grandmother's grandmother."

At least it wasn't anything *I* had caused to happen. "But you said—"

"It's mostly ruins," the girl said. "The timbers burned, and the roof caved in, and the walls collapsed. But the way the stones fell, there are tunnels. And if you can find it, one of the tunnels leads down to the catacombs."

Catacombs might be useful for hiding stuff.

"Have you ever been down to these catacombs?" I asked.

The girl glanced at her mother. "No."

Neither the mother nor I believed her. The mother twisted the little girl's ear until the poor child squealed. The mother said, "I told you to stay away from there. That's no place to be playing—it's too dangerous."

"Yes, Mama," the girl squealed.

"You wait until your father gets home," the mother warned. "You are in *so* much trouble."

"Excuse me," I said. "We're not finished yet. Are you saying children play in the catacombs?"

"No," the girl said, but her mother still had a grip on that ear and warned, "Better not."

155

"*Other* children," I clarified.

Still, the girl said, "No. It's too scary. We peeked in once or twice. *Ow!* The boys sometimes dare each other to run in, circle the marker, and run back out again. *Ow! Mama!* But they always run as fast as they can, in case of ghosts. Nobody ever goes past the first room. *Ow!*"

"How many rooms are there?"

The girl shook her head that she didn't know. The mother shrugged. "The church is in front of the hill, and the hill is where we buried our dead before we started the cemetery."

I said, "We're willing to pay if you can show us how to get to that first room."

"Pay with what?" the mother asked. "You had to borrow for what you've promised us already. Speaking of which . . ." She held out her hand.

I glanced at the guard to see if he had any more coins with him. He shook his head.

"Can you describe the way to us?" I asked the girl. She nodded, and I handed over the penny to her mother.

THE GUARDS didn't have any money, but they *did* have the supplies to fashion the torches we'd need if we were going to be exploring underground.

The church was, as the child and her mother had indicated, in ruins. I could see why the mother was frantic to keep her daughter away.

We found the larch tree she said marked the opening that led under the rubble. Crawling in was the tightest squeeze. After that, the pathway, though cramped, was well-worn enough by hands and knees, that we easily found our way through: right turn at the fallen and burned beam; right turn at the darker stone that was shaped like a round loaf of rye bread; ignore the wide way, which looked like where you should go but dead-ended a few feet beyond; left turn under the slab of rock as long and wide as a man.

The biggest danger was crawling while carrying torches—the risk of those in back burning the butts of those in front. Crawling in a dress five sizes too big was no fun, either. I was worried I was going to crawl right out of it.

Suddenly the stone rubble ended and we were on a dirt floor, the ceiling just high enough that the second tallest guard could stand upright. I readjusted my dress the best I could.

I saw the marker the goose girl had talked about the town boys having to circle, if they dared. It looked like a waist-high stone pedestal on which rested a stone coffin. *Was* it just a marker, showing what lay beyond, or was it, in fact, the final resting place of the first dead person?

Too late to be grossed out by that. Beyond the marker, the walls had been scooped out and wooden shelves had been built into them, three high, lining both sides. But these had begun to decay and disintegrate, and many had tipped or collapsed entirely. What the shelves had held was, of course, the stuff and purpose of catacombs: dead bodies. Just within our torchlight, we could see a doorway. Another room. Presumably more bodies. They had been laid head to toe, one after another after another, three tiers and a half-dozen sets of shelves on either side, with just enough room to let pass a small wagon through the center. My feet wobbled on the ruts the wheels had made, carrying generations' worth of Fairfield citizenry to their final rest.

Some of the bundles were wrapped in linen, badly tattered now so that I could glimpse hints of hair and mummified flesh. Other bodies hadn't been wrapped so well, or the shrouds had deteriorated more. There were bones lying on the floor—either flung by the collapse of shelves or scattered by scavenging animals. The place smelled of humans returning to dust: a lung-coating, throat-clogging smell that wasn't the same but reminded me of the nursing-home room where my grandfather had died.

One of the guards stepped forward and shone his smoking torch on the side of the pedestal on which the coffin rested.

Janine de St. Jehan didn't know how to read, but Giannine Bellisario had had enough years of Catholic education to know that *Requiescat pacem* means, "Rest in peace."

The guard knew more than I did. He rattled off the rest of the Latin words then translated: "Rest in peace. Let none but the dead pass through here."

The guards looked spooked.

I was, too. Still, "The dead didn't rest themselves here by themselves," I told them. "It must be safe for living people to *pass through*."

I took the lead, trying to ignore the shadows that my torch sent dancing on the walls.

No sign of treasure, which made sense, since Rawdon wouldn't have risked an especially daring Fairfield child stumbling upon his hoard. It had to be hidden farther in.

We walked through into the second room, which was identical to the first, and then the third. Some of the remains had been scattered at a time when people had still been visiting, for bones were piled up along the sides: the skulls resting on the floor, their empty eye sockets watching us. But that wasn't the important thing about the third room. The important thing about the third room was that there were two doorways leading out of it.

Uh-oh. I shone the torch into the right-hand room. In the gloomy distance, I could make out three doorways.

The guard who had shone his torch into the left-hand room said, "Five."

Five? I looked, just in case he could read Latin but couldn't count. Yup, five. So, eight possible ways to go.

A quick look showed that all the routes had the wagon tracks and footprints of the people—now long dead themselves—who'd brought the bodies in. None of the footprints stood out as being fresher than the rest, so it was impossible to tell which direction Rawdon had taken.

Oh, boy. A maze. And here I'd been hoping the topiary maze was the only one I'd have to deal with.

"All right..." I said. People around here weren't too good at thinking on their own or making suggestions; that was supposed to be my job. "First thing we'll need to do is go back to where the rubble was and get some stones so that we can scratch marks into the doorways. That way we can tell where we've been and not get lost. We'll divide into three pairs. You"—I pointed to Latin boy—"and I will go together. Whenever we have two choices, we'll take the right-hand route, and we'll mark the doorway with an arrow to show which way we passed."

To the second pair, I said, "You two will always take the left-hand route. When you make *your* marks, make two arrows—one on top of the other—so that your mark will be different from ours and we can all immediately see who's passed, going in which direction."

I subdivided the last pair of men. "You will wait in the first room with a supply of torches we can come back for in case we're in here long enough to need them"—*I hope not, I hope not,* I thought—"and in case one of the search parties actually finds the stolen booty." *Please let it be soon.* To the last man, the tall one, I said, "And you will wait outside the church, so you can flag down the wagons when they arrive."

It was, I think, a good plan. The guards didn't disagree with me, but then, they probably wouldn't have, no matter what.

My partner and I went from room to room to room. Rawdon wouldn't have hidden the stolen money one coin at a time on individual corpses. Spreading the treasure out like that would make it too difficult to recover. Or so I told myself so that I wouldn't have to frisk the dead bodies. Already I suspected bugs were gathering on my dragging hem, and I worried about bugs dropping down the front of my dress—bugs that had been crawling on and eating corpses.

And then we came to a room just like all the others, except that there were bodies not only on either side but on the third wall also, the one opposite the doorway by which we'd entered. And there were no other doorways.

Just as I was turning back, convinced we'd reached a dead end, my partner whispered, "What's that?"

And at that moment I, too, caught the flutter of movement just beyond the glow of our torches.

But there was nothing there.

I was leery of approaching, but if something was moving, that might be a sign of a secret doorway. *You HAVE to look,* I thought, and forced myself to lean in close over one of the bodies. I held my breath against the stale, dusty smell, and kept the torch up and away from the cobwebs that hung thickly. *Let it be a current of air,* I hoped, *and not a swarm of maggots.*

Something brushed my arm.

I squealed and just barely managed to keep from dropping the torch onto a corpse.

Cobweb. Just a loose piece of cobweb, despite my precautions.

My partner hadn't fled, but neither had he come closer to make sure I wasn't under attack by Rawdon, the undead, or any other threat.

There were no maggots; there probably couldn't have been on such a long-dead body. Nor was there any breath of air indicating a room beyond, no marks on floor or ceiling where an otherwise hidden door might scrape.

So what had moved?

"Nothing here," I told him. "We have overactive imaginations."

He sighed. I sighed. I realized we'd both been holding our breaths.

We backtracked through the maze, then took the next unexplored path, to begin again.

It didn't get any better. Over and over in various rooms one or the other of us would jump, sure we saw something, sure we felt something brush against us, sure somebody or something was watching. But every time we looked directly, we never saw anything.

Probably nerves, I told myself. Probably a trick of the eyes, where torchlight and shadow met. Probably.

We could also hear what sounded like whispers.

Probably the other team, I told myself....

Until our paths crossed, and with none of the four of us speaking, we once again heard—just at the threshold of sensation—what may or may not have been voices.

No wonder the Fairfield kids were afraid of ghosts.

It must be some strange acoustical property of the interconnecting caves, I thought, *the guard, left behind to make torches, talking to himself to help pass the time*. But when we went back for more torches, I didn't ask him if he was.

The wagons arrived sometime between our second and third torches, and still no sign of Rawdon or the treasure.

I considered whether I should order the rest of the men to join the search but worried that if there were any tracks farther in, they'd get trampled.

Some of the tucks and gathers of my dress had come loose, and I was dragging what felt like yards of velvet brocade along the packed earth path. At one point when I thought I must have picked up about five pounds of dirt, I turned to shake out the dust and saw that I had, in fact, snagged part of somebody's rib cage. I shook it loose and kicked it toward the wall, where I wouldn't step on it on my way back through here.

I was sure we'd been looking for at least the three days of game play.

Even if Rawdon had become worried that we would be on his trail, I assured myself, he couldn't have removed the entire treasury from here and relocated it in the brief half-day he'd had. It *must* still be here.

I *had* to have the treasure to be able to keep the guards working for me, which I obviously needed to do. But I was hot and sweaty despite the chill air, and I was cranky and I was tired and I was hungry.

It was so frustrating, I wanted to bite someone.

And the thought of biting made me think of Wulfgar.

We couldn't see any trace of Rawdon's passing down any of the passages we'd searched. But that didn't mean Rawdon had passed without a trace. Surely someone with wolf-keen senses could smell where a living man had walked among the dead.

Couldn't he?

CHAPTER EIGHTEEN

Calling in the Reinforcements

I didn't want to call off the search entirely, just in case. So I ordered two new pairs of guards to take over while the original searchers rested.

No rest for me, of course. I knew how far I'd get if I sent a messenger to ask Wulfgar—at the crack of dawn, no less—to make the two-hour trip to Fairfield to help me.

So I headed back all by myself. It was eerie, riding my horse across the darkened countryside while the world slept, except for the occasional barking dog and an owl, which swooped so close I almost had a heart attack. The wind whispered in the trees and brushed against my arms, startling me over and over. I arrived at the castle at about the same time as sunrise. I'd made it to the second day. *Hallelujah.*

Penrod must have talked some of the guards into remaining, because two of them guarded the raised drawbridge. The trouble was, they didn't recognize me. They insisted I was a beggar and told me to come back later in the morning when the gates were open.

I argued calmly.

Then forcibly.

Then irritably.

Then I yelled at them, "Get Captain Penrod now! He'll tell you who I am."

"Sorry. No. Can't do that," they said. "Captain's asleep. Come back later."

I was so tired and frustrated and angry, I didn't know what to do. So I screamed. I screamed and screamed and screamed—like a teenage victim in a cheesy horror movie—hoping to wear them down, or to wake up somebody who would verify I was who I said. It sure scared my horse, and the castle's many dogs began to howl.

Screaming continually is actually very tiring, and in less than a minute, my throat was suffering. At about two minutes, I could tell my volume was definitely going down. After three minutes Sister Mary Ursula strolled out from the bushes. She was wrapped in two towels—and only two towels: one around her; the other turban-style around her head. Believe me, under normal circumstances a seventy-year-old nun dressed in two towels is *not* a welcome sight, but I was delighted to see her.

"Such a fuss," she said, shaking her head at me. "If you had cleansed your soul with me this past night, you wouldn't feel this way, I'm sure."

The guards called down to her, "Be careful of the crazy girl, Sister!"

"That's all right," Sister Mary Ursula assured them. "I know her."

So they lowered the drawbridge and let the two of us in.

I glowered at the guards as we passed. People in this world, I was coming to learn, were only able to think for themselves if it inconvenienced me.

As I walked toward the castle, I heard a guard give the order for the bridge to be raised. A few moments later, he repeated the order. And then again.

I went back to see what was the matter.

"It's stuck," the guard manning the mechanism said.

"How's it supposed to work?" I asked.

He showed me the cogwheels and the chain that let the door down so that people could cross over it, and raised it for security at night and when the castle was under attack.

I'm not an engineer, but it was immediately obvious that the drawbridge's natural position was *up* not *down*. The counterweights had to be lifted to lower the bridge so people could get in, which I guess makes sense from a defensive point of view. You don't want the bridge sticking down and open if an invading army is running toward you, screaming and waving weapons. All of which meant the bridge should be easier to raise than to lower—the exact opposite of what seemed to be the case now.

Just what we need, I thought, *with the barbarians on our doorstep.*

"Could it have been sabotaged?" I asked as the guard fiddled with the mechanism.

"I don't see how." He pointed. "Nothing wrong here. The chain is fine. And there's nothing blocking there."

"Except it won't work," I said.

"Except it won't work," he repeated. "It's like something is holding the bridge down."

The trouble was, we could plainly see nothing was.

The bridge wasn't caught on anything, either in the ditch that surrounded the castle, or on the farside, where the drawbridge lay.

Other guards came to see if they could do better, two pulling at a time, though the first guard said it wasn't supposed to be a matter of strength.

"*You* should be able to do it," he said.

He probably meant, "Even a weakling like you," but I said, "Yeah, like King Arthur being the only one who could pull the sword out of the stone."

"What's this Arthur king of?" the guard asked. "And why did he keep his sword in a stone?"

"Never mind," I said. But I tugged, anyway.

And the bridge started to come up. Easily.

Some of the guards who'd come to see and give their advice backed away suspiciously. But most cheered and congratulated me.

Strange, I thought, but since it ended well, I wasn't going to complain.

They took over raising the bridge the rest of the way, having no trouble now, and I went to find Wulfgar.

In the castle the servants were already up and working: preparing breakfast, opening the windows to air out the rooms, heating water for the laundry. The royal family was *not* yet up.

I banged on Wulfgar's door.

No answer.

I banged again.

There was a sleepy mumble—probably he told me to go away.

I kept on banging. The servants who had been in the hall ran for cover.

Wulfgar flung open the door. He had on a nightshirt, and his hair was all askew, and his eyes were still puffy from sleep. *"What,"* he growled, "is the meaning of this?"

"Knocking on a door?" I asked innocently. "That's an ancient custom among many peoples of the world signifying: Please let me in."

Wulfgar drew his lips back from his teeth but retained human form.

"I need your help," I told him, "to get the treasury back."

"Ask *fascinating, remarkable, wow!-imagine-that* Abas."

Was that the way I sounded? "I need you." I could see he was winding himself up for a sarcastic comeback, so I added, "And your special talents."

He raised an eyebrow and waited.

In this lifetime I hadn't seen him turn into a wolf. I said, "I understand you were raised elsewhere."

"Yes." He gave a definitely wolfish grin.

"I need you to track down Rawdon."

"No," he said.

"He stole our treasury."

"Raise our taxes."

168

No time. Plus, of course, that would make the peasants even surlier. "Please," I said.

He closed the door in my face.

I untied the magic ring from its makeshift necklace. I banged on the door some more. This time when it flew open, I said, "Take this ring."

Wulfgar's eyes grew wide and frightened. No doubt he had no desire to take the ring, and yet he found his hand moving to take it. He *knew* he was bespelled.

He took the ring and slipped it onto his finger.

I said, "First, I need you to protect me from harm."

His expression didn't become any less murderous, but I knew that now I was safe from him—and from others while he was beside me.

"Next, I want you to come back to Fairfield with me and help me find where Rawdon has hidden the treasure."

Wulfgar stepped out into the hall.

"You may get dressed first," I told him.

I figured men can always dress faster than women, so there wasn't time for me to get into something more practical, even if I knew where to get it. Sure enough, Wulfgar wasn't long. He wore such a fierce expression that the castle dogs whined and slunk away from us, their tails between their legs.

The guards lowered the drawbridge again for us to cross. I called out for them to keep the bridge up, even during the day, in case of attack. After we'd gone over, I heard the guard yell that we were clear.

No sound of a raising bridge from behind us.

"Raise the bridge!" the guard yelled.

Nothing.

Well, I couldn't close it from this side. Something else for me to look into when I got back.

IN FAIRFIELD, people from the town had gathered at the burned and tumbled remains of the church, drawn by the presence of the wagons and the squad of guards. Seeing that the wagons were empty and the guards were mostly lazing around, I gathered that there still was no sign of the treasure.

I led Wulfgar through the minimaze of rubbled church to the first room of the catacombs. Both pairs of men I had set to search were there, along with the man assigned to make torches. The searchers started explaining—before I said a word—that they'd just come back for replacement torches. I figured I'd returned faster than they anticipated and I'd caught them taking a break. I'd been gone four hours—which was probably about how long their break had lasted.

"That's all right," I said. "Stay here. Prince Wulfgar and I will search now."

Taking a torch, I led Wulfgar through to the third room, the one where the catacomb maze started. "I want you to find Rawdon's trail," I said. "We will go together. Don't try to lose me." I had another thought. "And if we *do* get separated, I want you to come looking for me right away. You are not to let any harm befall me."

"You already said that about no harm," Wulfgar said.

"Just reminding you."

Wulfgar didn't say any magical words that I heard; and I didn't see him make any magical-looking gestures.

He simply suddenly shrank, fell forward, and transformed into a wolf.

Too late it occurred to me that the ring was bound to fall off the toe of his paw. Would that stop the spell? But the ring kept hold, even when Wulfgar padded on all four feet to the left-hand door.

He walked at a steady pace that kept me at a breathless half run.

If you slow down, he'll have to slow down, too, because you commanded him not to lose you, I told myself. But I wouldn't give him the satisfaction of knowing that I couldn't keep up.

There wasn't any pattern to our path, and there were too many intersections, with most of the rooms too similar to be distinctive. Sometimes the dead bodies had mummified; sometimes they were simply bones; sometimes the bones were scattered on the floor; sometimes they were mostly in their carved wall niches. (The wooden shelves were only for those rooms closest to the entrance.) We went through one section where an underground stream must pass near, for several of the rooms were damp, and in two of them we had to wade through puddles that came up to my ankles. There had also been cave-ins in several of the rooms, which I sincerely hoped had happened a long time ago.

Long after I'd given up trying to make sense of our direction, Wulfgar suddenly stopped. He'd slowed down two or three times before, to sniff at the tunnels, but now he suddenly reverted back to human shape.

"What?" I asked.

"Counselor Rawdon," he said.

I lowered my voice to the faintest whisper, just in case Rawdon hadn't heard us coming or seen the light from my torch. "Where?" I asked because there were two possible doorways, plus the one we were closest to, which had collapsed—though surely Rawdon wouldn't have wanted to make his way over that pile each time he came, I thought.

Imitating me, Wulfgar whispered dramatically, "There."

For a moment I thought he meant that Rawdon was in the room beyond the pile of stones and dirt where the doorway had collapsed. But then I saw the foot that was sticking out of the pile, the foot that was neither bone nor mummified flesh. Proof that cave-ins happened as recently as within the last day.

"Do you think he's dead?" I asked.

"No, I think he's napping."

"He could just be injured," I protested.

Without answering, Wulfgar scrambled up the pile of collapsed catacomb, ignoring the body. He had to duck to squeeze through what was left of the opening.

I was going to say, "Not so fast," but when I got to the top, I could see into the next room. Wulfgar hadn't moved on, but stood among dozens of sacks that were stacked on top of one another. Beneath my feet, protruding from this end of the cave-in, was a small hand-pulled cart onto which several of the bundles had been loaded. The force of the cave-in had knocked some of the bags off, and one had split open, scattering gold coins, which glinted in the light of my torch.

"He must have been trying to move the gold out of

here," Wulfgar said. "He might even have been heading for one of the seaports, to hire a boat and leave the country. I'm guessing he rushed too much."

That was my guess, too—that Rawdon had accidentally smacked into the doorway with his overloaded cart, not realizing that this entire area was weakened by the moisture of that nearby water.

That was something for me to remember and be careful of.

"All right," I said. "This time we need to go slowly so that I can make scratches with my stone to mark the way for the guards to find their way here." I'd use double arrows, one after the other, to identify the correct way. "We'll let the men dig this out, gather the money, return it to the castle in the wagons at whatever speed they can make. But the two of us won't wait—we should be getting back as soon as we can to check on the situation with the barbarians."

Wulfgar used the toe of his boot to poke at the stones covering Rawdon. "One of us hasn't had breakfast," he grumbled.

Even with all the trouble Rawdon had caused, I refused to consider letting Wulfgar snack on him. "Neither of us has," I assured him, tugging on his arm. "Don't you dare even think about that."

"Even magic can't control thinking," he said wistfully.

BY THE TIME I had carefully marked out the route and given instructions on how many men to have carrying the treasury out and how many men to have guarding the treasury that had been carried out, so that the people of Fairfield didn't walk off with it, I had a crisis of faith— not over my trailblazing abilities or even my troops' mental abilities, but over how hard it would be for the average guardsman to remain honest in the face of so very much money. They could easily decide that a kingdom's treasury, divided among the fifty of them, was more money per guard than any of them was ever likely to see again.

"Wulfgar," I ordered, "you'll have to stay behind. Keep an eye on the men. Make sure they don't take any of the money for themselves. Then help guard the convoy on the way back."

"I haven't even broken my fast yet," Wulfgar complained again.

Well, none of us had.

"Send a few of the men into town to buy provisions for everyone," I said. I knew Wulfgar was only cooperating because the ring compelled him to, so I specified: "Don't be excessive with spending the money, but pay a fair price. And return to the castle as quickly as you can in safety."

I couldn't think of any loopholes I'd left. Which didn't mean Wulfgar wouldn't find one.

"No plotting against me," I added.

Wulfgar saluted then spat on the ground, just barely missing my toes.

BY THE TIME I made the two-hour trip back home, I had a strong suspicion that lunch was probably over.

I could see that eventually they'd gotten the bridge up without me, though now they had to lower it once more.

Captain Penrod was standing on the castle wall as I approached. I waved and held up the one sack of gold I'd brought with me in case any skeptical guards needed proof that the money *had* been found. Penrod returned my wave, and I heard a cheer from the guards as word of my success was passed.

My horse clattered over the drawbridge, and the eager guards gathered around.

I tossed the bag to Penrod and said, "That's the first of it. The rest is about a half-day behind."

Penrod handed the bag over to one of his lieutenants and helped me dismount. I had a sore butt from all the riding I'd done, Lady Bliss's red gown was stiff and stinky with sweat—not to mention tattered and muddy—and I'd had absolutely no sleep last night and no breakfast this morning.

We watched as the guards were unable to reraise the bridge.

"Any idea what that's all about?" I asked Penrod.

He shook his head. "They say it's as though the bridge is weighted down, but then that weight goes away after a little while."

"That 'little while' could be the death of us in case of enemy attack," I warned. "Can a new mechanism be made?"

Penrod passed that down to his men as an order.

"How are things going?" I asked him.

"Not badly," he answered, but so hesitantly I knew he wasn't telling the truth.

"You might as well tell me now," I said.

"The messengers you sent to find the barbarian camp returned."

Because of his dismal expression, I guessed, "The barbarians didn't accept our offer of peace?"

"The messengers returned without their heads."

That sounded like a definite *no* to me.

Now what?

"All right," I said. "I absolutely need to lie down, just for a bit. I'm so tired I can hardly walk straight, much less think straight."

"Oh," Penrod said.

"'Oh' what?"

"It's just that the meeting has already started."

"What meeting?"

"With the magic-users—Uldemar, Orielle, and Xenos."

I was pleased to hear they'd arrived, but, "Who are they meeting with?" I asked.

"Queen Andreanna," Penrod said.

I guessed there wasn't time for a nap, quick or otherwise.

CHAPTER NINETEEN

Magic Realism (without the Realism)

When I got to the Great Hall, the doors were closed and two guards stood in front, which I gathered was Queen Andreanna's subtle way of letting me know I wasn't invited.

"Make way for the king," I commanded, never acknowledging a *thought* that they wouldn't.

Assertiveness sometimes pays off. The guards were so quick to open the doors that the little guy with the trumpet didn't have a chance to blow a fanfare.

"Oh," Andreanna said as I entered, "look. It's the pig girl."

"Sheep," I corrected automatically.

They were all sitting around one of the dining tables—no serving side this time: the queen, Abas, Kenric, two guys I didn't know, and one woman I didn't know. Actually, the woman wasn't sitting at the table; she was sitting on Kenric's lap, though there was plenty of room on the bench, particularly since I'd left Wulfgar behind in Fairfield. She looked like any teenage boy's fantasy: a Barbie-doll figure that defied gravity, a super-model's face, lustrous black skin, and about fifteen pounds' worth of cornrowed hair fastened off with tiny golden bells. Her outfit was composed exclusively of leather, lace, and strategically placed metal. Wulfgar had said Orielle was better-looking than the other magic-users. I would be willing to bet my college fund that Orielle was better-looking than 99 percent of the world's population.

There was no sign of Sir Deming or Sister Mary Ursula—apparently the queen didn't feel she needed advisers.

"Please send for the royal advisers," I said to the guards.

The queen was making an irritated face, but for once it wasn't about me. "Close the doors, you incompetent fools," she ordered.

I turned and saw that although the guards were tugging on the doors, the doors weren't moving.

The queen sighed.

The page put down his trumpet and joined in the guards' efforts to close the doors. Nothing. Even when all three men concentrated on one door and hurled their weight at it, it wouldn't close.

Don't tell me the castle itself is rebelling against me, I thought.

"Abas, can't you do something?" the queen said.

"I can do lots of things," Abas protested.

The queen sighed again. "Can't you do something about the door?"

The guards moved out of Abas's way. He pushed. Nothing. He pushed harder. Still nothing. He moved around to the other side and pulled. The doorknobs and the ornate metal plates to which they were attached yanked out of the wood. Abas handed them to the guards, then returned to our side of the doors and once again pushed. I saw the muscles on his arms bulge, the muscles on his back ripple, the muscles on his thighs expand like they were about to pop. There was a creaking noise of wood protesting. Then the huge oaken doors cracked, split, and fell in shards. Without the hinges having budged.

What was going on?

"Well, that was quite useful," Kenric said.

Abas shrugged and returned to the table.

The queen gestured for the guards and the page to leave.

As they picked their way through the pile of splintered wood, the page reached behind him—it must have been mindless force of habit—to pull closed the piece of door that was still attached to the hinges. It swung easily.

The people at the table looked at me suspiciously.

Luckily, with such a limited number of them, they couldn't crowd me out this time. I would have preferred to sit on the same side of the table as the any-other-female-would-feel-like-a-poster-child-for-the-criminally-ugly-compared-to-*her* Orielle, so I wouldn't have to look at her; but she was sitting on Kenric's lap, and he was sitting on Andreanna's left, with Abas having returned to Andreanna's right. If I wanted to sit on that side, I would have had to sit directly next to Orielle. There was a space between the two men who sat on the other side of the table, as well as more room at either end of the bench they shared. I decided on the middle seat, to avoid what might be interpreted as favoritism.

"This," Queen Andreanna said in the same tone someone would use to point out a backed-up toilet, "is Princess Janine. Princess Janine"—she managed to look down her nose even though she wasn't quite facing me—"these are Orielle, Uldemar, and Xenos."

"Hello," I said to the wizard on my right, Xenos.

He was dressed in a brown monk's robe, with the hood pulled up around his face.

Shy little guy, I figured. I made a point of smiling at him until he looked up at me. I noticed the pointy, hairy ears about the same time I realized that what he was pulling out of his pocket and popping into his mouth were live centipedes. He glared as though he was sure I was just waiting for the chance to grab his lunch away from him.

I edged toward Uldemar, who announced in a booming voice: "She brings the stench of the dead with her."

Talk about getting personal.

I turned to face him. He was the wizard I'd glimpsed in the coming attraction. I'd noticed that he was very tall and that his head was shaved. But now, close up, I gulped, for I saw what I hadn't had time to see in the promo: His eyes were like Ping-Pong balls—totally white, with no pupils or irises.

Stammering, I said, "I—I've just come back from the catacombs. There *were* dead people there." *Of course there are dead people in the catacombs,* I mentally chided myself. *They know that. Stop blathering.* I said, "I—I've recovered the stolen treasure." I'd kept a handful from the bag I'd given to Penrod, and I placed this on the table to prove my story.

Uldemar sniffed. But when he spoke, his voice—though deep and elegant—was no longer intimidating. "So pleased to meet you," he said.

"Good to see—" I started, my mouth a full syllable ahead of me. How could I be so thoughtless as to bring up *seeing* to a person who was obviously blind? If somebody else had said it, I would have kicked her. I was tempted to kick myself. "I mean," I corrected myself, feeling my face go all hot and red—but his eyes *were* the most disgusting things I'd ever seen, and my stammer came back, "I—I—I—" which I realized sounded like "Eye, eye, eye." For something to do with my hands, which had developed a sudden tendency to flutter, I folded them and went to place them on the table in front of me.

Except that I banged the edge of the table, and when I jerked back, I knocked one of the gold coins onto the floor.

I leaned down to get it, but it was too far under the table, so I pushed the bench back. Wood on stone made a loud screeching like fingernails on blackboard. Xenos leaped to his feet to get away from me, and Uldemar—who couldn't see what I was doing and had felt the bench beneath him move—grabbed for the stability of the table. The bench stopped so suddenly, I nearly slid off.

Again I reached under the table, this time smacking my forehead loudly against the wood. Before my eyes cleared, I accidentally latched onto Xenos's ankle— which was as hairy as his ears.

He shook me loose impatiently.

At last I located the coin, put it back on the pile, and folded my hands on the table in front of me, though at this point the bench was so far back I had to stretch to reach. But I figured I better leave well enough alone. I didn't want to draw any more attention to myself by touching the bump I could feel already swelling over my left eye.

Eye reminded me of Uldemar.

He was still waiting, a pained look on his face.

"Hello," I said.

"Oh, I see what you mean, Kenric." Orielle giggled. "She *is* all that you said."

Well, excuse me. We can't all be naturally gorgeous, polished, and coordinated.

Abas gave a tittery laugh. He was carving his initials into the table with a dagger about the size of a small garden hoe. For all that I had chosen him to be my ally, I was aware that he could just as easily carve his initials into me.

Andreanna sighed. "Well now that *she's* here, I suppose we'd better ask her what she wants to do."

"About what?" I asked, sure I'd come in during the middle of something.

"About new drapes for the windows," Andreanna purred, then snapped, "*About the threats to the kingdom, of course, you absurd little ninny*. Have you been too busy twiddling your thumbs to be aware that the kingdom is in danger on several fronts?"

"No," I said. "I mean, yes. I mean, I *have* been busy, and I *have* been thinking about our problems. I just didn't know what particular problem you were discussing before I came in." *Stop trying to excuse yourself to them,* I told myself. "OK," I said, "what are our problems? First—"

Uldemar interrupted, "You smell of the dead."

"Yes," I said, "I know." I didn't point out that he'd told me so already. "First," I repeated, "the drawbridge."

"What are you talking about?" the queen demanded.

"The drawbridge—it keeps getting stuck on open."

The lovely Orielle said, "It worked when I came through this morning."

Xenos, biting off a centipede's head, grunted and nodded, which I took to mean that he'd had no problem, either.

Abas said, "It worked fine when I went to let in Uldemar."

"It gets stuck," I insisted. "Ask the guards." I sounded pathetic, begging to be believed. "It got stuck when I came in at dawn, and again when I left a little bit later, and just now when I came back. It gets stuck, then it suddenly works again. Just like these doors."

"You mean the Great Hall doors, which worked perfectly well for the rest of us?" Kenric asked.

"You *saw*," I protested. They couldn't deny seeing it, when the broken rubble Abas had generated still cluttered the way. "You saw that the doors wouldn't close."

"I did," Kenric agreed. "I'm just wondering why both the drawbridge and the Great Hall doors stick for you, and only for you."

Uldemar said, "She carries the dead with her."

"Enough already with the dead!" I yelled at him. (All right, all right, I yelled at a blind guy.) "I know I stink. I haven't had a chance to bathe yet. Surely you can put up with it while we discuss more urgent matters."

Uldemar said, "I didn't say that you stink. I said that I could smell the dead about you."

I paused to work this out. "You mean, like..."

"They must have followed you," Uldemar said. "From the catacombs."

So much for assuming I was the victim of an overactive imagination.

Sister Mary Ursula picked that moment to come climbing over the debris of the doors. "Ewww, dead people walking around, following live people. Have you been performing more of your necromancy, Uldemar?"

"Not me," Uldemar said. "Simply ghosts."

"I don't like ghosts," Sister Mary Ursula said. "They hang around watching you when you can't watch them, and they make rude comments. Everybody's fat from the perspective of someone who's been dead a hundred years."

Well, that put a whole new perspective on taking a bath.

Sounding put out, as though I'd invited the ghosts to

follow me specifically to annoy her, Queen Andreanna asked, "How many are there?"

Uldemar leaned closer to me and sniffed. "Several hundred," he estimated.

"Are they dangerous?" I asked.

"If they're all standing on the drawbridge so that it can't be closed while we're under attack, yes," Uldemar said. "Mostly they're annoying—howling at night, rattling chains so that it's impossible to get a good night's sleep. As Sister Mary Ursula pointed out, they do have a tendency to watch when people don't want to be watched, and to make rude remarks. The majority of the living can't hear them unless a whole bunch of ghosts are yelling together, but it isn't fun to know that people— even dead people—are sniggering at you."

As the queen of all sniggerees, I could empathize.

Kenric flashed that distracting smile of his at me. "They do seem to have developed a fondness for you," he pointed out. "If you stay away from the drawbridge so that they don't cluster on it, we should be fine." He gave just the slightest emphasis to his "we." *They* would be fine so long as the ghosts concentrated on harassing me.

"How do we get rid of them?" I asked.

Xenos made a noise halfway between snort and laugh. When he saw me look at him, he pulled his hood down farther over his face, and he jammed a centipede into his mouth to stifle the sound, but I could see his shoulders shaking with his silent glee.

I assumed this did not signify good news.

Uldemar said, "Understand, ghosts get bored. They

don't sleep, they don't eat—day after day, year after year, sometimes century after century. If they've decided that it will be fun to haunt you—"

I squealed as a bony finger that I couldn't see jabbed me in the ribs.

Xenos shook with silent laughter.

Uldemar finished, "—it will be difficult to distract them."

Queen Andreanna said, "We don't have time for this nonsense."

"I once had to do battle with an undead ogre," Abas said, but before he could tell us the details, Sir Deming entered the room.

"What's she done now?" Deming demanded, making a big show of looking at the broken doors—as though I could have knocked them in.

"Ghosts," Orielle told him, and blew him a kiss.

Deming sat down next to her, where he could get a good look down the front of her dress. He said to me, "You didn't need to bring ghosts; I said you could bring the sheep with you if you got lonely."

Deming, I thought, *would make a fine ghost.*

"All right," I said. "Let's get the meeting started. Sister Mary Ursula, why don't you have a seat."

"Oooo, no," she said, shrinking back. "I could never sit down next to a wizard or a necromancer or a witch. They are not One with anybody or anything. They are like buttoning your coat and not noticing till you get to the bottom that you're one button off, or a hot ember that burns your skin, or a piece of doo-doo that you step in while you're wearing sandals."

Xenos pulled back his hood to make kissy-lips at her, and she shrank farther away.

"All right," I said, trying to regain control of the meeting, "we have to decide what to do about the barbarians."

"What about the barbarians?" Uldemar asked.

"I killed three of them," Abas said. "First—"

"Abas," I interrupted, "later." To the three magic-users, I explained, "The barbarians sent a raiding party into the courtyard, and Abas did kill three of them."

"Saving your life," Abas emphasized.

"Saving my life," I agreed. "Before the last one died, he said that one of the others had been their king, and that the reason they were attacking was because King Cynric had taken a crown made for their first chieftain, Brecc the Slayer."

"*Won* the crown," Abas corrected. "You're not very good at telling stories."

I ignored his criticism and turned to Xenos. "Did you make that crown?"

Xenos spoke for the first time, his voice as sweet and melodious as the sound you get when you accidentally telephone a fax number. "Yes," he said.

"The barbarians want that crown back," I said. "And I'm told Cynric gave it to a dragon who was ravaging the south."

Rather than replying, Xenos popped another centipede into his mouth.

"We sent messengers to the barbarian camp to let them know we were willing to return the crown if we could get it, but the barbarians killed the messengers."

Andreanna turned to Abas and whispered loudly, "Big surprise."

"I wasn't surprised," Abas said. "If I was a barbarian, I would have killed the messengers, too."

"I think," I said, "that we are in imminent danger of the entire barbarian camp attacking." I looked at my advisers. "Any thoughts?"

Sister Mary Ursula said, "To forgive and to be forgiven are two sides of the coin of Harmony."

When it became clear she had no more to say, I said, "Yes, well, anybody else?"

Deming said, "Though yesterday's raiding party was small, they *did* bring an entire armed camp into our lands. Presumably that was in case the smaller group did not succeed. If they were willing to wage war to get the crown, I can't believe they'll forgive the killing of their king—regardless of how many sides of coins forgiveness covers."

I said, "So you're saying to forget retrieving the crown, to concentrate on defending the castle."

Deming nodded.

"Still..." I said. I had to believe that if Rasmussem included a dragon, I was supposed to have *something* to do with it. "How difficult would it be to track down this dragon?"

Uldemar said, "I could find him in my scrying glass."

The blind guy, I thought.

"Sure," I told him.

Uldemar was wearing a pendant that he took off from around his neck and laid on the table. It looked like a

188

slice of onyx—flat and about the circumference of a cross section of a baseball—in a gilt frame.

I bent closer. It *might* have been glass, but it was totally black. I could see myself and part of the room reflected in it.

Uldemar arranged his hands so that all ten of his fingers rested on the edge of his scrying glass, which left only a small area open in the middle.

As I watched that space, a swirl formed beneath the surface, as though thick black liquid were being stirred. But the swirling got lighter, as though the invisible stirrer were adding a lighter substance, like someone adding cream to melted licorice. Then more and more cream. I glanced up at Uldemar and almost squealed. The exact opposite was happening to his eyes: His white eyes were aswirl with darkness.

A bony finger jabbed me in the side, and I came close to becoming airborne. But it wasn't one of the ghosts; it was just Xenos, who was so pleased with himself for startling me that he practically choked up a piece of centipede.

Still, Andreanna found fault with me rather than Xenos. "If Cynric hadn't been so fevered and delirious when he was dying," she announced to all, "he never would have chosen her."

Finally, Uldemar's eyes and the scrying glass were reversed: The glass was smooth as white porcelain, and Uldemar's eyes were totally black, without any definition or detail at all. Unsettling as it was, I couldn't look away. After several long moments, Uldemar closed his eyes, probably for about five seconds. When he opened them, they were once more featureless white. The scrying glass had resumed its former blackness.

He said, "The dragon is in the southern province, in a cave on a mountaintop known as the Old Hag."

Andreanna said, "How is this little sheep-tending person going to overcome a dragon?"

I glanced at my good old ally Abas, who could—single-handed—overcome wild boars, undead ogres, and princess-kidnapping barbarians.

"I don't do dragons," he said.

Of course not. Since it was *my* game, naturally *I* would be the one to have to do it.

Orielle said, "If you can get close enough to the creature, I could give you a potion that would poison it."

"Wonderful." Xenos chortled so hard I expected to see centipedes come flying out of his nose. "She could present the dragon with a doctored ham-and-cheese sandwich: 'Here, Dragon, why don't you eat this before you eat me?' Fast-acting is this potion? Or did you have in mind something that would be absorbed through its skin? 'Care for a massage before I die, Dragon?'"

Orielle smiled as though she found his comments amusing even though they were derisive. Then she gestured with her finger, and Xenos's ear fell off.

It sat, hairy and warty, on the table.

"Put it back," he screamed at her. "Put it back now."

"What?" She tapped her own delicately shaped ear. "Can't hear you."

"Stop fighting," I told both of them. "We need to stick together or we're likely to all die together."

Orielle sulked but made a dismissive gesture to the hairy ear. Xenos snatched it up and slapped it against the side of his head. It stuck immediately, and I figured it was best not to mention that he'd put it on upside down.

"Uldemar," I said, "do you have any ideas on how to overcome the dragon and regain the crown?"

"No," he said. "I'm mostly a finder."

"Yeah," Xenos complained. "And mostly he's good at finding dead bodies. That's probably how he found the dragon—by the leftover bits and pieces of those who went before you to kill it."

"That's true," Uldemar admitted.

I rubbed my hand over my face. I was having trouble concentrating when I was so tired and no one was cooperating. "There has to be some way," I said. "But I haven't slept or eaten in ages, and I can't think straight. I'm going to take a nap and..."

What was all that racket coming from down the hall? *Probably the ghosts,* I thought, *already practicing sleep prevention.*

But it wasn't.

A guard came scrambling over the debris of the broken door. "Attack!" he yelled. "We're under attack!"

SUBJ: URGENT--Bios
DATE: 5/25   04:12:57 P.M. US eastern
        daylight time
FROM: Nigel Rasmussem
        <nrasmussem@rasmussem.com>
TO: dept. heads distribution list

These readouts are alarming. G. B.
doesn't have much time left. Premature
disconnection may be the only option,
and the technologists warn this could
result in severe brain damage likely
to leave G. B. in an irreversible
vegetative state.

***The translation software garbled
Japan's last message. Japan, please have
something for us. Reword and resend
ASAP.

CHAPTER TWENTY

Siege

Kenric, Abas, and Xenos were fastest. I was right behind them as we ran down the hallway. From outside I could hear yelling, but when I reached the doorway to the courtyard, I could see the drawbridge was up, which was a pleasant surprise. A flaming arrow hit the doorframe inches from Xenos's head. He yelped and went into reverse, treading my toes.

"Never mind," he muttered, slinking past me, past Andreanna and Deming, who were on my heels, back into the safety of the hallway. Orielle had stopped far enough back to be out of danger of stray arrows, and Sister Mary Ursula had just rounded the corner, huffing as she waddled in our direction. We'd forgotten poor Uldemar back at the table.

Just as I was about to peek out of the doorway, Kenric and Abas came racing back from outside. I stepped out of their way barely in time to avoid a collision. Abas paused only long enough to grab the burning arrow out of the wooden doorframe and fling it to the ground, where it would burn out harmlessly. Kenric threw open a side door, and both brothers dashed up a steep spiral staircase.

I took a moment to see what was going on in the courtyard. Some of our guards were there, lugging buckets of water to put out fires that had caught in the thatched roofs of the surrounding outbuildings—like the barracks and the well housing. But most of the guards were up on the walls. Assuming that was where the stairs led, I followed after Abas and Kenric.

The noise of men shouting became louder.

I came out onto the wall that surrounded both castle and courtyard. I know I'd been over it when the barbarians had carried me, but at that time, I hadn't been in any condition to notice much. Now I saw that the walls were wide enough to accommodate men running back and forth, trying to defend the castle. There was no safety rail on the castle side—which made my twenty-first-century self cringe at the possibility of injuries and subsequent lawsuits—but the side that faced out had that typical solid-then-open pattern, like a jack-o'-lantern smile with every other tooth missing, that my medieval self recognized as battlements. The guards could hide behind the upright sections, the *merlons,* then shoot arrows through the openings, or *crenellations*. The trouble was that *enemy* arrows also could fly through the openings. Dead and wounded men lay where they dropped, stepped over by guards intent on keeping the barbarians from scaling the walls.

When I'd been in the barbarian camp, I'd had the impression that there were a lot of them. They looked like even more now that they were running toward the castle waving their swords, firing their arrows, and battering at the upright drawbridge with a tree trunk long enough to reach over the ditch. They had catapults, too. I was just in time to see the first bombardment, huge rocks wrapped with rags that had been soaked in something flammable. Two of the rocks landed in the courtyard, where they didn't inflict much damage; but the third landed on the battlement itself, crushing one man and burning those who tried to go to his rescue.

Abas and Kenric had taken up bows and were firing into the advancing crowd of barbarians. I hovered uselessly, worrying that the ghosts that had followed me from the catacombs might find it amusing to give me a little shove while I was standing in this precarious place. The smells of blood and pitch were making me woozy, and the smoke stung my eyes.

"Princess Janine!" one of the guards called above the screams of men, some attacking, some dying. "Lady, this is a dangerous place for one not trained in war craft. Best for you to find a more secure position within."

He was right. Even if my personality had provided me with the inclination to participate, Rasmussem had not provided me with the skill for fighting. But I couldn't believe my role in this battle was merely to seek a suitable hiding place—even though that *was* my inclination.

I had to fight every instinct I had. "What can I do to help?" I shouted back.

For one who had been so concerned about getting me to safety, he was quick enough to point to one of the pages who was dumping a basketful of arrows to replenish the stock the archers were using. "Show the princess where the supplies are kept," the guard ordered the page.

And so I started running up and down the stairs, bringing load after load of arrows to the archers, delivering them to different stations on the wall to make sure nobody ran out. Apparently the ghosts were diverted enough by all the activity that they didn't feel called on to trip me or knock me down.

Despite my ongoing terror, things went well until I dropped a basket of arrows between Abas and Kenric. The area was slick from water used to douse some burning debris, and as I turned, one of my feet slipped. No amount of frantic arm-waving was enough to regain my balance. I could tell I was sliding toward the edge, like an out-of-control skater. I had time to ask myself, *Can I possibly survive a fall from this height?* and to answer myself, *Not likely,* before my right foot cleared the edge, then my left—and then someone had hold of me around my waist and hauled me back up onto the wall.

That someone was Kenric. I saw the surprise on his face as he took in my damp, sooty appearance and recognized me, and then he gave that grin that—even under the best of circumstances—made my knees weak. "Thank you," I managed to whisper.

"You're welcome."

Too bad he was my half brother. Too bad he wasn't real.

Behind him a barbarian who had shimmied up a rope anchored by a grappling hook cleared the top of the wall, and Abas took his head off with a swipe of his sword, then he sliced through the rope to prevent anyone else from climbing up.

I looked down the dizzying height and saw a cluster of barbarians holding their shields above the heads of other men to protect them from the arrows our archers were raining down on them. "What are they doing?" I asked.

"Sapping," Kenric told me.

My Rasmussem-provided subconscious told me that meant they were digging a tunnel so that section of wall would collapse.

"Are we in danger?" I asked.

"Not imminent danger. It will be worse at night, when we can't see them so well. Meanwhile..." He nodded beyond me, and I saw that Captain Penrod and some of his men had emerged from a nearby doorway, carrying a huge cauldron that I could only assume held something hot and nasty.

The barbarians must have had a lookout for just such a thing, for as our men tipped the cauldron, a trumpet or horn sounded, and the barbarian sappers ran from their place by the wall so that the burning oil spilled only on the slowest of them.

Then suddenly their horn sounded again, and all the barbarians fell back.

"What's that all about?" Kenric asked suspiciously.

"Dunno," Abas answered. "No reason for a retreat."

Back and back the barbarians pulled, until they were out of range of our archers. Then one man, bearing a white flag, approached on horseback.

"Surely they're not surrendering?" I said, though I very much hoped they were.

"Parley," Captain Penrod told me. "They want to talk—though I don't know why. They weren't winning, but neither were they losing."

Watching with barely suppressed strain as the barbarian messenger approached, the castle guards waited, their arrows notched and trained on him.

Finally within shouting range, the barbarian reined in his horse and called up to us, "Return that which is being ours or we will be killing you all."

Kenric, Abas, Penrod—everyone—was looking at me. *Oh, my turn again to do something?*

I stepped closer to the edge of the battlements. Clutching the upright merlon to steady myself, I scanned the ground below, deserted now except for the bodies of the dead and wounded. If a ghost tickled or shoved now, I was a goner. If one of the supposedly dead barbarians below was faking, I was an open target. Still, I raised my arm so the messenger could see me, and I shouted down to him, "That offer was made to you already. You returned our envoys without their heads. If you killed them before they spoke, this is what they were sent to say: We don't have the crown of Brecc, but we are willing to help you find and reclaim it."

The messenger said, "That is being well and good. But firstest you must be turning over to us that one of you which is being responsible for the death of our good king Grimbold. Otherwise we will never-ever be giving up until everly one of you is being dead."

Everyone was looking in our direction.

I reassured Abas, "Don't worry. I would never turn you over to them."

Kenric made a sound, which, after a moment, I realized was a stifled laugh. Abas scratched his head, obviously confused by what I'd just said.

What? I thought.

Captain Penrod shuffled his feet and told me, "The ranking officer is responsible for the actions of all in his or her command."

For a second I thought *he* was taking responsibility. But he didn't outrank Abas. I did.

"Oh," I said. *I* was responsible for Abas? And Andreanna? And Kenric and Wulfgar? That hardly seemed fair when they were so intent on killing me off.

There was a *whizz* and a *thunk,* which I figured was that hypothetical decoy left on the field to pretend he was dead until he got a clear shot at me.

But it wasn't. It was one of our men, shooting down toward the barbarian. The arrow had struck about a handspan in front of the horse and stood quivering in the ground while the rider tried to control his mount, which was rearing in fright.

Lucky he didn't hit him, I thought, for surely breaking a truce by murdering an unarmed messenger was not right. But before I could take responsibility for my men and yell, "Don't kill him!" another arrow flew from the battlements and struck the ground inches from the horse's leg. And then another. And another. And another. And not a one hit horse or man. Their feathered shafts formed a line in the dirt between him and us.

Despite the threat of death, my men were saying they would not turn me over.

Which was a big relief to me.

The horse was turning in tight circles, but at least he was no longer rearing. The envoy spat on the ground and yelled, "Then be preparing to being dead!" and he spurred his horse back in the direction of his own lines.

"Janine! Janine!" my men began chanting, sounding for all the world like fans cheering their favorite baseball player. For a delicious moment, I forgot this was all make-believe and that my life was in danger—not from barbarian invaders but from computer overload. For a moment I knew what it was like to be popular. Then I remembered that this was merely one step toward surviving this game.

Captain Penrod was saying, "The men are with you because of your courage."

Courage? I'd been scared stiff every moment I'd been up here.

Penrod must have known what I was thinking. He said, "You stayed. You helped. You did what you could."

"Well," I said, "so did all of you."

"The queen didn't," Penrod pointed out.

Abas and Kenric shared a sour look over that rebuff to the royal family name.

By then the barbarian messenger had made it back to

his own lines. The rest of the barbarians gave a great yell and shook their swords and spears and bows in our direction.

I expected them to storm the castle, but they didn't. In fact, they seemed to be settling down where they were.

"They'll wait till nightfall," Penrod said. "They'll be able to accomplish more under cover of dark. Still, we'll need to keep alert in case of raiding parties."

Could I be crowned as king tomorrow if we were still under siege? It didn't seem likely. I couldn't believe I was just supposed to wait until we wore the barbarians down or the barbarians wore us down. I would have asked Kenric and Abas their thoughts, but they had melted into the crowd, and there was no sign of them.

Penrod was ordering his men: "We must tend to our injured during this respite. Sergeants, count up the casualties so that we can set up a schedule for resting and watching."

"I'll be back," I promised Penrod.

I felt the presence of the catacomb ghosts crowding me as I went down the narrow stairway back to the Great Hall. Apparently the other times they had stayed on the battlements, watching the attack. But now that there was a lull, they wanted to hang around me some more. *Oh boy.*

We climbed over the broken doors of the Great Hall and had another meeting. Uldemar had fallen asleep and had to be nudged awake.

"I," Queen Andreanna announced as she walked into the room, "was seeing about provisions for our men.

There was no need to be making unfounded speculations about my courage."

Well, someone had run to Mama fast with news of all that was said.

And I didn't believe her excuse, either. How long does it take to run down to the kitchen and tell the cooks, "We're under attack, so prepare portable food"? But I didn't point that out. I just said, "Good. Thank you. That's one thing less for me to have to worry about." *One VERY SMALL thing* . . .

We didn't wait for Sister Mary Ursula, whose size and age pretty generally made her the last to arrive. Eventually she would catch up.

"Any thoughts?" I asked.

"You could sacrifice yourself for the good of the many," Andreanna suggested.

Of all people, it was Sir Deming who came to my defense. "The way the barbarians would see it is that if we're weak enough to offer up our king, we're weak enough to be conquered. They would not be satisfied with just her death."

"It was only a suggestion," Andreanna pouted.

"How vulnerable are we?" I asked.

Kenric said, "We have enough food to last for two weeks, longer on half rations. The well is supplied by groundwater springs—no way they can befoul that—so, an unlimited supply."

Which would have been good news if *I* didn't have only until tomorrow to settle this.

"The sappers?"

Abas answered, "If the guards are alert, the sappers can be kept at bay." He cracked his knuckles, which—if it was meant to show how tough he was—didn't impress me.

"Any back way I should know about?" I asked. "Secret passages into the castle?"

Deming rolled his eyes. "What's the purpose of fortified walls and a drawbridge if you're going to have a little door marked SECRET ENTRANCE—ATTACKERS PLEASE STAY OUT?"

"Is that a *yes* or a *no*?" I pressed.

"No," he said. "No secret ways in."

"OK," I said. "So, for the moment we're in no immediate danger. Is there anything we can do besides having our archers pick them off one by one?"

"You mean by magic?" Uldemar asked, his eyes as blank and disconcerting as ever.

"That would be a possibility," I said. "What can you do?"

"I can smell the ghosts you brought with you," Uldemar said. "I can use my scrying glass to find people or other living creatures. I can transform my shape, and I can reanimate the dead."

"Reanimate the dead?" Finally this was sounding like good news. "You mean you can bring back our men that were killed during the attack?"

Uldemar was nodding, but Orielle said, "But they'll still be dead, and they'll keep on decomposing, which, personally, I find disagreeable in someone I'm trying to carry on a conversation with."

It did sound like a serious drawback. "What do *you* do, Orielle?" I asked.

She smiled, showing off perfect teeth that I would bet never had an overbite or suffered from tartar buildup. "My specialty is potions," she said. "I have one that will give a man, or a woman, great strength and stamina. If you'd like, I could mix up a batch for all the guards, so each man could fight as though he were two."

"Sort of like an Abas clone," I said, wondering if she'd given some of her potion to my middle half-brother, or if he'd come by his strength solely through diligent self-absorption.

Orielle blinked and processed my anachronistic statement and said, "Like a miniature Abas, yes."

"Except," Xenos said, obviously delighted to be the bearer of bad news, "for that slight little complication."

Orielle made a bad-smell face.

Of course Xenos would find the flaw in anything. "What complication?" I asked.

"It only lasts one hour," Orielle admitted, "so you'd have to calculate exactly when would be the best time to administer it to the men."

"*And . . .*" Xenos prompted.

Peeved, Orielle pointed out to him, "Your ear's on upside down." Sullenly, she admitted to me, "After it wears off, the person will be so weak, he won't even be able to stand up. That stage lasts two hours."

Not a good thing if the battle isn't quite over on schedule.

Xenos was tugging his ear and frowning, so Uldemar

had a chance to say, "Hardly better than one of my dead people, eh?"

I asked, "Xenos, what do you do?"

Now he was ticked off, too. "Apparently I sit here all afternoon with my ear on upside down, and nobody tells me."

"Can you fix it magically?" I asked, trying to be helpful, as well as trying to get a feel for what he was capable of.

"You ignorant little nobody, you," he snapped. "I make artifacts. Like crowns that get stolen away from perfectly nice barbarian kings by unscrupulous civilized kings and then stupidly given to nasty dragons." He jumped to his feet. "So I, for one, have no need to worry about the barbarians tearing down your walls or starving you out, for they hold me in high esteem and will let me pass without harm."

"Perhaps," I told him. "But unfortunately we won't be able to lower the drawbridge to let you out—"

"I don't need you"—he glanced around the room to include all of us—"or your drawbridge." He muttered something I couldn't make out, then walked through the wall with as much ease as someone walking from sunlight through shadow.

"Now you've done it," Uldemar said. "Now you've really irked him."

I guessed so. Annoying as the beastly little guy could be, I asked, "Can you stop him?" because I might need him later on in the game.

"I can only try." Uldemar reached into his robes and

pulled out a vial from which he poured a powder into his palm. This he tossed into the air in front of himself. As soon as the powder touched him, he transformed into a bat. Either that, or he disappeared and the powder itself transformed into a bat—it happened too fast to be sure of anything, except that it was one of the scenes from Rasmussem's promo. Only then it had been an eagle. With a cry disconcertingly like a squeal, the bat flew out the window.

Queen Andreanna said to me, "Well, you've gotten rid of two out of three of the people most likely to help us out of this disaster you've caused. What are you going to do next?"

I caused this? What about Abas's input into the situation?

Luckily, I didn't have to answer, because at that moment Sister Mary Ursula entered the room.

Unluckily, what she said was, "Bad, bad, bad news. Bad news. Prince Wulfgar and the squadron accompanying him and the treasury are now One with the barbarians."

CHAPTER TWENTY-ONE

Back to the Battlements

Queen Andreanna screamed and threw herself backward like a Victorian lady having the vapors. But I figured it was calculated drama, for she didn't lose herself to the moment enough to fall off the back of the bench.

Orielle rushed to her side to fan her and to say, "There, there," which might have meant that Orielle was easily fooled, or—more likely—that she was smart enough to *pretend* she was easily fooled.

"What happened?" I asked Sister Mary Ursula.

"Wulfgar was returning from Fairfield, leading the wagons bearing the recovered gold," Sister Mary Ursula said. She paused and considered. "Gold..." She shook her head disapprovingly. "True, it is of the earth and comes from the earth, but if ever there was a thing which caused more division rather than Oneness—"

"Sister Mary Ursula!" Andreanna bellowed, having recovered, at least, the strength of her voice. "Get on with what's happened to my son!"

"He must have been feeling a certain sense of Oneness," Sister Mary Ursula said, refusing to be put entirely off, "for he didn't send scouts ahead, and so he stumbled into the barbarian camp and was captured."

"*I* would have sent scouts," Abas grumbled, "no matter how *One* I felt."

"Yes, dear," Andreanna said, "but that's you."

I was thinking that Wulfgar, being what he was, should have had a certain advantage in a surprise attack. Not sure how many people knew of his ability to transform into a wolf, and not wanting to give away anything that I shouldn't, I said, "Perhaps Wulfgar, being the clever person he is, might have managed to escape..."

Sister Mary Ursula asked, "You mean by turning into a wolf?"—which goes to show that not every situation calls for subtlety. "No, the barbarian messenger specifically said that didn't work."

"'Messenger'?" I echoed. "The barbarians sent a messenger?"

"Well, of course there's a messenger. How else would I know what had happened? Captain Penrod sent me to ask you to come up to the north battlement."

Again my brothers moved faster than I could—one of the disadvantages of wearing a dress, particularly a dress that's five sizes too big. But I was ahead of Andreanna, Deming, and Orielle, and way ahead of Sister Mary Ursula and, once again, Uldemar.

Looking over the parapet, I saw the barbarian messenger had walked this time, and he had one of our guards as prisoner. The guard was holding a sack, and a pile of gold was poured out at his feet—proof that the man was not a simple deserter but one of the group that had been accompanying the gold.

I called down, "If you think *that's* Prince Wulfgar, you're mistaken."

The barbarian spat. People in this world seemed fond of spitting. He said, "Wulfgar is being the one what can be changing his self into a wolf. He is being our captive."

"We take your word for that?" I asked.

The barbarian gave his prisoner a shake. "Tell," he commanded.

The guard was nodding. "The prince is alive," he assured us. "He was asleep in one of the wagons when the barbarians surrounded us. He changed into a wolf but was struck in the shoulder by an arrow. Though he's injured, he will recover."

Sure, one of us got some rest, I thought grumpily, though it was hardly a fair grievance considering that now he was captive and wounded. I also thought, *Am I the only one in this kingdom who DIDN'T know Wulfgar could take on the shape of a wolf?*

Meanwhile, I called down to the barbarian, "What are you offering?"

"The life of the prince for the life of the princess."

To my surprise—and gratification—there was a roar of protest from my men on the battlements.

Before I could get too smug, Abas, sentimental softy that he was, nudged me and said, "Ask if that trade includes the gold, too."

Deming said, "The situation is more emotionally

wrenching than before, but we cannot give in to their demands."

Thank you, Deming.

I was glad to have a refusal that sounded like a political stance rather than cowardice. I yelled down, "We do not bargain with extortioners. But remember this: Harm Wulfgar and you lose any chance to negotiate later."

The barbarian spat—which came as no surprise—and slit the throat of his hostage—which *was* a surprise.

Our men released a flurry of arrows, deeming he had broken the truce first, but he was at the border of their range and quickly sprinted back to his own lines.

Andreanna said to me, "That's what they'll do to Wulfgar, too. And it's all your fault."

I half expected her to spit, too, but fortunately she didn't. She turned and headed for the stairs. "Out of my way, you old fool," I heard her say.

Sister Mary Ursula hefted herself up the last step, huffing like a beached whale. Andreanna pushed past her, and Abas and Kenric followed, with Orielle close behind, and Deming behind her. Sister Mary Ursula asked, "Did I miss anything?"

I ignored her and asked Penrod, "Did you see Xenos come walking out of the castle—through the walls—a short while ago?"

Though that should have been hard to miss, he said, "'Through the walls,' Princess?" and shook his head. "No, Princess."

"Or did you notice a bat, maybe?"

"A . . ."—Penrod hesitated—"bat?"

I waved my arms to indicate flapping wings.

210

"Hard to say, Princess," Penrod said. "Usually bats don't come out till dusk."

It didn't make any difference. I doubted Uldemar could get Xenos to return—even if, as a bat using his sonar sense instead of eyes, Uldemar could find him.

Perhaps thinking I'd become mentally unbalanced, Penrod said, "You should take what rest you can now, Princess. When the sun sets, they will resume their attack."

Would a two-hour nap make me feel like a new person, or would it just give all my overworked muscles time to stiffen? Better, I thought, to stay in the guards' view, helping—getting their attention in a good way lest they reconsider how much they had to gain by turning me over to the barbarians.

"Let's get these men fed," I told Penrod. "There'll be little enough time for that later."

Sister Mary Ursula said, "Oh no, not the stairs again."

"Sorry," I told her. I tried to think of something useful to occupy her. "Could you organize the ladies into making bandages?"

"I am One with the chickadee," she answered. "I am mother and sister and child of the deer the moment before the hunter's arrow pierces its heart."

I had no idea if that meant yes or no, or if she was simply declaring that she was a vegetarian.

THE GUARDS stayed on the walls, in case the barbarian attack came sooner than we expected, so their food had to be brought up to them.

I tried to help the pages, but frankly I was more bother than benefit because I had to hold my skirts up out of the way going up those stairs—and that's hard to do while carrying a heavy tray of food—and because the ghosts kept getting in everybody's way in the crowded stairwell.

"Maybe," the head page suggested, "it would be best if you stayed up here, helping to distribute the food."

I ended up doling out the mead, which had to be the best job I could have to make them appreciate me, for they seemed to like drinking better than eating.

But all the while, the shadows were lengthening and the edge of the sky got pink, and the pages scurried to clean up before the battle began and the trays and barrels and dishes became a hazard to the men who would be defending our lives.

I pounded the lid back onto the barrel of mead with the butt of a knife one of the men loaned me for that purpose.

"And did *you* take time to eat?" someone asked from behind me.

I turned to see Kenric, but my happiness at his concern was diminished by the sight of Orielle standing by him. He was carrying a huge wicker laundry basket filled with rags, and he put this down by my feet.

Ah, I thought, *Sister Mary Ursula's bandage brigade has been at work.*

Kenric said, "Orielle, go fetch Janine something to eat before they bring everything back to the kitchen, will you?"

I thought she might bristle at being spoken to as though she were a servant, but she only said, "Certainly," and went to intercept one of the pages.

Kenric nodded toward the bandages and said, "Orielle has doused these in a potion that will help promote healing."

"That was kind of her," I said.

Kenric grinned. "Orielle doesn't do things out of kindness," he said. "She works for pay."

Well. So maybe the two of them weren't as cozy as I'd thought.

Orielle came back bearing a bowl of stew and a hunk of bread. "You aren't being very kind," she complained to Kenric. "I don't *always* demand to be paid." She handed me the bowl. "I very much admire how you're handling yourself," she told me. "To go from the quiet life you've been used to ... I can't imagine. My father ran out on us when I was born with the witch mark on me." *Another no-account father,* I thought as she held up her palm, showing a pentagram that seemed etched into her skin. "My mother tried to drown me when I was seven, and I was raised in the gutter. I'm used to betrayal and deception and people trying to use me. But you're doing this all on your own, not needing anybody, not having to play *men's* games..." She drifted off, and I knew she meant "not having to flirt and act sexy," which I figured I couldn't have done, anyway, but I didn't think she was putting me down for not looking like a cover girl. It didn't sound as though her fabulous looks had given her a happy life. In fact, she said, "I envy you *so* much."

Somebody who looked like Orielle envied *me?*

"I've got an idea," Orielle said. "How about if we send Kenric away, and then we can discuss what's wrong with men and the way they run the world?"

"I beg your pardon," Kenric said. "What's wrong with men?"

"Nothing," Orielle said. "Nothing is ever wrong with a man—it's always someone else's fault."

"That's a stereotype," Kenric pointed out.

It was, but I couldn't help throwing in a joke I'd heard: "If a man is all alone in the forest with no one to hear him . . . is he still wrong?"

Orielle laughed.

"So," Kenric said, "should I just leave the two of you on your own, then?"

We waved him away and sat down on the battlement. "This stew," I said, "is the best thing I've eaten all day."

"It's the *only* thing you've eaten all day," she pointed out.

It was venison, which I wouldn't have chosen even before Sister Mary Ursula's comment about poor hunted deer. But I was hungry enough that I was willing to eat Bambi's mother.

Watching Kenric, who had gone to stand by Abas, Orielle said, "I'll admit those three are good-looking . . ."

"They are that," I agreed.

"But if I hear Abas brag one more time about how many roast ducks he can eat in one sitting or how many cows he can lift with one arm . . ."

I said, "Do the words *Spanish steel* mean anything to you?"

In unison and with a great deal of pomposity we both said, "Toledo," then giggled as though we were safe in a school cafeteria.

Orielle said, "And, of course, you can't trust Kenric."

"So I've heard," I said, thinking of Nigel Rasmussem's warning.

"And Wulfgar—come the full moon and he's impossible."

"I can imagine."

Orielle sighed. "But their looks *are* distracting."

I nodded, but I shifted uncomfortably. The stew seemed to be sitting in a lump somewhere between my throat and my stomach.

"Is something wrong?" Orielle asked.

I set down the bowl of stew. "I think I ate too fast after not eating for so long." I tugged on the neckline of my dress. "And I really should change out of this velvet monstrosity. I'm *so* hot." The day was ending. Shouldn't it be cooling off? My lips felt parched, and I went to lick them, but my tongue was so dry and heavy, I couldn't move it. I tried to say, "Isn't it getting awfully hot?" but my voice came out thick and garbled. Besides, I could see that it wasn't hot. Some of the men had put on cloaks against the evening chill.

Though my body was still hot, my heart went cold. *It's not fair!* I thought. *I'm doing well. I'm going to finish this game in this lifetime.*

But I'd taken too long to get here.

The damaged Rasmussem computers were overloading my brain. I was beginning to die.

"No!" I tried to cry defiantly, but it was little more than a moan.

"Let me get you something to drink," Orielle offered.

I saw her stand, but I felt as though I were looking through the wrong end of a telescope. And either she was tipping, or I was. *Must be me,* I reasoned, for the parapet was at an odd angle, too.

Kenric came up to Orielle and put his arm around her waist. "Not feeling well, is she?" he asked.

"Fevered," Orielle said, "and delirious."

"Ah, what a pity," Kenric said, not looking or sounding the least bit pitying.

Neither did Orielle, come to think of it.

Captain Penrod came rushing over. *He* did look distressed. "Princess!" he cried. He took hold of me and sat me up straight—I know only because I could see him do it. I couldn't feel his hands on my arms. My neck was no longer strong enough to hold my head up.

I couldn't feel anything, and I told myself, *Don't panic. It could be worse. Not feeling anything is better than feeling pain.* But that didn't truly help.

Abas must have joined the group. "What's the matter with *her*?" I heard him ask.

"Fevered and delirious," Kenric said.

"Just like Father," Abas commented dryly.

"Just like Father," Kenric echoed.

And then I *did* feel something. I felt fizziness engulf my body.

CHAPTER TWENTY-TWO

Did Someone Say Déjà Vu?

They'd *poisoned* me, dammit. Probably to trade my dead body to the barbarians for Wulfgar's safe return. Or maybe just for the fun of it. Both Sir Deming and Queen Andreanna had insisted King Cynric had been fevered and delirious before he died. They'd brought it up as a rationale for why the king had named me his heir, but now I wondered what had killed *him*.

And Kenric. Deming had declared him much too interested in magic. Yeah, right. Much too interested in a certain user of magic. I should have asked Orielle *why* her mother had tried to drown her.

I stood up on the hillside overlooking St. Jehan and screamed in frustration—which scared Dusty, though she still came up to me, just slower than usual, her tail giving a tentative little wag. I was glad that I wasn't being deep-fried by the computer, but I *would be* if I didn't figure my way out of this convoluted, backstabbing, mean-spirited game.

"Is everything all right, dear?" my mother asked when I got to the bottom of the hill.

"I am One with the morning," I told her. "And my chosen adviser knows her meats."

"That's nice," my mother said, and she introduced me to Sir Deming, and I met my father—who was my favorite person in this game—and I went to the shrine of Saint Bruce the Warrior Poet.

I spent my travel time working on remembering the poem I'd recited last time. I was beginning to suspect that Saint Bruce would accept any poem a player made up, but I knew for a fact that he had accepted "An Ode to Saint Bruce." *I* didn't think it was good poetry, but who was I to argue with a saint with a sword in his hand? So I recited it again:

> *"Saint Bruce was a warrior poet.*
> *He lived in a cave, don't you know it?*
> *He wrote sonnets and verses,*
> *But never said curses.*
> *He'll give you one chance—please don't blow it."*

Feordina whimpered and flung herself out of the way, but then she always did.

I was waiting for her to say, "He must be in a good mood. Lucky you; he's accepted your poem," when I saw the sword begin its fatal swing down.

```
SUBJ:   URGENT--Deadline
DATE:   5/25   04:17:06 P.M. US eastern
        daylight time
FROM:   Nigel Rasmussem
        <nrasmussem@rasmussem.com>
TO:     dept. heads distribution list
```

Our numbers concur with Japan's:
Giannine may or may not have time
to complete one more lifetime. There
definitely won't be another chance.

She is making a valiant effort but may
not be able to make up for time lost in
her initial attempts to break through
level 1.

Medical personnel standing by.

Members of the press are aware that
there is a situation but do not have
details. Please remain calm and refer
all questions to Jim in PR, who is
preparing a statement.

I will try to remain calm, too, but I
am sick at heart.

CHAPTER TWENTY-THREE

Will the Guilty Party Please Step Forward?

OK, so apparently when Feordina warned that Saint Bruce had a good memory, she didn't just mean he would recognize published poetry—apparently she meant a player had to make up a new poem each time.

Thanks a lot, Nigel Rasmussem.

OK: hill, Deming, Dad, shrine... The next time I stood in front of the statue, I recited:

> *"A poem in a cave:*
> *Offering up all my hopes*
> *On butterfly wings."*

Feordina didn't wince and duck. She smiled and said, "Haiku."

"Yes," I said.

"Saint Bruce likes haiku."

"Well, good."

"Except..."

How had I known there'd be an "Except..."?

"Except, haiku's so *very* short..."

"Succinct," I corrected.

"Good word," she told me. "Haiku's so *very* short that if a poet offers up haiku poetry, Bruce *does* like two." She smiled her brown-toothed smile at me.

A *second* poem?

"Did I mention the time limit?"

So, on the spot, I made up another haiku:

> *"The statue of Bruce,*
> *Silent but waiting to strike:*
> *Poem, do not fail me."*

Feordina and I watched the sword.

"Not quite as good as the first one," she said. "But he must be in a good mood. Lucky you."

If I were lucky, my father would have forgotten my birthday.

But apparently, I thought as I hid the ring in my bodice, I had to make my own luck one step at a time.

So when, at the castle, Rawdon introduced himself, I wouldn't let him go. "No, you come into the Great Hall with me," I told him.

"Oh, but you're meeting your family for the first time," he said. "This should be a joyous private occasion."

I could have said, "Yeah, well, we both know it's not going to be and, anyway, I know where you're off to, you larcenous little weasel, you." But I didn't. I just said, pleasantly, "I insist. As your new king."

The royal family didn't care that I brought a witness with me; they were just as irritable and snide as ever.

I'd been thinking about which family member I needed to choose as an ally. They'd each had a crack at killing me: Abas had taken my head off in this very room; Wulfgar, in his wolf shape, had killed me both in the topiary maze and in the barbarian camp; and I was sure Kenric had arranged for me to be poisoned—whether or not he was also behind the death of King Cynric.

So, who to choose this time?

Wulfgar was unpredictable unless I used the ring on him; so if I needed the ring later on, I'd be out of luck.

Abas had prevented the barbarians from kidnapping me—which I had to believe was a good thing—except that, in saving me, he had killed King Grimbold, which the barbarians seemed exceptionally reluctant to forgive. Was there a way to get Abas to fight off the barbarians more . . . gently?

"Abas" and "gently" in the same sentence: *Right.*

Bringing me back to Kenric, who had been my first choice all those tries ago, based on his good looks— which were, come to think of it, what had gotten me into this game to begin with. *Kenric.* Well, Mr. Rasmussem had warned me away from him. Or maybe not. "Kenric and Sister Mary Ursula don't work well together," he'd said. Maybe all he had meant was that that pairing needed extra work.

How many more times could I afford to be wrong?

"Kenric," I called as the royals dispersed. "May Counselor Rawdon and I walk with you?"

At which point Rawdon said, "You know what would be nice? Why don't the two of you have a cozy little chat—"

"No, no." I linked arms with both him and Kenric.

"Let's all three of us walk together and get to know one another. Tell me, each of you, your impressions of King Cynric."

They both looked startled and maybe a bit worried at that thought.

I said, "Rawdon, you first."

"Oh," Rawdon blustered. "Well. Ah. What do you mean?"

"I haven't had a chance to know my father. It's very difficult to grow up without a father, you know. So many things make no sense if you don't have your dad— those mushy Father's Day cards every June, Father Christmas, 'Our Father who art in heaven...'"

They were looking at me as though my brain were dribbling out of my nose.

"Not that I'm bitter or anything. Was he a good man? Fair? Did he have any faults, like, was he overly trusting, perhaps?"

By then we were out in the courtyard. There was the supply wagon, though no barbarians were lurking behind it for the moment. And there were Captain Penrod and the other guard, yet again dragging the poacher boy between them.

"Oh, look," I said. "I wonder if this is something we need to make a decision about. Hello, Captain. I'm Princess Janine. What's happened here?"

Penrod said, "We caught this boy poaching. He killed a deer. The usual punishment?"

Before Kenric could ask me what I thought, I turned to Rawdon and asked, "What do *you* advise, Counselor?

Are you an advocate of strict interpretation of severe laws to deter crime?"

I saw Rawdon gulp. His voice faint and maybe wobbling just the slightest bit, he said, "The law is the law."

The boy sniveled, "No. I didn't do nothing. I found 'im dead already. I was dressing 'im down so's the meat wouldn't go to waste, but I didn't kill 'im."

I pressed Rawdon. "So there's no room for compassion for one who has foolishly done wrong, then come to sincerely regret his crime?"

"I wouldn't say that," Rawdon whispered.

No, I wouldn't think you would.

I saw that Kenric was watching Rawdon appraisingly, no doubt wondering what had rattled him. I said, "Of course, in this case, we don't even know for sure that the accused is guilty. Or do we?" I turned to Penrod. "Did any witness actually see him kill the deer?"

"No witnesses," Penrod admitted. "But look at his hands."

I said, "Good point. But then, he admitted he was dressing down the deer once it was already dead. This is a difficult decision without witnesses. Do we know for a fact how the deer died, and how long it had been dead?"

"There was an arrow in its gut," Penrod said. "And the body was still warm."

"You're very good at details," I told him. His manner was friendlier, too, once I didn't simply dismiss him and declare him wrong and the boy free. "Was the boy carrying a bow?"

"Yes," Penrod said.

The boy hastily said, "I found it. It was just layin'

there, like, on the ground, at the edge of the clearing. And I, uh, picked it up before I started in on the deer. Which was dead already. Killed by someone else. Who probably heard me comin', and thought it was you, and fled before I got there. Before *you* got there, too."

"That's not a very likely story," I told him. "But on the other hand, I don't see any way to disprove it." I looked at the men around me, none of whom was saying anything. I said, "I'm inclined to say that—since we can't avow that this boy is the culprit—it is better to err on the side of compassion."

Penrod looked about to object, so I added, "But neither can we be seen to let people flaunt the law. Still, killing the boy serves no purpose. The deer is already dead, whether by his doing or another's—and his death will not bring the deer back. Cutting the boy's hand off will only make him unlikely to find gainful employment, and he'll become a drain on society. If we jail him, we have to feed him and take guards off their regular duty in order to watch him. I think the best solution is to put him to work—for a period of...a month?" I looked at Rawdon. "What do you think?"

"That sounds fair to me," Rawdon said weakly.

"Interesting," Kenric said, whether at my line of reasoning or at Rawdon's response.

"Captain, you decide what chores you think would be best to set for this boy. Keep in mind his age and his strength, but assign him whatever duties you see fit."

Penrod nodded. He ordered the other guard, "Bring him to the crew that's fixing the smithy roof."

"Meanwhile," I said to Penrod as the second guard

led the boy away, "I want you to come to me if there are any problems you or the other guards have with the way anything is done here."

"Yes, Princess," Penrod said.

"Anything," I repeated. "You and your men are the backbone of this castle. The work you do is invaluable, and I see that you run things smoothly, efficiently, and fairly, and I want you to know how much I appreciate that."

"Thank you, Princess," Penrod said.

"You know what?" I turned to Rawdon. "Here we are starting a new kingship, with a new way of interpreting the laws, and I think something else we need to do is give a better salary to our hardworking guards. What do you think?"

"Well," Rawdon huffed, but that was all he could get out.

I smiled at Penrod. "How much and how often do you get paid?"

"Actually," he said, "there seems to have been a problem with that lately. We've been shorted several times the last months, and we haven't yet been paid for the past fortnight."

"Really?" I said. Kenric was already looking at Rawdon, so I turned to him, too. "Who's in charge of the men's pay?" I demanded.

"You see," Rawdon told me, "as the king was getting weaker these past weeks, I began to worry that someone might take advantage of the situation, and once the king named you his heir, I thought, *Well, but the king's wife and her sons might refuse to acknowledge the king's wishes,* and I thought, *If they have access to the king's treasury, there's no telling*—"

Kenric took hold of Rawdon by the scruff of his neck. "Have you done something with the treasury?"

"No," Rawdon said. "That is, I just moved it—for safekeeping."

"Where?" Kenric demanded.

"I didn't mean that I mistrusted *you*," Rawdon assured Kenric. "Of course, I knew *you* wouldn't try to make off with the money, but sometimes your brothers—"

Kenric gave him a shake.

"Fairfield," Rawdon admitted.

Kenric shook him even harder.

"How much did you steal?" I asked, because in this lifetime there was no way for me to know. "All of it?"

"No," he said as though that thought was ridiculous. "Just some. Just a little."

"Uh-huh," I said. "You've seen my mercy with the boy accused of poaching. I will spare your life, too, if you show us where you've hidden the treasury. You will be dismissed as counselor and instead will be put in charge of..." What was something bad, but not so horrible he'd rebel? I thought of our neighbors in St. Jehan and finished, "...in charge of raising the pigs."

Rawdon dropped to his knees, kissed my hand, and said, "Thank you, Your Gracious Highness."

"Good job, Princess," Captain Penrod said to me.

"Yes," Kenric acknowledged. Was he actually looking at me with respect? Yes, I was pretty sure he was. *Surprised* respect, but still...

I said, "Penrod, you take Rawdon and keep him

under guard, while Kenric and I determine how much of the treasury is gone."

Penrod saluted, while Kenric held his hand out for Rawdon's keys.

I said, "And, Penrod, the queen mentioned the possibility of barbarian unrest. My instincts tell me this is a very serious danger. Double the guards around the castle wall, and make sure everyone is alert."

"Yes, Princess."

As Kenric and I turned back to the castle, I just barely caught a glimpse of Sister Mary Ursula as she reentered ahead of us. Apparently, if I didn't simply let the poacher go, she didn't approach me. Either that, or the fact that I was with Kenric kept her away.

"Who was that?" I asked since, in this lifetime, I hadn't met her.

"That is the singular Sister Mary Ursula," Kenric told me.

I let it go at that.

Naturally, when we got to the treasury room, there was quite a bit more than "some" of it missing. All that was left was what he would have made off with this day. "The first thing I think we should do is put Sir Deming in charge of counting out exactly how much is left," I said. Obnoxious irritant that he was, I had no reason to doubt his honesty; and Sister Mary Ursula had made clear her distrust of and disliking for gold. For all I knew, she might toss what was left into the lake to make the gold One with the water. "Then I want the guards paid, and I want them to get a bonus for their salaries being late, because the last thing we need is to lose credibility with them. Then we'll need to get wagons and guards to travel to Fairfield to retrieve the money."

"How many?" Kenric asked.

"I'll leave that up to you," I said, to make him feel I valued his opinion. If he suggested something significantly different from what Penrod had in the previous game, I could always overrule him.

"And will you go to Fairfield yourself," Kenric asked, "or will you send a representative?"

"What do you suggest?" I asked.

"*I* don't care."

OK. "Well, then," I told him, "probably I'll go." I didn't think anything was scheduled to happen at the castle in the afternoon that I would miss. All I'd done the previous time was get cleaned up and fitted with that awful red dress. Then I'd lost a lot of time searching in the catacombs, running back and forth to the castle. . . .

Oh, yeah, the catacombs. I suddenly remembered the ghosts. If I *didn't* go, the ghosts wouldn't be able to follow me—surely a good thing. But I worried that, without me, the game would arrange for *something* to happen so that whomever I sent wouldn't be able to find the money.

We went back down to the courtyard to assure Penrod there was enough left in the treasury to pay the back salaries. Though I could see the extra guards posted, I remained alert for barbarians, glancing back and forth and over my shoulder—for I was fairly certain Rasmussem would have them get in even if I ordered *all* the guards out.

229

Kenric finally asked, "Is something wrong? You seem to be doing an awful lot of twitching."

I couldn't admit what I knew, so I said, "Fleas."

"Charming." Kenric sighed.

Sure enough, when we got to the wagon, I saw a shadow that shouldn't be there. I shoved Kenric out of the way, hit the ground rolling, and yelled, "Attack! We're under attack!"

CHAPTER TWENTY-FOUR

Fast Forward

An arrow whizzed through the air where a moment earlier Kenric and I had been standing.

"Attempt to take prisoners!" I shouted. I kept rolling, reversing direction, this way and that, trying to make myself an unlikely target for the barbarian archers.

Our guards manning the walls fired a flurry of arrows into the area behind the wagon. They were also firing over the wall—which must have meant that the rest of the raiding party had come out of hiding when they realized their compatriots in the castle compound were in trouble.

I stopped rolling, figuring that the three barbarians who were behind the wagon had enough other worries that they were unlikely to be concentrating on me. Besides, if nobody was shooting at me, I must look incredibly silly rolling all over the courtyard.

Some of the guards went behind the wagon, and they

dragged out two bodies and led out a prisoner. For the moment, I was too dizzy to focus on his face.

Kenric helped me to my feet and held on to me as I staggered toward the wagon. The survivor *was* King Grimbold. I sighed heavily, and Kenric tightened his grip, no doubt convinced I was about to faint. Penrod was on my other side, though I'd been unaware when he'd joined us. One of the guards on the wall yelled down, "Captain, about a half-dozen barbarians took off into the woods."

"Should we pursue them?" Penrod asked me.

"No," I said. "We'll question this man first." I gave my most regal look down my nose—though I was no competition for Queen Andreanna and her *what*-is-that-bad-smell? glare—and I demanded, "Who are you? And why did you sneak over our walls and attempt to do harm to me and my men?"

Grimbold spat—big surprise—and announced, "I am being Grimbold, King of the North, and I have comed here to claim that which is being mine that has been stoled."

I gave just the hint of a bow of my head—only enough to acknowledge his status as a king. "King Grimbold, I am Princess Janine de St. Jehan, due to be crowned as the new Shelban king in two days' time. I wish that we could have met under better circumstances. Surely this"—I waved my hand in the direction of his two dead compatriots and all my guards with bows still trained on him—"this is not the way for neighbors to meet."

The fact that I was speaking calmly, without threats, had a positive effect on the captive king.

"My peoples," he explained, "have never been having good luck speaking to your peoples."

"I am sorry to hear that," I assured him. I gestured for our guards to put their weapons away. There was little Grimbold could do to harm me unless he made a suicidal leap forward to throttle me, and my show of good faith could only make him obligated to me. "What is this item of yours that you believe we have?"

"The crown of our firstest chieftain, Brecc the Slayer, made for him by the wizard Xenos."

"Do we have such a thing?" I asked those around me.

"Yes," Kenric admitted.

"We *stole* it?" I tried to sound as appalled, as though I were only hearing it for the first time.

"Not exactly."

"I think," I said in my best Solomon voice, "we need to settle this immediately. King Grimbold, I regret the death of your companions. I wish that you had known me well enough to have felt you could approach openly."

He inclined his head, which I very much hoped meant he was taking responsibility for the death of his own men.

"Meanwhile," I said, "let us discuss this matter indoors. Shouldn't it be almost time to eat?"

There were lots of enthusiastic nods from my men.

"Then let us go in."

Neither those guards who were scheduled to eat at that time nor Grimbold waited to be invited twice, leaving me alone with Captain Penrod and Kenric.

Penrod dropped to his knees and offered me his sword. "Obviously, I didn't post enough guards, Princess

Janine. You could have been killed, and it would have been my fault."

"No." I shook my head for emphasis and refused to take the sword. "They were determined and would have gotten in no matter what. I have the utmost trust in you."

He bowed, with a murmured, "I am indebted to you."

Kenric said, "As am I. I owe my life to your vigilance."

"To my fleas," I corrected, "that made me restless."

Kenric smiled. "Nevertheless..." he said, and took my arm again—this time not to steady me, but to escort me into the Great Hall.

When I entered the room on Kenric's arm, Queen Andreanna wore an expression as though she'd just put a pickled eyeball into her mouth. Kenric ignored his mother's scowl and smacked Abas on the arm, indicating for him to move in closer to Wulfgar, so that I could sit at the high table with them.

"We need room for King Grimbold, too," I said.

Abas had already gotten as close to Wulfgar as comfort would allow, but neither Wulfgar nor Andreanna budged.

"That is being all right," Grimbold announced. "I will be seating myself here, next to this handsome woman." And with that he plunked himself down on the edge of the bench beyond Andreanna, which—under normal circumstances—would have accommodated only the tiniest of persons. Grimbold wasn't tiny.

Andreanna scooted closer to Wulfgar faster than I'd ever seen her move.

"Hello, there, my lovely," Grimbold said to the queen. "I be guessing you still being fit enough to be breeding children."

"I beg your pardon!" Andreanna was practically on Wulfgar's lap, trying to gain more distance from Grimbold.

Grimbold, who hadn't spoken quietly before, now shouted, "I said, 'I be guessing you still being fit enough to be breeding children!'"

"King Grimbold," I said by way of introduction, "this is Queen Andreanna, the widow of King Cynric. Queen Andreanna, this is King Grimbold, whom I have invited to dine with us while we discuss matters of state."

"Ah!" Grimbold shouted the length of the table down to me. "The queen, is she? Probably one of them delicate sorts—is that what you be telling me?"

I nodded.

He turned his attention back to Andreanna. "All right, then," he assured her, "I be acting refined around you." He nudged her in the ribs with his elbow and winked. "I don't be believing in making my women skittish."

For just this once, things only got better.

Grimbold explained that King Cynric had taken the crown that rightfully belonged to him and his people.

Abas explained that his father had won it in a tournament.

Grimbold and Abas debated the finer points of tournament rules till the rest of us were just about facedown asleep in our bowls of leek soup before Abas conceded that perhaps his father had been a bit overly lenient in his interpretation of what was and was not allowed.

Queen Andreanna protested, "He won it fairly!"

Grimbold said, "I be liking a woman what defends her man."

Next I asked where the crown was likely to be—of

course, nobody knew—and we invited Sir Deming and Sister Mary Ursula to join us. Grimbold moved in even closer to Andreanna and said to Sister Mary Ursula, "Come over here and sit next to me, you sweet young thing," though she had to be thirty years older than he was.

Sister Mary Ursula giggled like a sixth grader.

Once again Deming remembered that King Cynric had given the crown to the dragon, and once again he speculated that one of the magic-users might know how to find the dragon.

I gave orders for the magic-users to be sent for, despite Sister Mary Ursula's warning that magic was nasty.

Grimbold assured her that he would protect her from any of magic's nastiness.

She giggled some more.

Grimbold said he would send word to his people that I was working on reclaiming the crown and that they should postpone attacking the castle.

"Give me three days," I told him, knowing I had only two days, at the most, before the game would end—with or without my having recovered the crown.

"One," Grimbold said, a hard bargainer despite the fact that he'd just eaten close to an entire roast pig at my table.

"Two," I countered, and he spat on the floor and slapped his palm on the table, which seemed to mean we had an agreement.

Queen Andreanna left the table before the pastries were served, murmuring something about having to watch her figure, despite Grimbold's assurance that he liked his women substantial enough to grab hold of.

In fact, we all left the table before Grimbold had finished eating.

I had decided it was safest if I accompanied Rawdon and the guards on the expedition to Fairfield, just in case of complications. I hoped that, with Rawdon leading us through the catacombs directly to where he had hidden the gold, I might avoid picking up any ghosts. But, just in case, I decided I'd better take a quick bath now and choose what clothes to wear. Who knew when the next time would be I could do so without witnesses?

I told Sir Deming I'd chosen him to be in charge of the treasury—what was left of it, plus what we recovered—and that made him almost pleasant. What he said was, "Good decision."

"Can you suggest someone I might borrow clothes from?" I asked, sending mental vibrations his way that said, *Not Lady Bliss, not Lady Bliss.*

Deming looked at me appraisingly, and I was sure he was about to make a disparaging remark. Instead, he said, "If you're going to be running around the countryside digging up treasure, you might do well to borrow one of the page's uniforms."

It struck me as a good idea, too.

After bathing and changing, and making a twine necklace to hold the ring, and handing out to the guards their back salaries and their bonuses, it was time to set off for Fairfield. This time we brought provisions in case we were there long enough to get hungry. I left Kenric in charge of the castle because that seemed a good show of trust in him at a time when, in fact, I was fairly confident nothing much would be going on. I brought Captain Penrod with me, since the castle was no longer in danger of barbarian attack.

Rawdon didn't cause any trouble on the way, being so relieved not to have received a death sentence that he kept trying to kiss my hand. Who would have guessed that such a thing could become excessive?

In the catacombs I still caught glimpses of things that weren't there and heard echoes of whispers that had never been spoken.

I didn't have high hopes for not accumulating ghosts.

It *was* much easier crawling around tunnels and exploring catacombs while wearing a page's tunic and breeches than it was wearing a red velvet gown made for a woman of the kind Grimbold would definitely have found substantial.

Rawdon led us to his hiding place. Despite all the trouble he'd caused, I even warned him that the doorway looked rather punky and that it needed to be shored up so it wouldn't collapse.

I stayed while the guards brought load after load of gold to the waiting wagons; but if any ghosts had attached themselves to me, and if they *were* going to make sleeping difficult, I knew I should probably get a head start home. Leaving Captain Penrod in charge of escorting the convoy home, I made it back to the castle at about midnight.

The guards recognized me this time—as well they

should, since I was the one who'd given them their money—so they readily let me in. As I walked to the castle, I heard them having trouble raising the drawbridge.

"Hello, ghosts," I muttered.

One of them poked me in the ribs, while another pulled my hair.

The good times were over.

CHAPTER TWENTY-FIVE

Morning Comes Early
When There's No Snooze Button

Just as I had been warned, the ghosts proved to be a nuisance all night long.

They moaned.

They wailed.

They rattled the window shutters.

They set the castle hounds to howling.

It wasn't that their noise was continuous. No, you can get used to just about any sound that *never* stops. Instead, they periodically grew quiet, giving the impression that they had worn themselves out or gotten bored or taken pity on the castle's inhabitants. I would start to doze. Then a door would slam. A long-dead person would scream. Cobwebby fingers would brush my face.

My brain knew that my body was lying on a total immersion couch at a Rasmussem Gaming Center, and that probably less than an hour had passed since I'd gotten there on a Saturday afternoon. Try to tell *that* to the body

I felt I was wearing, which was convinced it had been tossing and turning all night.

I gave up around dawn. A servant had left a bedpan, and a pitcher of water to clean up with. I used both beneath the cover of my blanket, and I dressed under there.

Despite these precautions, I was pretty sure I heard ghostly laughter.

While I'd been away at Fairfield, someone had left an elegant gown for today's use, but I once again chose the page's outfit. The way this game had shown a tendency to go—breeches and tunic were a more practical choice than a dress.

I stuck my head out the door to see if anybody else was up yet. In the hallway, bleary-eyed servants stumbled about their early-morning tasks. And Sister Mary Ursula, wearing her fetching two-towels outfit, was just returning from her skinny-dipping trip. "My soul is refreshed, and I am One with the world," she announced.

"Congratulations," I mumbled. "Do we go to the Great Hall for breakfast, or is it brought up to our rooms?"

"Whatever you decree, dear," Sister Mary Ursula said. "You *are* our next king."

"In my room would be nice," I said, heading back to bed, too exhausted to check whether she or any of the servants had heard.

Apparently the ghosts had truly quit come sunrise. I awoke at a slightly more reasonable hour when a sleep-deprived servant came in carrying breakfast. Buttered chocolate Pop-Tarts would have been nice, but I made do with fresh bread and honey.

"Could you ask Sister Mary Ursula and Sir Deming to meet me in the solar when they finish their breakfasts?" I said.

The servant, yawning, nodded and shuffled her weary way out.

I fought the inclination to put my head back down. Surely someone who hoped to be crowned the following day had more important things to do than sleep—no matter how tired I was. There would be time to catch up *after* I was king.

I knocked on Kenric's door. Though he was dressed, I wouldn't have sworn he was truly awake. "Somehow or other we seem to have picked up ghosts," he told me.

I didn't tell him how or who. I said, "We recovered the gold."

He nodded. "I heard the wagons come in some time between the banshee wailing and the chain dragging."

So had I. I'd figured if there was any problem, Captain Penrod would have sent for me, despite the hour. In fact, I suspected that the guards who had fetched the gold had an easier night than those of us in our beds in the castle.

"I'm going to interview the advisers," I told him, "to see which one to name my official appointee. Any suggestions?"

As I reflected on past games, I saw that Sister Mary Ursula did sometimes give good advice, as when she had warned against trusting Rawdon or eating the venison stew. The trouble was, most often I couldn't tell what she was saying until after the disaster struck. Of course, she had clearly cautioned me regarding magic and Kenric, but I was willing to ignore that. So I thought for a change I'd ask Deming, whom I'd already placed in charge of the treasury. I was pretty sure Kenric would pick him, too—considering that Mr. Rasmussem had warned against choosing both Kenric and Sister Mary Ursula—and that would give me the chance to seem like I was seeking out his advice while I was, in fact, doing what I wanted.

Kenric said, "All things considered, Rawdon wouldn't be my first choice—though he was my father's counselor. And Sister Mary Ursula is a bit..."—he paused and then came up with—"mystical...for my taste. Deming is a bit of an obsequious toady, but on the whole he's steady."

Obsequious? Doesn't that mean the kind of person who says, "Yes, sir. No, sir. Please let me grovel at your feet, sir"? Maybe he was obsequious to some of us in the royal family...

I tried to look thoughtful as I said, "Deming. Hmm."

Kenric was probably waiting for me to go so he could lay his head down for a few more minutes, so I took pity on him and left.

In the solar, Sister Mary Ursula was doing tai chi exercises: those slow-motion, almost dancelike stretches. She had changed out of her towels to another outfit; the accent pieces looked like stuff that was either left on the beach by high tide or blown by the wind against a fence. Sir Deming wasn't there yet.

"Hello," I said. "We haven't had much of a chance to

talk." We hadn't—not in this lifetime. Of course, I *had* been actively avoiding her.

She didn't stop her exercises, but she said, "I am One with my body."

"Well, that's good," I told her. "Meanwhile, I was hoping that you might stay while Sir Deming and I discuss matters of state—"

"Oh no, no." This time she *did* stop. "Oh dear, no. One counselor is all you need. A unicorn only needs one horn to be a unicorn and not a horse or a goat. A blank sheet of parchment only needs one drop of ink before it is no longer blank. A pretty girl only needs one wart on the end of her nose before she doesn't want to leave her house. One counselor is enough, my dear."

I really liked the idea of getting multiple possibilities laid out before me, so I pointed out, "Only if the counselor is the right counselor. I want to be One with wisdom."

Sister Mary Ursula said, "Don't we all?" and resumed her exercises.

Sir Deming came in then. He raised one eyebrow in surprised disapproval at my boys' clothing. "Didn't Lady Patrice bring a dress for you?" He looked ready to turn right around and search for Lady Patrice to complain that I was dressed inappropriately.

"Yes," I told him. "But this seemed better suited to me."

"Oh," he said. I was surprised he could speak at all with his lip so curled in superior disdain. "This is a fashion statement rather than an oversight. I see."

"Good. Because my wardrobe is not what I'm seeking advice on." I smiled to show I was joking. Yeah, right. "But I *do* need advice on just about everything else."

We discussed every detail I could think of concerning the running of my kingdom. We started with taxes: how much the people were charged, how often they paid, what services were provided in return for payment. (Sister Mary Ursula, despite her contention that I didn't need her advice, gave a very loud *Hmph!* when I didn't abolish the tax system.) We discussed every single law on the books. (Though Deming pursed his lips disapprovingly and said I was asking for anarchy, Sister Mary Ursula hummed approvingly when I abolished capital punishment in favor of fines and community service.) We made plans for the improving of roads and the establishing of schools (who could have ever guessed I'd end up in favor of schools?) and the forming of a trade fair to be held every autumn in the town of Fairfield. I called for riders to announce the proclamations from town to town, hoping that my new way of running things would settle the peasant unrest.

Deming and I had our midday meal in the solar since we didn't want to stop in the middle of things. That, and I was worried about the ghosts, who were periodically knocking over piles of paper and had already spilled one jar of ink. If they messed up our notes or walked off with something we'd been working on, I was sure we'd never be able to get it right again afterward.

Sister Mary Ursula had gotten bored and left while we'd been discussing gross national product—which sounds like it means something interesting, but I'd learned in Participation in Government class that it simply means how much, totally, a country owns and produces.

Deming and I were just finishing when Kenric came by.

"I thought you'd like to know," he said, "that the magic-users have all arrived, and Mother is even now meeting with them."

"Well, how kind of her to ask you to tell me about it," I said, knowing—even before his grin—that she had not. "Sir Deming, would you please find Sister Mary Ursula? I'd like the two of you to attend with me. Tell her I know she mistrusts magic, but I would very much appreciate her counsel. And Captain Penrod, too."

Deming nodded, and I went with Kenric to the Great Hall.

CHAPTER TWENTY-SIX

Keeping Everybody (But Me) Happy

The guards in front of the Great Hall doors didn't wait for me to order them to let us in—which might have had more to do with Kenric than me. Whatever. They saluted and opened the door, and the page blew the trumpet to announce us.

"Oh," Andreanna said as I entered, "look. Someone has hired a stunted, shoddy little page to help us out. Oh dear; my mistake. It's only Janine."

Abas gave his surprisingly tittery laugh.

I asked, "Has lack of sleep made some of us cranky?" though I knew she could sleep as long as Rip van Winkle and still wake up grouchy.

As last time Xenos and Uldemar sat on one side of the table. The queen, Abas, and Wulfgar sat across from them. This time Orielle was sitting on Wulfgar's lap. I wondered if she had moved to him when Kenric left to fetch me, or if she had only chosen Kenric last time because

Wulfgar hadn't been there. I liked to think that Kenric was her first choice but he had told her, "No way. I'm looking for Janine instead of you."

Uh-huh.

Not that I would sit on his lap. Not unless, of course, he asked me.

Andreanna ignored my superior comeback to her ill-tempered jibe and turned her sour face to the guards, ordering, "Close the doors, you incompetent fools."

"Just leave it for a few moments," I recommended to the men who were pushing, pulling, and throwing their weight against the unmoving doors.

Now, if you were a castle guard, who would you be more afraid of: me or Queen Andreanna? The guards continued trying to close the door.

I went to the table and introduced myself. "Hello, I'm Princess Janine. I'm guessing you're Orielle." Orielle gave a dazzling smile that was sure to melt the heart of any young man and to make just about any female want an appointment with a plastic surgeon. I turned to the two men. "And Uldemar and Xenos."

Uldemar nodded at his name, though Xenos was hiding in his monk's cowl.

"Welcome," I told all of them. I realized I hadn't properly greeted them last time. "Thank you for coming on such short notice. I truly appreciate your willingness to help."

My words must have made Xenos feel at home, for he reached into his pocket and tossed a centipede into his mouth.

Kenric sat down next to Abas, making sure that there was enough room for me to sit beside him.

At the other end of the room, the ghosts must have finished squeezing through the doorway, for the guards were suddenly able to shut the doors—which slammed with two solid thuds.

Uldemar took the opportunity to announce, "She brings the stench of the dead with her."

Because we had all been kept up all night, Andreanna knew exactly what he meant. "Oh, you're the one who let the ghosts in, are you?"

"Yes," I said. "I'll tell you my plan for them later." Of course, I had no plan, but suggesting I did *might* be a way to get the queen off my back.

She gave a suspicious, "Likely, I'm sure!" but didn't demand details.

One of the ghosts, however, poked me in the ribs.

It's hard to look self-assured and in command when you've just given a sudden squeal and jumped about a foot out of your seat. "If we're quite ready to settle down..." I said. Nothing from the ghosts, but Sir Deming chose that moment to come in.

"Sorry to interrupt." Instead of sitting, he cleared his throat. Twice. He had either developed a twitch, or he was trying to signal me about *something,* giving his head a sideways jerk toward Queen Andreanna. But when she noticed, he immediately stopped and pretended to be scratching his neck.

Andreanna snapped, "I hope she hasn't brought lice, as well as ghosts."

Deming, practicing his obsequious toady manner, said, "No, I'm sure not. Sorry. Just a crick in my neck."

Andreanna glowered as though the fact that he didn't have lice was a personal affront to her.

I asked, "Will Captain Penrod and Sister Mary Ursula be joining us?"

Deming sat down—how could any male resist?—next to Orielle. He told me, "Captain Penrod said that as a simple military man, he could not possibly attend a state meeting. He assures you that he will steadfastly follow and defend whatever policies you set."

Meaning: "I can carry out instructions, but I can't make suggestions." Silly me.

"And Sister Mary Ursula..."—Deming sneaked a glance at Andreanna, saw that she wasn't at the moment looking at him, and gave me that look-over-*here* nod that signified I-had-no-idea-what—"Sister Mary Ursula is on her way." Nod, nod. Seeing both my baffled expression and Andreanna's increasingly impatient one, Deming shrugged.

Probably just another disaster, I told myself. "OK," I said slowly, "well, then, why don't we get started? I've asked all of you here so we can have a chance to get to know one another, but most pressingly because of the problem with the barbarians."

"Excuse me," a familiar voice interrupted from the doorway, "but it is not *we* that are being the problem."

I looked up and saw that King Grimbold had arrived, with Sister Mary Ursula on his arm.

Oh, so that's what Deming was trying to warn me

about: Queen Andreanna's new beau had invited himself.

"I'm sorry," I said. "Terrible wording on my part. The problem is not you and your people; the problem is how to win the friendship and gain the trust of you and your people by recovering that which has been taken from you."

Grimbold gave a solemn bow to indicate he accepted my explanation.

"Please have a seat." I gestured to the bench across the table, where only Xenos and Uldemar sat.

But Grimbold squeezed himself in between Abas and Andreanna. "Have you been missing me as muchly as I have been missing you, you delectable woman you?" he asked Andreanna.

"Wulfgar," Andreanna demanded from between clenched teeth, "*do* something."

Trying valiantly to swallow a grin, Wulfgar said, "Sorry, my hands are full."

She-with-whom-Wulfgar's-hands-were-full winked and blew a kiss to Grimbold.

The barbarian king smiled and said, "Hello, young lass," but his attention was all for Andreanna.

"Sister Mary Ursula," I said, "have a seat anywhere."

"Oh dear, no," she said. "The room is One with ghosts, necromancers, wizards, and witches. No, no, I couldn't possibly sit down, no."

I wasn't sure how standing made the situation better for her, but I wasn't going to argue. I said, "I thank you for coming despite your dislike of magic."

"Well, you asked so nicely," Sister Mary Ursula said.

Score one for being polite.

I said, "Xenos, my understanding is that you made a crown for the first chieftain of Grimbold's people."

"Yes," Xenos said in his fingernails-on-blackboard voice.

"Brecc the Slayer," King Grimbold reminded us.

"And then King Cynric..." I hesitated and Queen Andreanna said emphatically, "Won," and King Grimbold corrected, "Stoled, my turtledove," and I compromised with, "*got* that crown from King Grimbold's father." Nobody argued, so I went on, "Then King Cynric gave the crown to a dragon who was ravaging the south, though we don't know where that dragon is now."

Sure enough Uldemar leaped in, offering, "I could find him in my scrying glass."

The process was no less disconcerting for knowing what to expect. After Uldemar cast his spell on the black glass, he announced as he had before, "The dragon is in the southern province, in a cave on a mountaintop known as the Old Hag."

Andreanna started, "How—"

And I interrupted, asking, "How far away is this mountain?"

"A week's journey," Andreanna said, obviously delighting in the bad news.

A week? When I only had this day and the next? If I was lucky. "Isn't there any shortcut?"

I looked at each of them in turn. From Deming's, "Nope. Sorry," to Andreanna's self-satisfied smirk to Kenric's gloomy shake of the head, there was no hope from my side of the table. Uldemar was checking his scrying glass again, but he, too, was shaking his head.

Xenos, however, had sunk so deep into his monk's robes that he was in danger of disappearing under the table. He looked, I thought, exactly like a kid mentally begging the teacher not to call on him.

"Xenos?" I said.

"No," he mumbled. "No shortcut." He popped a centipede into his mouth.

"Any idea how to get from here to there and back to here in, oh, let's say a day and a half?"

"Theoretically or actually?" Xenos asked.

Uldemar said, "Come to think of it, how did *you* get here so soon, Xenos? When I contacted you through the scrying glass, you were at least two days' journey away."

"I walk fast," Xenos said.

"He's got boots!" Sister Mary Ursula cried. "That is *so* like a wizard! You are so not One with the world!"

"'Boots'?" I repeated.

"Seven-league boots," Kenric interpreted for me.

"Ah!" I looked under the table. Xenos tried to cover his boots with his robe. "May I borrow those?" I asked.

"And am I supposed to go barefoot meanwhile?"

"I'm sure we can get you some nice slippers to use," I said. "And there's a boy working for us who's interested in wildlife"—I didn't explain about his being a poacher—"and if you'd like, I would put him in charge of finding all the centipedes you could possibly want the entire time I'm away."

Xenos considered for a moment. "I like spiders once in a while, too."

"Certainly."

"Chocolate covered?"

I forced myself not to shudder. "However."

Xenos took off the boots. "They work as regular boots unless you say, 'Seven leagues.' Then they'll take you one step. If you want to go another seven leagues, you have to say, 'Seven leagues' again."

"Gotcha," I said. "Thank you."

Andreanna said, "And I don't suppose you're even going to fumigate them before putting them on."

I took off my shoes and put on the boots, which were green leather and knee-high and *did* give off a smell like the school's locker room on a bad day. But at least they fit.

Andreanna curled her lip at me. "All those hideous boots are going to do is get you there and then—once you see how truly terrible the dragon is—get you out of there quickly. That's *if* you're lucky enough to see the dragon before it sees you. Of course, if *we're* lucky, you'll get up such a momentum of seven-leaguing, you'll walk right by us and get lost in the wilds of the north."

Grimbold patted her arm and said, "Now, my precious, you should na be speaking so harshly to the princess. She be doing her best."

I smiled to show I appreciated the thought. "Does anyone have any dragon-slaying ideas?"

Orielle said, "I could give you a potion that would poison him, if you can get close enough to him."

Xenos started chortling, but before he could go too far, I asked, "What other kinds of potions do you have?" I knew, but not in *this* lifetime.

"I have one that will increase a person's strength and stamina—giving him, or her, the ability to fight as two, or to work for twice as long."

"Any drawbacks?" I asked before Xenos could get a word in.

"It lasts only one hour."

"That's not so bad," I said, which made her admit, reluctantly, "And . . . after it wears off, the person will be so weak, he won't even be able to stand up. That stage lasts two hours."

"Very useful," Xenos taunted.

Before Orielle had a chance to turn on him, I pretended his words had been meant earnestly. "Yes, it might be, if I time things perfectly. Please mix me up a batch, Orielle, just in case. What's the price?"

Orielle paused to consider. "The hand of Wulfgar in marriage."

"What?" Andreanna screeched.

"Just the hand?" Xenos asked innocently.

Wulfgar, I saw, did not look displeased. "Wulfgar?" I asked.

He didn't need long to think it over. "Yes," he said. So, "Agreed," I told Orielle.

"You . . ." Andreanna sputtered, "you . . . you . . ."

Grimbold patted her hand again. "They be making a mostest attractive couple," he said trying to calm her. He nudged her and winked. "Just like us."

Andreanna leaped to her feet to get away from him. "How dare you give away my son?" she shouted at me.

"She asked," I explained, "he agreed."

Grimbold tugged on her arm. "Sit down, sweetest, before you be hurting yourself," he advised.

Andreanna sat down because there really was nothing she could do.

Sister Mary Ursula clapped her hands in glee. "Oh, I love weddings: two people becoming One. And it gives all of us the chance to wear our best clothes."

In her case, I could only imagine.

Still, none of it *really* helped. Was I supposed to take Xenos's boots to get to Old Hag Mountain, then use Orielle's potion to make me strong enough to fight the dragon? I wasn't a fighter, and I couldn't imagine how I could succeed in killing the dragon when trained knights had failed. I was sure—or, at least, I was hoping—this situation called for thinking, not brute strength. I asked, "What weaknesses does this dragon have?"

"None," Andreanna snapped. "It's big, and it's fierce, and it's ruthless. Only my husband stood between it and destruction of our entire kingdom when it began raiding the towns and villages eight years ago. It would have killed us all if Cynric hadn't faced it down, then convinced it to take the crown and leave." She turned on her sons. "Perhaps you were too young to remember when it came to our very walls and we were within one dragon's breath of dying."

"I remember," Wulfgar said.

"And now you, you foolish little would-be king, you want to take that crown back?"

Well, I thought, maybe I *wasn't* supposed to get the crown. I asked Grimbold, "You have to have *that particular crown* back?"

"Yes," he said.

"You wouldn't accept anything else?"

"No," he said.

I looked at Wulfgar and Orielle. I looked at Grimbold and Andreanna. I said to Grimbold, "Like, perhaps, the hand of—"

Queen Andreanna interrupted, "Don't you dare even suggest that."

"Tempting as the offer is being," Grimbold told me, "I have been telling my people I would be returning our crown to us." He kissed Andreanna's hand. "Forgive me, my pumpkin."

She wiped her hand on her gown as though removing something very foul and very sticky.

I could give him the ring and compel him to accept Andreanna in trade for the crown. But I had the feeling that solution would cause more problems than it solved.

I was going to have to face the dragon.

CHAPTER TWENTY-SEVEN

Preparations for a Journey

I declared the meeting at an end. "I will leave as soon as Orielle provides me with the strength potion," I announced.

"Good riddance," Andreanna said, which I gathered was the closest she would come to wishing me luck. She stalked out of the Great Hall in a huff.

Grimbold, poor lovesick puppy, followed.

Orielle needed to gather some herbs from the garden; and Wulfgar—another lovesick puppy—went with her.

Abas said, "Past time for my aerobics."

And Xenos announced he was going to look for those slippers I'd promised him, and then he was going to find that centipede-catching boy.

"I'll help you," Deming said. "As for you," he told me, "now that King Grimbold is gone, let me be more free in my advice."

"Yes. Please. Thank you," I said.

"You'll never succeed in killing the dragon," Deming said. "Kill Grimbold instead, then have our army take on the barbarian army."

"But I promised. And he's our guest. And that's just so . . . so . . . dishonorable and underhanded."

"Hey," Deming said, "you pay me for my advice. Take it or leave it." He followed Xenos.

"Sister Mary Ursula?" I asked. "What do you think?"

She pinched the bridge of her nose and hummed. "I think I will check if my blue dress with the pieces of rose quartz sewn around the neckline and the shedded-yak-hair cuffs is clean enough to wear. It's a bit warm for summer but very slimming."

That left just Kenric and Uldemar. Uldemar, I saw, had fallen asleep.

"Any advice?" I asked Kenric.

"You have advisers for that," he told me.

Yeah, except neither of them had any useful advice.

Except, I suddenly remembered, except I *did* have three advisers.

"I think," I said, "I'll see what ex-Counselor Rawdon has to say."

Kenric and I found him sitting on the wooden fence of the pigpen, tossing vegetables that were past their prime to the pigs.

"Princess Janine"—he jumped off the fence to kneel at my feet—"thank you for sparing my life."

"Everyone makes mistakes, Rawdon," I said, "and mistakes need to be paid for. But if I ordered your death, that would be *my* mistake. Do well here, and eventually you may once again work your way up to your old position." *Minus the treasury key,* I mentally added.

He bowed to indicate he accepted my words.

"Rawdon," I said, quite loudly because the pigs were making complaining noises that their feeding had stopped, "as the late king's official adviser, you might have information that would help the kingdom."

"What would you like to know?" he asked.

That was the problem: I didn't know what I needed to know. At least he hadn't answered, "Fat chance I'd do anything for *you.*"

I said, "Do you know anything about the dragon to whom King Cynric gave the crown from the barbarian king?"

Rawdon nodded. "After threatening to wipe out the entire castle eight years ago, it was ... let's say *turned back* by King Cynric, and it swore never to visit these lands again. It resides in the south, somewhere. I'm not sure exactly where."

Kenric said, "Uldemar says it's at Old Hag Mountain."

Rawdon nodded. "Then what's the question?"

I told him, "Xenos gave me seven-league boots to get there, and Orielle is mixing up a potion to make me stronger. Do you think that's the best way, trying to physically overpower the dragon?"

One of the catacomb ghosts tossed a head of lettuce into the pigpen, bouncing it off the head of one of the pigs, but the pigs didn't seem to mind the manner in which the food was delivered.

Rawdon said, "You are aware that this dragon is

something on the order of ten times as tall as you? And that it breathes fire? And that it will not readily give up one iota of gold? Dragons *love* gold."

"Yeah," I said.

"I'm glad it's not me," Rawdon said.

"I'm glad it's not me," Kenric echoed.

I'd known better than to even ask him.

"What do you suggest?" I asked Rawdon.

"You said Xenos is here?"

I nodded.

"You know that he puts magic into items, such as those seven-league boots."

It suddenly occurred to me where Cynric had gotten that ring I currently had tucked beneath my tunic.

"Xenos has other such items," Rawdon told me. "I'm guessing he probably has something that would be useful to you in this situation. It's just that he doesn't like to part with them, so you may have to twist his arm a bit."

"Thank you," I said. "That was very helpful. I'm going to recommend an immediate promotion for you." I asked Kenric, "What's one step up from tending pigs?"

"Tending chickens?" Kenric suggested.

"Would you prefer that?" I asked Rawdon. When he nodded, I promised, "I'll see to it."

As we left, he once again sat on the rail and began tossing produce to the pigs.

KENRIC AND I found Xenos in the barracks, describing to the poacher boy the attributes of prime centipedes.

I waved the boy away.

"Are you still here?" Xenos demanded.

"As you see. I understand that your specialty is magical artifacts?"

"I already gave you the boots," he complained.

"Yes, and I'm very grateful. But I was just thinking: If I'm wearing them when the dragon steps on me or eats me, you won't get them back."

"You could take them off," he suggested. "Before you go into the dragon's lair."

"But I'll be alone," I pointed out, "since obviously nobody would be able to keep up with me while I'm wearing them. So there won't be anyone around to return them to you."

Xenos pouted.

"Do you have anything else I could use that would help me survive my encounter with the dragon, so I could come back here and return your boots to you?"

"You're trying to trick me." Xenos folded his arms across his chest. "You're a tricky talker, just like your father."

I needed a moment to remember he was talking about Cynric and not Dexter the peat cutter or my own dad back in Rochester, New York.

"I'm not trying to be tricky," I assured him. "If, for example, you have a second pair of seven-league boots and you want to come with me so that you could bring the first pair back..."

"No," Xenos admitted sullenly.

"Or something else to help me defeat the dragon?"

"No," he repeated, but I didn't believe him.

"OK, then. Well, thanks for the boots." I held one foot

up admiringly. "Maybe, somehow, they'll get back to you. Come on, Kenric, let's see if Orielle's potion is ready."

"All right, all right," Xenos said. "I know of something that may be able to help you. But I don't *have* it. I was telling the truth when I said I didn't *have* anything to help you. My father has it."

His father? When he'd been around to make the crown for the first barbarian king? How old could this father be?

"What is it?" I asked.

"A hat."

"What kind of hat?"

"A hat that lets you slip between the moments of time."

Kenric and I exchanged a puzzled glance.

"Excuse me?" I said.

Xenos explained, "You can keep on moving, but all around you everyone and everything else stays at the moment when you first put the hat on."

"It stops time?" I asked incredulously.

"Obviously, you don't understand the concept at all," Xenos scoffed. "It only *feels* as though you've stopped time. You're slipping through the time stream." He shook his head and muttered in disgust, "Amateurs."

"This sounds like it would be very helpful," I said.

"I should think so," Xenos sneered.

"And all I need to do is go to your father and ask him for the hat, and he'll give it to me?"

"Yes."

Somehow I doubted it would be that simple. Somehow I suspected that Xenos knew something—in fact, probably a lot of somethings—I didn't.

While I was worrying about that, I had a sudden inspiration. I said, "That crown you made: Is that magical, too?"

"Maybe," Xenos said.

"Do you want me to shake him a bit?" Kenric offered, sounding for a moment like his brother Abas.

"It grants the Midas touch," Xenos said.

"You mean whoever wears it can turn things to gold?"

"*Thing*," Xenos corrected. "It only works one time for each owner. The barbarian kings have slowly been building their wealth. King Cynric, of course, thought big. King Cynric used it on the tallest tree in the forest."

I finished, "But once he'd used up his 'once,' he gave it to the dragon."

Kenric said, "The fact that the dragon was about to make dinner out of all of us would have helped in that decision."

So much for Andreanna's claim that Cynric had scared off the dragon—he'd *bribed* it. This also explained why Grimbold wasn't willing to accept Andreanna in exchange for the crown.

"Do we know what the dragon used the crown on?" I asked. "Or if, in fact, he's used it yet?"

"Don't know and don't know," Xenos said. "But even if he's used it, he *still* won't be willing to give it up. Dragons love gold."

"So I've been told," I said.

ORIELLE MET US back in the Great Hall, where she handed me an earthenware vial about as big as a medium-priced bottle of perfume. "It isn't my best-tasting potion," she apologized.

Naturally.

She said, "But I added mint to make it more palatable."

I wondered if that was just coincidence, or if somehow the people at Rasmussem knew that I hate mint. But I thanked her, even so.

"One hour," she reminded me.

Uldemar woke up then and asked, "Have you thought of any way I can help you?"

"You've been a help already," I said, "contacting everyone for me, and finding the dragon."

"Still..." he said.

"And Xenos has me going to his father to pick up a magical hat that will help me."

"Well, then, let me bring you to his father."

"I have the seven-league boots," I reminded him.

"But what if his father doesn't live seven leagues away?"

"Excuse me?"

Uldemar explained, "The boots take seven-league steps. No more, no less."

Seven leagues, I calculated—no doubt helped by Rasmussem's subliminals—was about twenty-five miles. "You mean I can't take, like, a half step? Maybe if I only wore one boot?"

"I'm afraid not," Uldemar said. He had taken out his scrying glass, and he set it on the table. He cast his magic spell and said, "I see he lives beyond Fairfield. I could take you there; then once you have what you need, I can calculate exactly how to get you to Old Hag Mountain in seven-league increments."

"All right," I said. "Thank you. How can you get me to Xenos's father's place?"

"I can turn into a horse and carry you."

"That would be wonderful." I thought about it for a moment. "Ahm, I hate to be rude or anything...but when you transform into an animal...ahm, does that mean you can...ahm..."

"I'll still be blind," he said. "You'll have to guide me."

Well, maybe *wonderful* had been a slight overstatement. Maybe this would be...OK, I hoped. "And what payment do you want?"

"Well, I certainly don't want to eat centipedes or to wed any of the queen's remaining sons. How about twenty-five gold pieces?"

It was expensive, but I said, "Yes."

We packed some food, since I'd seen that these things always took longer than I guessed.

"Good-bye," Kenric told me. "Good luck."

"Keep everybody out of trouble while I'm away," I said to him.

Uldemar turned into a handsome bay horse, already saddled. His eyes were still disconcertingly blank.

I climbed on and blew kisses to those who came to see me off, which was Kenric, Orielle and Wulfgar, King Grimbold, and Captain Penrod.

We rode over the drawbridge, and—after we'd passed—I heard the guard order the bridge to be taken up.

Nothing.

Oh boy. The ghosts were coming with us.

CHAPTER TWENTY-EIGHT

Xenos's Dad

Actually, Uldemar was very surefooted; and if we didn't make as good time as I had with the horse I'd ridden last night, we made better time than I would have walking.

"Let me know when you get tired," I told him.

He threw his head and whinnied.

We rode through Fairfield at a time my subconscious insisted was between midafternoon and vespers, though I would have called it somewhere around five-thirty of a summer afternoon.

For a blind guy, Uldemar was certainly good about landmarks. Periodically he would return to his own shape to say something like, "We should be coming upon a pond ahead and to our right." And, "We'll be going through some scraggly trees, but there's a meadow beyond." And, "As soon as we reach the stream, we'll turn to travel into the sun."

"Have you been here before?" I asked.

"No," he answered. "I saw it all in my scrying glass."

It took about an hour beyond Fairfield before Uldemar said, "The house is on a hill after the lightning-struck elm. It isn't," he added, "much of a hill."

And there it finally was, a neat little house with a little garden around it, all on top of a grass-covered hill.

Reverting to human shape, Uldemar put his hands to the small of his back and stretched. "Does it look promising?" he asked.

"Hard to say." I turned him so he was facing in the right direction.

The hill was about fifteen or twenty feet tall, steeply inclined except in front of the house, where it sloped more gently and there was a flagstone walk.

"There's a path," I told Uldemar.

"Lead on."

I took one step onto the walk.

And couldn't take a second.

I could lift my foot up, but I couldn't put it down. I felt like a mime walking into a giant wind. Something I couldn't see was keeping me from moving my foot forward.

"Princess Janine," Uldemar said, "there appears to be something in my way."

"There appears to be something in *my* way, too," I said. "But I can't see what it is."

"Drat! Has it gotten to be night already?" Uldemar asked.

"No. I can see perfectly well, but when I try to move

my foot..." I still couldn't move it forward. I tried to one side. I tried to the other.

The other worked.

"Oh," I said. "Here we go." I took another step forward. But then I was blocked again. "No, wait," I said.

I looked down at the walk. Each flagstone was big enough to accommodate a person's foot. They were various colors, set in what appeared to be a random pattern: a heathery blue, rose, gray, black, and cream. I was currently standing on a rose-colored stone, and the stone behind me was rose, too. The one directly behind that was cream, but the one I had crossed over from was another rose. I took a step to the left, onto another rose stone. "I think this path is color-coded," I said.

"Lucky me," Uldemar said.

There wasn't another rose touching the one I was on, but there was one two over. I stretched my leg and stepped onto the new stone.

"It seems," I said, "as though we can only step on the rose-colored stones." But then I looked back and saw that he was on a gray one. "Or maybe not. Uldemar, can you take a step, not exactly to your right, but halfway between forward and right?"

He did, and he was able to move.

I revised my analysis of the situation. "It seems as though whatever stone we first step on, after that, that's the only color we can step on."

Uldemar went back to his original stone, then backed off the path entirely. "I'm going to let you handle this," he said.

"OK." I made my way more or less forward for about a dozen more easy steps. The path even let me jump over three stones to get to one that was rose. But when I tried to leap over four stones, I bounced back as though a rubber band attached me to the previous rose-colored stone. There were no other rose ones to step on from where I was, so I had to back up and find my way down another pathway. After following that for a bit, I once again came to a place from which I couldn't step or jump to another rose stone. From where I was, I looked toward the doorway of the house. All the stones near the stoop were cream, black, or gray. No wonder I wasn't getting anywhere on the rose path. I made my way back to the start.

Uldemar was sitting on the lawn. "Back already?" he asked. "Did you get the hat?"

"Not yet," I told him, and started again, this time using the gray stones.

But no matter how I tried, there was one stretch I couldn't get beyond—where there were too many rose, blue, cream, and black stones in between the grays.

Again I made my way back.

Again Uldemar turned his face expectantly in my direction.

"I'm trying the cream ones now," I explained before he could ask.

What was it with the Rasmussem people and mazes?

But this time, eventually, I made it to the front stoop. "I'll be back as soon as I can," I called to Uldemar.

He waved cheerily.

I knocked on the door.

A little boy answered.

I realized I didn't know Xenos's father's name, so I was left to say, "I'm looking for Xenos's father."

"That's me," the kid said. He looked about five.

"Not Xenos's child," I said, creepy as that idea was. "Xenos's father."

"That's me," the kid repeated.

Cute. Like when people let their toddlers record the message for their answering machines. I hate that, too. "Is there an adult home?" I asked.

"Look, honey," the kid said, "if I gotta tell you one more time, I'm going to slam the door in your face and go back to smoking my cigar in peace: Xenos's father—that's me."

He *was* holding a cigar in his pudgy little hand, I noticed.

OK.

"I'm sorry," I said. "You took me by surprise. Xenos said to go to his father—that would be you, I see now—to get the hat that allows the wearer to step out of the time stream. Or was it step *into* the time stream?" I tried to remember what Xenos had said. "Something like that. It doesn't stop time, but it makes it *seem* as though time has stopped. To an amateur."

"Honey," Xenos's father said, "you've got to learn to stop dithering. I know what hat you mean." He held the door open for me, and I stepped into a tidy hallway. There was a hat rack with an assortment of hats on it, and I was already sure the one I was going to get was the ugly pink faux fur with the rhinestones and the ratty peacock feather.

"Stand here," Xenos's father said. He pointed to a spot where there was a big red X on the floor.

"Why?" I asked suspiciously.

"I'm bored," he said. "Humor me."

I stood on the center of the X.

"Now I'm going to ask you three riddles," he said. "If you answer them correctly, I'll give you the hat."

"And if I don't answer correctly," I guessed, "that coatrack is going to come over here and beat me to death."

Xenos's father shook his head in obvious distaste. "You have an unhealthy imagination, young lady—anybody ever tell you that? No, if you don't answer correctly, you get another chance."

"One chance?" I asked.

"As many as you want."

My suspicion must have shown on my face.

"I'm an old man," Xenos's father said, despite his appearance. "Nobody ever comes to visit *me*. Everybody comes because they need to pick up something Xenos promised them." He gave a baby-toothed grin. "Humor me," he said again.

Well, I could just give him the ring and demand the hat, but what if I needed that ring later?

"All right. What's the first riddle?"

"The first riddle is this: You see those woods outside this window?"

I nodded.

"That part wasn't the riddle," Xenos's father explained.

"I already guessed that," I said.

"Kids today. Anyway, you see the woods. My question is this: How far can you walk into those woods?"

I had no real sense of where I was, much less how big the woods were. And what did he mean, how far could

I walk into those woods? Was there something blocking the way, a river or a cliff, something or someone dangerous? Or did he mean how far could I walk before I tired out? Or how far in one day?

I decided it was time to clarify the rules. "I don't have just one guess?"

Xenos's father smacked his palm against his forehead. "If I was a stickler, I would call that your answer. Once the riddle is asked, you aren't supposed to say *anything* except the answer to the riddle. Haven't you ever done this before? You're lucky I'm a patient man. And I already told you, you can try as many times as you want. Now: How far can you walk into those woods?"

Anything I said would be just a guess. So, remembering my boots, I answered, "Seven leagues?"

The floor opened under me, and I went flying down the fastest, slickest slide I'd ever been on, through a black tunnel, popping out a hole at the bottom of the far side of the hill the house stood on. Several of the catacomb ghosts had been caught at the same time I was and had made the trip down with me. *They* liked it—I could tell, picking up their excited psychic energy. *They* didn't have to worry about concussions or contusions.

I rubbed my bruised elbows and said the kind of words my grandmother grounds me for. Shakily, I got to my feet and walked back around to the front of the house.

Uldemar asked, "Got the hat?"

"Not yet. Xenos's father likes riddles. He wants to know about these woods here. Do you have any idea how big they are?"

"Square acreage?" Uldemar said, and I realized that

would be no help at all, because the woods could be long and skinny, or a square, or who-knew-what? "Do you want me to check my scrying glass?"

"No," I said sulkily.

"What, exactly, did he say?"

"He said, 'How far can you walk into those woods?' And the trouble is, I don't know these woods."

"The trouble is," Uldemar corrected me, "he's not asking you a question; he's asking you a riddle."

I thought about it and groaned. I went back to the flagstone path and once more picked a way, using only cream-colored stones, to the front stoop. It was faster this time than last, but I still had several dead ends and reversals. I banged on the door.

Xenos's father opened it. "Hello," he said. "Care to play a riddle game?"

I followed him indoors, and he once again positioned me on the X.

Looking satisfied with himself, Xenos's father once more said, "The first riddle is this: How far can you walk into those woods?"

"Halfway," I answered. "After that I would be walking *out* of the woods, not into them."

"Very good!" Xenos's father cried. "See, you aren't hopeless after all. All right, the second riddle is this: Two great armies are about to do battle, the Great Army of the North and the Great Army of the South, and they meet exactly on the equator. After the battle is over, the bodies are too mangled to identify. Where do the survivors get buried?"

"Well," I said, "but which army won the battle?"

Too late I remembered his warning that I wasn't supposed to say *anything* except the answer to the riddle. The floor disappeared from under me. I tried to grab for the edge, but I was already going down that slide so fast it felt as though my butt was about to catch fire. This time, I could definitely hear a whispery ghostly, "Whee!"

After I hit the ground and the dizziness passed, I went back around to the front of the hill. Uldemar was sitting on the lawn, trying to make music with a blade of grass. I said to him, "Two armies meet at the equator and fight a great battle. After it's over, where..." I sighed, having caught up to myself. "Never mind." The ghosts could have told me that one.

Once again, I picked my way up the front walk and knocked on Xenos's father's door. I was beginning to get faster at this. "Are you enjoying yourself?" I asked.

"Immensely," he admitted.

He stood me on the great red X and said the long sad story again: "The second riddle is this: Two great armies are about to do battle, the Great Army of the North and the Great Army of the South, and they meet exactly on the equator. After the battle is over, the bodies are too mangled to identify. Where do the survivors get buried?"

I said, "The survivors don't get buried."

Xenos's father gave a great drag on his cigar. He said, "I haven't had this much fun since Xenos had a cold and was sneezing centipedes. All right, here's the third riddle: Where was Moses when the lights went out?"

That one I knew. "In the dark."

"There. See," Xenos's father said. "I don't know what you were worried about."

I said, "Those riddles were hardly the quality of the riddle of the Sphinx."

Xenos's father shrugged. "Egyptian humor. Personally, I don't get it. Now for your hat." Sure enough, he picked up the awful pink one. But then he reached into the crown of the hat, and pulled out another, a crumpled knitted ski cap the color of March slush. "So, I'm assuming Xenos told you all about this. Don't bother answering; that's what's known in the business as sarcasm, dearie. The hat lets you keep moving when all about you is still—that part he told you, I'm sure. What he probably left out is that once you put the hat on, whatever you're doing—whether it's stealing money from the poor box in church, or spying on the boyfriend when he's out without you, or sneaking back into the house so your parents don't know you climbed out the bedroom window—"

I interrupted. "Those are pretty lame reasons to be using a hat that lets you avoid the time stream."

"Do I criticize you when you're giving examples? All I'm saying is that whatever you're doing, you only have a limited time to do it. Ironic, isn't it? Get it? Time/time?" He shook his head. "You don't get it."

"I get it," I assured him. "How long do I have?"

"If you count like this," he said at a leisurely pace, "one Rasmussem Enterprises, two Rasmussem Enterprises, three Rasmussem Enterprises . . . then you'd get to three hundred Rasmussem Enterprises, and the hat comes back here."

Nothing like a little bit of blatant self-endorsement. And what he was saying was that I had five minutes. Five minutes.

"The hat..." I said.

"Comes back here," he finished.

"With me?"

He shook his head.

"Leaving me..."

"With your hand in the poor box, or your face pressed up against somebody else's window, or climbing up the stairs to the second floor while your father's sitting there watching you."

Or, in my case, face-to-face with the dragon.

"Yeah," Xenos's father said, taking another drag on the cigar. "I didn't think he'd told you. Any questions?"

I sighed, but said, "No."

Yet again the floor swallowed me, and I went skittering down that slide through the hill and out the other side. Luckily, I managed to keep hold of the hat. But I was going to be a mass of bruises even before meeting the dragon. More and more ghosts were joining me for each ride.

I picked myself off the ground and yelled up to the house, "Ever wonder *why* nobody ever comes to visit you?"

Still staggering, I rejoined Uldemar. "Got it," I told him.

He had the decency not to say, "About time."

CHAPTER TWENTY-NINE

A Journey
of a Thousand Miles
Begins with a Single Step
(and Other Trite Nonsense)

Sitting at the bottom of Xenos's father's hill, Uldemar did his calculations of exactly where I had to step to have the seven-league boots take me to Old Hag Mountain. The trouble was that the direct route was not divisible by the seven leagues each step would take me, so I had to head off southwest to a certain point, then turn and head due east. There was also a minor detour to avoid a step that would have landed me directly in someone's kitchen.

"That's not a physical problem," Uldemar told me. "As you're moving, the boots pass through solid objects." Which explained how, in the previous game, Xenos had walked through the wall but then was not seen by Penrod's men outside. Uldemar continued, "But it would be unsettling to those seeing you. Out of fear, they might harm you."

"What if I land inside a tree?"

"You can't. You'd land on top of it. I'll try to keep you away from trees."

We decided it would be best not to have the boots take me directly into the dragon's cave. If the creature was home, it might kill me before I had a chance to get my bearings.

"This route will take you to a flattened area between the summit and the base of the mountain," Uldemar said. "It should be climbable."

Should be. Don't you love it?

It was getting to be dusk, but I decided to start, anyway. Once I got to the mountain, I could make up my mind if it would be better to continue up at night or wait there till morning. Dragons, Uldemar told me, were like cats, taking a lot of little naps throughout the day and night so no time was better than others to try sneaking up on it.

I tucked the hat I had riddled for into the bag that held my evening meal and Orielle's potion, and I looped the bag over my belt.

"Good luck," Uldemar said. "Remember to always walk straight in the direction you're facing." He'd already said that about seven times. "Don't try to take big strides—just walk normally. The boots will take care of themselves." *That* he'd said about nine times.

"Will you be all right?" I asked him. Maybe I'd asked him once or twice before but I felt guilty leaving him.

"I'll be fine," Uldemar assured me.

So I took a deep breath, said, "Seven leagues," and put my right foot forward.

When I'd tried to make too big a jump on Xenos's father's front walk, I'd felt as though a rubber band had yanked me back. Now I felt like the rubber band itself, all stretched out, with my vision a meaningless blur and an awful rushing-of-air sound so intense I was sure my eardrums were about to burst. I was tempted to bring that right foot back, canceling the seven-league step so that I could try again later. But I knew it wasn't going to get better. I moved my left foot forward.

And found myself in a totally different place from where I'd just been.

Instead of Xenos's father's hill on an otherwise flat area bordered by woods, I saw gently rolling hills coming down to an immense lake.

Thank you for not landing me in the lake, I thought to Uldemar.

I took another step and found myself in yet another landscape: farm country, with fields of barley and rutabaga.

And another, this time landing in a rocky, desolate place. That was where I was supposed to turn ninety degrees to the left to avoid the unpredictable kitchen. I stepped onto a seashore.

Step after step I took until finally, as the sky turned dramatically pink, I found myself partway up what had to be Old Hag Mountain.

Amazing! I had never, in my heart, actually believed it would be so easy.

I left a whole bunch of broken sticks so I would be sure—if I survived my encounter with the dragon—to be able to start my return trip from the exact right spot.

Next was climbing up.

It should be climbable.

Yeah, right.

I had to find handholds and toeholds and trust my life to an anemic tree that didn't have the sense to grow out of horizontal ground.

This would be a lot easier, I told myself as my arms began to ache, *if I was stronger.*

Which was when I remembered Orielle's potion.

One hour of being as strong as Abas, followed by two of being as weak as Dusty at her arthritic worst.

Should I take it now? I looked up the remainder of the way I had to go. It was getting dark, so I wasn't able to see clearly. I *thought* that if I was stronger I could make it up in less than an hour—if I didn't fall off the mountain first from not being able to see. But what then? Then, with night coming on, I would have to find my way into the lair, avoid the dragon, locate the crown, and hope that my two hours of total helplessness didn't strike while I was still in there. It was the same thing I would have to do if I waited until morning, but my chances had to be better if I could see what I was doing.

I found a cozy little crack in the stone, and I settled in for the night, hoping the catacomb ghosts wouldn't think it a good joke to roll me out and over the side while I slept. Thinking about the ghosts, I suddenly realized I had no sensation of them around me. *They weren't able to keep up to those seven-league steps,* I thought. *Ha!*

They were probably still at Xenos's father's house, riding down that slide. *Double ha!*

I ate my meal of bread, cheese, and cold mutton, with an apple tart the castle cook had packed for dessert. For drink, I had warm water from a clay jar. I was happy for the tart, but a double-cheese pizza and a milk shake would have been even nicer.

I HEARD the dragon several times during the night, moving about, snoring occasionally, once singing—I *think* it was singing—in its dragon language. To me it sounded like a recording of a cough, played backward at slow speed.

Once it got to be light—my third day in this adventure (my, how time flies when you're having fun)—I ate the last of my bread and drank almost all of my water, saving a bit for just-in-case.

I started climbing back up that mountain, but it wasn't any easier today than it had been last night. When I almost fell because my fingers cramped, I realized it was time to try Orielle's potion. Pressing myself onto a ledge big enough for about half of one foot, I got out the vial, took out the stopper, and downed the whole thing in one excruciating gulp. Not one of her best-tasting potions had Orielle said? Imagine a ninety-five-degree August day, and a construction worker slaving away on the melting asphalt. Then imagine licking toothpaste out of his armpit.

But a moment later, that didn't matter. I had a hot flash that caused a tremor in the leg on which I was balancing all my weight. In another moment that was gone, leaving a warm, tingly glow all over, from toes to fingertips. That, and the foul taste in my mouth.

I reached for a handhold, and pulled myself up as easily as an Olympic gymnast doing a chin-up.

Up and up and up I went, so easily that I asked myself why I hadn't taken the potion earlier.

Then I remembered why, for I'd come to right below the ledge of the opening to the cave where Uldemar's scrying glass showed the dragon lived.

When I was securely positioned, I got out the hat so that I could slap it on my head at a moment's notice. I held it in my teeth, so that it wouldn't accidentally brush off as I swung myself up onto the ledge.

Then I swung myself up onto the ledge.

There, close enough to spit on—if I'd been a barbarian and inclined to spit—was the dragon.

CHAPTER THIRTY

Dead Oxen and Gold

Andreanna and Rawdon had been right: The dragon was enormous. Even though I'd been prepared for its size to stun me, its size still stunned me.

The creature had its head on its paws, and its eyes were closed—which meant that it was either sleeping or trying to lull me into believing that it was sleeping, at which point it would jump on me and either eat me in one quick swallow (I could only hope it would be one) or incinerate me or squeeze the life out of me.

I fought the inclination to seven-league my way straight out of there. I fought the inclination to slap Xenos's magic hat on my head and make time stop moving for the dragon.

I knew both inclinations were stupid. After determining that I *had* to get the crown and struggling my way up that mountainside—what would running accomplish? If I didn't succeed in this, I would stay hooked up to Rasmussem's computer equipment until my brain fried. That made getting fried by a dragon look slightly ... well, not better, just less bad.

And what if I put on the hat while the dragon was asleep? That would waste its power.

Anyway, why would the dragon pretend to be asleep? If it saw me, wouldn't it simply kill me right away?

Except I remembered Uldemar explaining how dragons napped like cats. What if, like cats, they also played with their prey?

But could the dragon have kept a straight face if it saw me, a girl dressed as a page, walking on the tips of my toes, looking as though I was about to eat a ski cap? I wondered if dragons shot flames out of their mouths when they laughed.

The dragon didn't twitch.

Scattered about this area were various bones. There was a gnawed-on ox over to one side, which explained that the awful smell was not entirely dragon bad breath. But not all the bones were animals—some still had scraps of clothing attached. I kept on moving. There was a second, bigger, cave beyond, and I could see the glitter of gold.

Luckily, there was room to circle behind the dragon without having to climb onto it. I nervously kept my attention on the creature's eyelids until I realized I was endangering myself by walking backward. I could easily trip or knock something over, and the noise would surely awaken a catnapper.

I turned my full attention to the piles of treasure.

The piles and piles of treasure.

The piles and piles and piles of treasure.

How could I ever find one crown amid all that glittering hoard?

I started pawing through mounds of gold. There were coins, there was jewelry, there were boxes, baskets, combs, and plaques. There were eating utensils, musical instruments, tools, toys, knickknacks, figurines, and a bigger-than-life statue of a Greek hero. (I could tell he was Greek, because he didn't have any clothes on, the way Greek statues never do.) There were even a pair of robes woven entirely of spun gold.

But was there a barbarian crown? Not that I could see.

I started unloading one of the overflowing treasure chests—there were seven or eight, probably more buried in that one corner where the gold was piled to within inches of the cave's ceiling.

It can't be there, I tried to convince myself. *THAT pile's been accumulating for generations, and King Cynric gave the dragon the crown only eight years ago.*

Unless, of course, the dragon had been moving things around, shifting stuff from one pile to another, handling the gold while gloating over it—and why bother amassing gold if you aren't going to gloat over it? Maybe the crown had been buried.

No, I told myself. This was a crown that could turn things into gold. Surely that would gain it a special place. Or at least not a place at the bottom of a pile.

I was putting things from the chest onto the floor so that I could get to the bottom, and there, finally, beneath a golden serving tray, was the crown.

Oops, no, wait. Wrong crown.

During our lunch King Grimbold had described his people's crown, and this wasn't it.

Maybe, over the passage of years since his father had lost the thing, *maybe* Grimbold hadn't remembered correctly?

Not likely, I knew.

I set the crown on the head of a waist-high statue of a monkey. If I couldn't find the right crown, maybe Grimbold could be appeased by this one, along with whatever other trinkets I could stuff into my now-empty provision bag. And Andreanna. I very much hoped I could give away Andreanna.

My teeth were sore from holding the hat for so long. I took it out to work my jaw. A watch would have been nice about now, to know how long since I'd taken Orielle's potion. My guess was about a half hour. I wondered if I'd have any warning, any sense of weakening, or if I'd just keel over.

I went to put the hat back in my mouth and somehow brushed against the monkey statue. The thing must have been hollow for it wobbled. I grabbed it just in time to keep it from going over.

But the crown fell off the back of its head.

A golden crown hitting a cave floor doesn't make all that much noise.

But enough.

The dragon was awake and on its feet in less time than it took me to glance in its direction.

For the moment, as I crouched beside the chest with the monkey statue between us, the dragon couldn't see me. But I could see it. I could see its nostrils dilate as it sniffed. *Sniff, sniff.* It took a step toward me, its massive belly dragging on the floor. *Sniff, sniff.* For a creature that slept next to an ox carcass that was at least a couple days old, surely it couldn't have a very well developed sense of smell. Another step. And then its huge head swiveled, and it was looking directly at me.

I jammed the hat onto my head, pulling it so low it stretched beyond my earlobes. I felt no change, but the dragon wasn't moving. Was it?

I peeked an eye open.

No, the dragon wasn't moving.

Slowly I got to my feet. I moved cautiously to the left.

Its glittering eyes didn't follow me.

I started breathing again. Then I started counting, "One Rasmussem Enterprises, two Rasmussem Enterprises, three..." I kept on counting as I hurled golden objects out of the chest, no longer needing to be quiet.

At "fifteen Rasmussem Enterprises," I got to the bottom of the chest, and there was no other crown. I moved to another chest. That took me to "sixty Rasmussem Enterprises," with no sign of a crown. Four minutes left— less, because I hadn't started right away. *Three hundred Rasmussem Enterprises* was looming close.

I kicked at a heap of gold sitting on the floor, scattering coins. A crown rolled out. I snatched it up. Then threw it down in frustration. Still not the right one.

The next chest was a big one with clumsily shaped heavy objects I had to lift out one by one, and it took me to "one hundred forty-four Rasmussem Enterprises" to find there was no barbarian crown in there.

There was a chest about the size of a two-drawer filing cabinet on its side. With my added strength coupled with the adrenaline of desperation, I held it upside down, scattering its contents on the floor. I threw the chest behind me and lunged for the crown I glimpsed, but it was the same one that had fallen off the monkey statue before. "One hundred sixty-seven Rasmussem Enterprises," and I was already looking twice in the same place.

Ignoring the other chests, I began pawing through the huge pile, convinced the crown had to be in the single hardest place to get to.

"Two hundred fourteen Rasmussem Enterprises... two hundred twenty-five Rasmussem Enterprises... two hundred thirty-seven Rasmussem Enterprises..." I kicked the Greek hero in frustration and glanced back at the dragon.

Not moving yet, but it would be soon. How many "Rasmussem Enterprises" had I lost while shivering under the unseeing gaze of the time-stopped dragon? Five? Six?

And what was the matter with me? I should have known better than to think other numbers while I was trying to count. Had I actually counted to "two hundred forty-five Rasmussem Enterprises," or had I skipped numbers because I'd been thinking the number five? I didn't actually remember saying, "forty-two," "forty-three," or "forty-four Rasmussem Enterprises," but maybe I had, and meanwhile, trying to figure it out, I'd lost more time.

Where was I? Never mind. I gave up counting entirely.

Once again I looked at the dragon. I had to get out of there, save myself now, try coming back later, with a better plan.

Yeah, right. If I was capable of thinking up a better plan, I wouldn't be here now.

That wasn't the same as being willing to let the dragon lunch on me.

I ran past the huge beast, back out onto the ledge, to the very edge overlooking the steep cliff with hand- and toeholds. I was going to have to go racing down there? . . . with my strength about to give out probably a few minutes after the hat spell gave out? . . . with a dragon sniffing after me?

The other choice was to hang around and wait for the dragon to gnaw on me like it had been gnawing on that ox.

I saw the gashes on the stone from the dragon's talons. I also saw two globs of gold on the ledge and realized what the dragon had done with its Midas touch—it had tried to turn Old Hag Mountain to gold, but instead had only gotten two golden rocks. No doubt it had been plenty ticked off.

Just like it's going to be now, I thought, suddenly aware of the breeze in my hair: *Good-bye, hat. Hello, dragon.*

I turned back to meet my fate.

The dragon was in the inner cave, facing the way it had been when, from its perspective, I'd disappeared. But now that I was on the ledge facing this direction, I saw what I hadn't seen before. The crown. Out here. The dragon had been sleeping with it tucked safely in the crook of its elbow, like a kid with a teddy bear.

I dove for the crown just as the dragon turned. A blast of flame frizzled the air at my back. I grabbed up the crown like an oversized bangle bracelet on my arm and looked over the nearest edge, which wasn't even the way I'd come up. How could I ever make it down onto flat ground with the dragon so close behind? Even now I could hear the grate of its scales as it heaved its massive body back out onto the ledge.

Without even turning back to look, I said, "Seven leagues," and stepped forward, though the ground was a mountain's height below me—hoping the boots worked in thin air.

CHAPTER THIRTY-ONE

Home Sweet Home
(Or Not)

I found myself on someone's thatched roof. I turned hurriedly, said, "Seven leagues" hurriedly, and stepped hurriedly, because my foot felt about to go through. Now I was in the middle of a field of something-or-other—I didn't take the time to make out what. I turned, said, "Seven leagues," and took another step. Now I was in a wooded area, having just missed a tree, which was good, because I was in no mood to have to climb down.

I'd just completed three sides of a square. One more and I'd be stepping back onto the mountain ledge I'd just stepped off of. Where the dragon might or might not still be sniffing around for the one who'd made off with its favorite crown. And even if the dragon had flown off, I'd have to climb back down. If my strength gave out while I was hanging from that cliff face, that would be the end of me. Instead I tried to estimate how to walk, in regular steps, to a point where after I turned and "seven-leagued," I'd be at the foot of Old Hag Mountain.

But landing on iffy ground was a danger. I'd do best to walk farther than I thought I had to. So I walked and walked and walked. And then all of a sudden I collapsed.

Oh, I realized, *the potion must have worn off.* I couldn't even move my legs to a more comfortable sprawl. My left arm, the one on which I'd been carrying the crown, was under me, and the tines of the crown were sticking into me, but there was nothing I could do. I did finally summon the energy to close my eyes.

I felt sweat trickle down my sides, I felt bugs crawl on me, I felt that miserable crown sticking into my rib cage.

I...felt...two...hours...pass...one...moment...at...a...time....

And then suddenly my right arm worked. I'd been concentrating on getting my hand to move—it only needed to cover about two inches before it could reach to wipe the sweat from dribbling into my eyes—and suddenly there it was, behaving like a perfectly normal arm with a perfectly normal hand attached to it, a hand whose fingers flicked away a drop of sweat that was about to roll into my eye and make it sting.

I sat up. There was no lingering weakness. I wiped my face with my sleeve and loosened my belt in an attempt to get some airflow under my clothes.

The crown was only slightly out of shape from my lying on top of it. I put it in the empty food bag tied to my belt.

I walked some more, until the sun was close to

overhead, maybe eleven or even eleven-thirty where people had normal clocks instead of canonical hours based on monasteries' prayer times. I turned. I took a deep breath, said, "Seven leagues," and stepped.

I was—at least I hoped I was—in the correct vicinity. There were mountains in the distance that I *thought* were the group of which Old Hag was one.

I did an about-face and tried to retrace the directions Uldemar had given me: so many steps straight ahead, turn (remembering to turn the opposite direction as I had coming here yesterday), some more steps, another turn. I knew I wasn't directly on course since I hadn't started from the place I had ended yesterday, and it was hard to tell if any of it looked familiar, though from a different angle, or if that was just wishful thinking.

Another step and I found myself treading water. Could this be the lake I'd seen after my first step? What would have been nice was if I could swim to the shore and walk a bit so that I could take one more step and find myself at Xenos's father's house. Of course, that all hinged on *if I could swim*. Which I can't. "Seven leagues," I managed to get out, in between taking in great mouthfuls of water. I moved my feet and found myself perched on top of a tree.

Luckily, it wasn't much of a tree, so I realized I wouldn't have a hard climb to get down. But I didn't even have to do that. While I was still busy coughing up water, there was a loud crack, and the branch I was on fell to the ground, taking me with it.

I lay dazed and bruised, looking up at the tree, vaguely wondering why it was in such sad shape that it broke under my weight. More exactly, I was wondering if it was in bad enough shape that it might fall on me as I lay there, helpless, with the wind knocked out of me.

The branches had no leaves, and the trunk was black, as though it had been through a fire. *Lightning struck,* I thought.

And then I remembered there had been a lightning-struck tree that had been the last landmark before Xenos's father's house.

I hiked and hiked and hiked, and just as I was telling myself that surely there were plenty of lightning-struck trees in the kingdom, there was the hill with Xenos's father's house perched atop it.

"Uldemar!" I called, seeing him, in horse form, grazing.

He had turned back to human by the time I reached his side. "I was beginning to worry," he said.

"Me, too," I admitted. "But I have it."

"Good for you!" he told me. "We should probably head back immediately."

Before I even had a chance to agree, the front door of the house opened. Xenos's father threw an old shoe at us and hollered, "And this time take your stinking ghosts with you!"

IT WAS PROBABLY after three in the afternoon, and we were almost back to the castle. I felt the press of ghosts around us, but for the moment they weren't poking, or pulling my hair, or otherwise being a nuisance.

We rounded a bend in the woods that bordered the castle lands, and there blocking our way were several woodsmen.

Now where have I seen these guys before? I wondered. Then I noticed their bows, and I remembered. *These are the poacher boy's friends or relatives.* The guys who had killed me in these woods once before.

For the moment their bows were at their sides, not up and pointed. Still, I dug my feet into Uldemar's sides. I wanted to yell, "Run them down," but they were sure to take offense at that. *No, no, no, no!* I was so close to the end; it was almost the close of the last day. All I had to do was hand over the crown to Grimbold, wish him and his people luck, and invite him to my coronation. This was no time to be running into surly woodsmen.

But Uldemar only made a hey-what's-with-those-feet? expression, and he stopped.

The thought flickered through my mind that I could jump to the ground, say, "Seven leagues," and be out of there. But I was sure Rasmussem would penalize me heavily if I abandoned Uldemar.

"Princess Janine," said the man whom I believed to be the poacher's father.

I figured it wouldn't do any good to claim he was mistaken—*See these clothes, I'm just a poor page out for a ride on a simple blind horse*—and besides, the man had, surprisingly, given a slight bow as he said my name.

"Yes," I admitted.

"You have my son in your custody at the castle."

"He was caught poaching," I said. "Under my new laws, he must work off the price of a deer, which is set at one month's labor. That means he has twenty-eight more days to his sentence." Under the circumstances, I was willing to consider this a thirty-day month rather than thirty-one.

The man did not rant or rave or demand an early release for his son. "I am indebted to you for changing the laws in time to spare my son's life."

"Oh." I had been expecting an argument. "You're welcome."

"The boy is wild," the man said. "His mother spoils him. I was sure he was going to be the death of all of us. I believe a month of hard labor—not backbreaking labor, understand, but hard, honest work—will benefit him."

"Hard, honest work it is," I assured him. "I hope it will benefit all." I gave Uldemar just the tiniest nudge to let him know I believed the conversation to be closed.

Uldemar took the hint, but the man shifted to remain in our way. "Princess Janine..." He licked his lips. "Don't go to the castle. Some of the peasants—*not us,*" he hastened to clarify, "but some troublemakers from the east—are planning to seize the castle."

"What?"

"They set out when they had news that old King Cynric was ailing. They believe it's time to live without a king."

Not during my reign, I thought indignantly.

The woodsman continued, "They don't know you, Princess. We tried to tell them about the new laws, but they've been on the road for three days. They don't dare return home empty-handed."

"I appreciate the warning," I said. "I truly do. But I *must* return. I can't let my people suffer a siege without me." *For one thing, they don't seem capable of tying their boot-laces without me there to tell them.* But I didn't say that, and the men finally moved out of my way.

"Good luck, Princess Janine," the man called after me.

In any case Uldemar had taken off at a gallop, aimed straight for a tree, and all my concentration was on holding on and directing him so that he wouldn't kill us both.

"Left!" I yelled. "Right! Left again! Duck!" Actually, if *he* had to duck, I would have been in serious trouble, but we both ducked, and we made it beneath a low-hanging branch.

As we got closer, I became aware of other people in the woods, also traveling swiftly toward the castle. A moment later we broke through the trees along with the first of them and could see the castle walls. We were in the front line of the invasion. All around us men were charging the clearing, waving bows and swords and knives as well as homemade pikes and staffs and clubs.

The guards manning the walls started raising the drawbridge. But then someone must have recognized me, and the bridge went down again.

The peasants were on foot, and Uldemar quickly outdistanced them. I rode low, for minimal wind resistance and to make myself a small target. An arrow flew close by my ear, and we weren't yet near enough to get covering fire from the castle.

And then suddenly Uldemar stumbled. I looked and saw a gash across his rump. But the arrow had only grazed him, and in a moment he took up his stride again, and after that we were beyond the range of the peasants.

"Drawbridge!" I warned Uldemar, and moments later, we clattered full speed across it.

"Raise the bridge!" I heard Captain Penrod yell from the battlements.

I reined Uldemar in, but I wasn't saying, "Whoa." I was saying another of those words that would get me in trouble with my grandmother.

"Raise the bridge!" Penrod repeated more urgently.

"You!" I yelled to one of the guards in the courtyard. "Tend Uldemar." I threw the reins in his direction and ran up one of the sets of stairs to the battlements.

Other men had taken up Penrod's cry of "Raise the bridge!" but we all knew it wasn't going to budge until those catacomb ghosts had finished crossing.

From the battlements, I could see the peasants were almost in range of my archers. There was no way the ghosts would be out of the way before the peasants reached the bridge.

"Men, ready your weapons," Penrod commanded.

All along the walls, guards raised their bows.

"No!" I shouted. "I can't begin my kingship with a slaughter of my people." *Even if they ARE ungrateful rebels*.

King Grimbold was in the courtyard and he shouted up to me, "My men are being just beyond the stream over there." Now that he pointed, I could make out their banners. "If you be having the crown, pull it out and hold it up for my men to be seeing. Then they be killing these peasants for you, and there be no need of yourself to be getting their bloodses on your hands."

"It's just the same," I protested. "I can't let your men kill them for me."

"Princess!" Penrod shouted, directing my attention to the peasants. In another few seconds they would reach the drawbridge, which was still held down by the weight of the ghosts. "Do we let them come in and kill us all?" Penrod asked.

"Ghosts!" I screamed. "Ghosts, listen to me! You're going to get us all killed."

Well, obviously, these guys wouldn't find that a particularly compelling argument.

I tried again. "Ghosts, you're from Fairfield. That's where your families still live—your children and your children's children. These peasants from the east will destroy not only this castle but Fairfield, taking over the fields you tilled, tearing down what you built. You heard my plans for an annual fair. That fair would make Fairfield a prosperous town. These men will prevent that from happening. All memory of you will die out with the slaughter and enslavement of your descendants—your children and your children's children. At best they will suffer and remain poor because of you." I was running out of things to say. "Rise up. Rise up and protect what's yours!" I wished I'd paid more attention to some of those patriotic speeches we'd read in school.

The fastest of the peasant army had reached the drawbridge. Their boots clattered on the wood. Momentarily. Then the men fell off on either side into the ditch.

But more men were coming up fast. Then they went into the ditch also. Their weapons rose up into the air and began beating them about the heads and shoulders.

Seeing this, the men behind began to slow down. Fruit seemed to suddenly fall off the trees in the castle garden—or to be plucked off by invisible hands—then those fruits sailed through the air to pelt the men still in the ditch. A banshee wailed, dogs began to bark, the peasants who were still on their feet backed away. Those in the ditch had a hard time getting out, with the ghosts harassing them.

But eventually, one by one, they managed to crawl out, to make their way across the clearing back into the woods.

We could hear them crashing through the trees, the ghosts still pursuing. If we were very lucky, the ghosts would be permanently distracted from us. And for once in this game, I truly did feel lucky.

Our men set up a cheer.

Grimbold's men began to approach.

I stepped out from behind the protection of the upright merlons and held up Brecc the Slayer's crown, and they, too, began to cheer.

Then somebody from within the castle courtyard screamed.

I could see one of the servants backed up against the wall of the castle, cringing and pointing up into the sky behind me.

I turned and saw the dragon.

CHAPTER THIRTY-TWO

The End

There wasn't time to run.

Not that running would have helped.

But *run*?—I couldn't even *duck*. I was frozen with fear. It was as though the strength potion had run out again, only this time leaving me standing, like a statue of a basketball player about to make a free throw.

The dragon had looked enormous in its lair. Now, with its wings outstretched and its taloned claws coming straight at me, I knew what *enormous* really meant.

I figured I also knew what *about to get her heart ripped out of her chest* really meant.

But at the last moment, the dragon pulled up short, landing on the parapet, its feet on two of the merlons right above where I stood. Standing upright, it breathed flame out over the courtyard—a warning shot over our heads, we would say in my regular era. But that warning shot had fire licking at the walls of the castle, a good hundred yards away, and the heat was enough to singe my eyebrows. Then the creature sniffed the air.

A moment later its face was a foot away from my face.

I realized the stench of its lair couldn't *all* be blamed on that ox carcass.

The dragon didn't breathe flame on me. It said, in a harsh, sibilant voice, "Seven-league boots are *not* impossible to track."

Oops.

"You have broken the covenant I made with King Cynric. Now I will take back that which is mine. Then I will kill you all." Its amber eyes blinked, slowly, like a lizard's. Then it said, "But I will eat *you* first."

For once I was hoping for the fizziness that signified Rasmussem's version of dying. I didn't want to feel a moment of that awful heat or those teeth ripping into me.

Idiot, I called myself as the dragon caught me up in one taloned claw and I suddenly realized what I should have done back at the creature's lair. "Dragon, take this ring," I said.

Would the compelling spell work with the ring hidden from sight beneath my tunic for safekeeping?

Apparently not.

The dragon continued to bring me toward its mouth—its mouth with its many, many sharp teeth— and I closed my eyes, not wanting to see my own end coming. *Three days. I had made it three days.* How many more chances could I possibly get?

And then I thought, *I don't NEED any more chances.* With my eyes still closed, I plunked the crown of Brecc the Slayer onto my head and pressed my free hand against the claw that held me.

I could feel the dragon stop moving.

I slitted one eye open a crack. Brightness nearly blinded me, and I shut that eye quickly, sure the dragon had tricked me into looking just as it was shooting flame out of its mouth.

But I didn't feel anything, heat or fizziness, and now my people were cheering, which I was fairly certain they wouldn't do if I was about to become a flame-broiled McNugget.

I peeked again.

That wasn't fire; that was the glint of sun off gold.

A lot of gold.

The dragon had turned into gold, a victim of my Midas touch.

Then began the rescue operation. With grappling hooks and small pikes, my guards were scaling the dragon's body to help get me loose of the golden statue's grip. It took a lot of undignified squirming and leg pulling and calls to suck in my stomach, but finally I popped free. Luckily, Captain Penrod had a good hold on me, or I would have dropped a hundred feet to the ground.

I took the crown off and handed it to Grimbold. His men were cheering like crazy. "Be careful with this," I warned.

He gave a look at the huge golden dragon perched on our battlements and said, "You been doing good."

"I been doing lucky," I corrected him.

People were coming up and giving me congratulatory slaps on the arms or rubbing my head for luck. Kenric gave me a hug, which was better than either. Even Andreanna had a kind word for me. She said: "I never thought we'd see *you* again."

I thought of how I'd set off with such low expectations with Uldemar...

"Uldemar!" I said. I searched for him in the crowd, but he was right beside me, and he took my arm, saying, "Well done, Princess!"

"You were injured," I said.

Putting his hand to his rear end he said, "Mostly in dignity."

Sir Deming, standing below in the courtyard, cupped his hand to his mouth and yelled up, "Why don't we take the celebration inside, where there isn't so much danger of someone taking a flying leap off the battlements?"

It sounded like fine advice to me.

"Head for the Great Hall," Deming shouted.

So I did, with my people clustering just as close about me as the ghosts used to do.

In the Great Hall, the tables were heaped with all sorts of delicious-looking food, including a huge cake shaped like the castle. The smell of roasting meat, of fresh peaches, of just-baked bread—it would have been irresistible even if I wasn't half starved.

"What's all this?" I asked.

"Your coronation feast," Kenric told me. He indicated the throne at the head of the room—presumably they'd put the second one in storage—and I saw a crown waiting for me on the velvet seat.

Queen Andreanna sidled up to me and said, "And you're late—what a surprise."

But she didn't have time to waste belittling me. She caught sight of Grimbold, who'd somehow or other gotten hold of a satin pillow and was walking around with the pillow on his arm, displaying his newly recovered crown, so that he looked like a hairy ring bearer at a giant's wedding feast. "Grimbold," Andreanna said with enough enthusiasm to indicate she'd been waiting all her life to greet him. She caught hold of his arm and looked into his eyes with newly established fascination. As she led him away, I heard her saying, "What a lovely crown! You know, my deceased husband never told me..."

I waved to Orielle and Wulfgar across the room. Orielle waved back, but Wulfgar had his attention captured by Abas, who was demonstrating one-armed push-ups.

Xenos came up to me, but only long enough to say, "Remember, those are *my* boots."

I wiped my brow with my sleeve and realized how dirty, hot, and tired I truly was. I blew loose the hair that was sticking to my forehead. "Should I change into something more regal?" I asked Kenric. A three-hour soak would have been nice, but I didn't know how long I had.

"Whatever you want." Kenric handed me a goblet. "You look hot."

"I don't really like mead," I said.

"I remembered. This is honey water."

It was overly sweet, but at least it was wet.

Sister Mary Ursula, wearing the most extravagant—and ridiculous—dress I'd ever seen, said, "I am One with happy endings," before the crowd carried her away.

In fact, the crowd, noisy and jostling, was beginning to get on my nerves, making me feel claustrophobic.

"Maybe," I told Kenric, "I should sit down."

I took two steps before my knees gave out. Fireworks seemed to be going off behind my eyeballs, the sound exploding inside my skull.

Stupid! Stupid! Stupid! How could I have accepted a drink from someone who had already poisoned me once?

Kenric knelt down beside me.

"How could you?" I asked, my voice a weak and raw whisper.

"What?" he asked.

"What did I do wrong?" I demanded. "Didn't I do everything I was supposed to? I can't go through all this again."

"You didn't do anything wrong," Kenric said, which I took to mean that my choices as would-be king were fine with him—he just wanted to be king himself. "I don't understand what you're saying."

It wasn't fair. I'd lived the entire three days. I'd saved the kingdom from barbarians, peasants, and dragon. And I had no idea what to do differently next time. If there was a next time. I winced against the sparks going off in my brain. "I trusted you. How could you poison me?"

Kenric protested, "I didn't."

To my embarrassment, I found that tears were leaking out of my eyes and rolling down the sides of my face.

"Janine," Kenric said, enunciating each word slowly and carefully, *"I did not poison you."*

If Kenric hadn't poisoned me, maybe this wasn't game

death. Maybe this was, finally, the long-anticipated brain overload. That would explain the fireworks.

I was aware that Kenric was holding me, cradling my head, while the crowd had pulled back to give me room.

I could barely get my mouth to work. "I don't know what to do," I said, aware that I sounded as though I had a mouthful of oatmeal.

"Give my mother the ring," Kenric said.

How did he know about the ring?

I saw Andreanna hovering with the crowd. I managed to get the piece of twine showing, and Kenric slipped it over my head. "Andreanna, take the ring," I mumbled.

Andreanna took the ring.

"Tell her to treat you fairly and not to incite her sons to rebel against you," Kenric told me.

"Treat me fairly..."—I licked my parched lips, and Kenric brushed my hair off my cheeks while I got up the energy to finish—"and don't incite your sons to rebel against me."

While Andreanna nodded, Kenric said, "Ask for the crown."

"Crown," I echoed.

Kenric forced me to sit up a bit more, and Sir Deming placed the crown on my head. "Long live King Janine," Deming proclaimed.

The world dissolved in a shower of glitters.

CHAPTER THIRTY-THREE

Satisfaction Guaranteed,
Or Your Money Cheerfully Refunded

Despite the special effects, I knew I hadn't gotten out of the game because I could feel that Kenric was still holding me.

On the other hand I was suddenly also feeling much better—I wasn't burning with fever, my head didn't ache, and the internal fireworks had stopped.

I could also smell popcorn, which struck me—in a vague, detached way—as odd.

Something, however, nearly ripped the skin off my head at my temples, and off either side of my neck, and off various other sites on my body.

"Got it," a female voice announced.

I opened my eyes and saw that the Rasmussem receptionist was leaning over me, holding a bunch of wires with suction cups at their ends—the wires that had formerly connected me to the Rasmussem computer.

"Are you here, too?" I asked, thinking that somehow

she had gotten sucked into the game. But then I realized I was in one of the rooms at Rasmussem, lying on a total immersion couch.

"Welcome back, honey," the receptionist said.

How could they make it so real? It was over, but I could still feel Kenric's gentle arms around me. The sensation was so vivid, I had to turn to look.

And there was Kenric, still holding me. "Yikes," I said, but without much energy because I was incredibly tired.

The guy holding me smiled—same glorious smile—but his hair was shorter, and he was wearing jeans and a RASMUSSEM GAMING CENTER shirt. He was also the source of the popcorn aroma. He lowered my head back onto the couch's pillow.

"Tell me you're not Kenric," I said.

"I'm not Kenric," the guy said obligingly. "I'm Nigel Rasmussem."

"No, you're not." I was confused, but I wasn't *that* confused. "I've seen Nigel Rasmussem. He's a short, round guy with glasses."

"That's my uncle David. I used his image to talk to you because I thought he'd look more credible to you. I used *my* physical appearance for Kenric."

"You certainly did." I considered for a few moments, then said, "But you can't be more than..."

I hesitated, and he supplied, "Sixteen."

Sixteen. Rasmussem Enterprises had been around for two years, which meant he had started his company when he was no older than I was now. I will probably *not* be starting my own company in the coming months. "So what are you?" I asked: "Some kind of computer genius?"

He said, "You gotta do *something* when your parents saddle you with a name like Nigel."

"Wow," I said. "And you came here because I was in trouble?"

Nigel Rasmussem shook his head. "Rochester, New York, is world headquarters for Rasmussem Enterprises. My parents regulate how much time I can spend with computers, so I work here after school and on weekends." He added—though I guessed it a moment before he said it—"At the concession stand."

The receptionist said, "Sit her up."

At first I resented her speaking as though I was totally helpless—but I *was* totally helpless. Nigel did most of the work of getting me to a sitting position.

The receptionist handed me a cup of water. "You're fine," she assured me. "You might be a bit disoriented at first, but that will pass."

"It wasn't like this the other times I played," I said, worried despite her calming words.

"The other times you played, there would have been a cooldown period between the game stimulus and the waking state."

"Are you sure?" I asked. This was, after all, the woman who compared games to soups.

"That's what they pay me for."

I was reassured until she started speaking to someone who wasn't there, rattling off a bunch of numbers and techno-jargon, then ending with, "Signing off, unless you say otherwise."

Another voice said, "You're fine." Then I heard a dial tone.

The receptionist leaned over and touched something on the wall behind me, and the speaker went off.

"Do you want to rest a bit, honey?" she asked. "I can dim the lights and put on some soft music. We called your grandmother, and she should be here soon. And, of course, there'll be a media circus waiting outside. So I really recommend the rest now."

"Yes, please," I said. Then, maybe begging just a little, I asked Nigel, "Could you stay a bit?"

He pulled over a chair, while the receptionist dimmed the lights, put on the music, and then pulled the door shut behind her.

I asked, "She's a technician here?"

"Actually, a total immersion technologist—as well as an emergency medical technician. Do you want to talk about what happened, or do you want to sleep?"

"Both," I admitted.

"We'll compromise," he said. "Lie down. Close your eyes."

I did.

"May I?" Nigel had leaned over and was holding my hand.

Yes! Yes! Yes! I wanted to shout, but I managed a refined, "Mmmm."

Nigel spoke in a quiet, soothing voice. "You were in the game for eighty-seven minutes, which normally would have been totally safe, except for the damage the CPOC people did. They're going to get their asses fried for endangering the welfare of a minor. But you did fine. You did more than fine. You did"—was that admiration in his voice?—"you did things in that game that I didn't think could be done."

"Mmmm," I said again, pleased though I hardly knew the guy. Then his words sank in. My eyes flew open and I almost managed to sit up. "You were watching me?" I demanded.

"Giannine," he said, "there were technicians on both coasts and in England, Japan, and Ukraine following your readouts."

Horrified, I asked, "You could tell what I was thinking?"

Sounding just as horrified, he answered, "No, of course not. That's not the way the equipment works. Reading someone's thoughts?" He said it so contemptuously, I had to believe he was speaking the truth. "We couldn't even see or hear *you*. We were getting a steady stream of biofeedback statistics and data on how the characters and setting were changing, which let us interpret what you were doing. Sort of like watching a solar eclipse, which you can't do with your bare eyes, so you cast an image with a lens, and that's what you see—a reflection."

"I'll take your word for it," I said. "What do you mean I did things other people didn't do? Wasn't I playing right?"

"Of course, you were playing right. You were just making unusual choices."

I was getting irritated. All right, he was gorgeous and a sixteen-year-old genius who was CEO of his own multinational company, but that didn't give him the right to mock me. "Well, my choices made sense to me at the time."

"I didn't say they didn't make sense," he answered defensively.

I settled back down on the couch and closed my eyes once more, wondering if it was too rude to tell him I'd changed my mind and that he could go now and tend his concession booth.

"It's just," Nigel said, "trusting Kenric is almost always a bad choice. I kept thinking, *No, no, no,* but you did...twice...and the second time it worked out... Thank you for letting me be a good guy for once."

I opened my eyes again. "You..."—I amended that to—"Kenric...helped me so much at the very end, when I thought it was all over..."

"Heir Apparent is a game," Nigel said. "It's supposed to be fun. Frustrating, sure, but fun. If a player starts crying, that's a signal something has gone wrong. The characters become much more helpful. It's what the programmers call The Secret Weapon."

"Oh," I said. "Well, Kenric was nice before, just especially nice at the end. And I don't usually cry. It's only I was worn-out."

Nigel smiled. "I could tell. That you don't usually cry. You're incredibly brave. And creative. And you were about to win, when the equipment began overheating."

I shuddered, remembering the fireworks, realizing how close I'd come to not making it. Sometime, later, I might be able to ask what they would have done if I wasn't at the end of the game when the equipment started shorting out. But for the moment, that was too scary. So instead I asked, "What did I do wrong?"

"You didn't do anything wrong."

"What did I do differently from other people?"

Nigel considered. I guessed there were a lot of things he could have chosen from when he said, "Most players give the ring to Sister Mary Ursula, befriend Grimbold at his camp, and get Xenos Senior to take on the dragon, rather than handling it personally."

I wasn't even close.

"But your way worked, so it wasn't wrong."

The receptionist-technologist-technician knocked softly on the door, then came in with the miniature dragon on its leash. It settled on the couch-side table that held the pitcher of water. Close, but not close enough to nip. It opened its jaws, revealing many teeth and a tiny flame about the size you'd find on a match head right before it fizzles out.

"Your grandmother hasn't arrived yet," the receptionist said, "but there's a man who claims he's your father."

My father?

My father had come *here*?

She had apparently demanded his driver's license, and now she showed it to me.

Despite my amazement, I got my voice to work. "Yes, that's him."

The receptionist said, "And the second question is: Do you want to see him?"

Well, he wasn't Dexter the peat cutter, but neither was he King Cynric. I braced myself. "Sure," I told her.

And I told the tiny dragon with the butterfly wings, "Your mother has bad breath, even without the dead ox."

Then I let Nigel help me sit up, though this time I really didn't need him, and I waited for my father.

If you've decided that this book and others like it are dangerous, clip along this line, glue this page to cardboard, and fasten onto a stick. Start your own protest demonstration!

Don't corrupt the minds of our children!

Down with fantasy!

CHAPTER 1

The Dangers of Higher Education

M Y MOTHER isn't normally the kind of parent who comes to school and has me yanked out of class because she needs to see me.

Never mind that the class I was pulled from was trigonometry, which is monumentally mind-numbing and—as far as I can tell—entirely useless to anyone except trigonometry teachers. It is rumored that, on a warm spring day three years ago, our trig teacher, Mr. Petersen, actually fell asleep during one of his own lectures. The speculation is that he has not awakened since, but is still droning on from memory, in a sleep-walking state.

I have never seen anything in Mr. Petersen's demeanor to make me doubt that rumor.

Generally speaking, I'd be eager for *any* excuse to get away from sine and cosine and whatever that third function is whose name I can never remember. But I felt a prickle of anxiety. Despite my mother's inability to come up with even one real-life situation where knowing the difference between opposite and adjacent, much less a hypotenuse would be a benefit to me, she does strongly believe in the theory of education. So I couldn't make sense of the note the messenger from the office interrupted the class to hand to me:

Grace Pizzelli
Go down to Mrs. Overstreet's
office right away.
Your mother is here

My brain instantly zipped to the West Coast, where Dad was attending a sales conference at a hotel I was suddenly convinced was the obvious target for arsonists, kidnappers, earthquakes, flash floods, outbreaks of Lyme disease, and/or killer bees.

My outlook wasn't improved by walking into Mrs. Overstreet's office. Mrs. Overstreet was wearing that I-smell-something-bad-and-I-suspect-it's-coming-from-you expression that must be taught in one of the required courses at principal college—a course that clearly would be more useful than trig.

But my mother had on sweatpants and a Milky Way Galaxy T-shirt she'd gotten when she'd chaperoned my Brownie troop's overnight at the Strasenberg Planetarium seven years ago. This is strictly at-home wear for her. Even for going to the grocery store, Mom's shoes need to match her purse. On this particular occasion, her shoes didn't match each other.

My prickly-all-over worry exploded into panic. "What's wrong? What's happened?" I asked. "Is Dad all right?"

My questions seemed to send my mother into a worse spiral than the one she was already in. "Dad?" she echoed. She glanced around the office, looking simultaneously dazed and frantic, as though not sure whether to level accusations at Mrs. Overstreet or the two strangers in the room—a man and a woman. She settled on the strangers and said in a squeaky voice, "You didn't tell me something happened to my husband!"

The man had a trim little beard, and excuse me, but if you were a casting director looking for someone to play the role of a debonair devil, you'd be giving this guy your card and asking him to come in for an audition. By contrast, the woman might well have been studying for that principal's course on intimidation through facial expression, but she was the one who spoke: "Mrs. Pizzelli, we don't even know where your husband is."

Mom's voice went even higher. "Tyler is *missing*?"

My feelings were bouncing all over the place because I didn't know if Mom was overreacting—which has been known to happen—or if she actually had a reason to suspect the worst.

Mrs. Overstreet went with option number one. "Mrs. Pizzelli, I'm sure your husband is fine." She didn't give my mother a chance to say more than "But—" before she continued, "When I go to conferences, the presenters always ask everyone to turn off their phones. I'm sure once they break for lunch, your husband will check his messages and return your call."

The other woman was nodding as though those were her thoughts exactly. "Please," she said, "now that your younger daughter is here, let's talk about Emily."

Emily?

Before I could ask "What's wrong with Emily?" the woman had stood up and offered me her hand to shake. She was very business-chic and sophisticated. "Hello, Grace. I'm pleased to meet you. Though not under these circumstances, of course."

The man, still sitting, smoothly interjected: "By which we do not mean to imply that Rasmussem Corporation or any of its employees is in any way responsible for those circumstances."

Ah, I thought, putting together that suave but slightly sinister look with his precise wording. *Lawyer.*

I finally noticed that they both had Rasmussem Corporation nametags, as well as school visitor badges.

The woman continued, "My name is Jenna Bennett, and I'm the chief technical engineer at the Lake Avenue Rasmussem facility. This is Alexander Kroll, from our legal department."

Mr. Kroll showed some of his teeth and added, "By which we do not mean to imply that this is a matter requiring adjudication."

Apparently, my principal didn't like lawyers. She leveled an I-am-picturing-doing-you-bodily-harm expression at him and said to my mother, "Yeah, yeah, so it's much too early to talk about suing the pants off them, but that's always a possibility."

Kroll's expression didn't change: proof, if anyone had needed it, about the sincerity of his smile.

Suing didn't sound good. People sue when something goes terribly wrong, and what did all this have to do with Emily—or me?

Ms. Really-I'm-an-Engineer-Despite-the-Fact-That-I-Look-Like-a-Principal-in-Training Bennett put on a pained expression.

But, fashionable and pretty as she was, she didn't know *pained*. My mother's eyes were red-rimmed and scared—*that* was pain. She took my hand and worked it like someone trying to soften up putty.

What a terrible person I am, I realized. *Something awful has happened to Emily, and here I am mentally moaning about a few squished fingers.*

Mom said to me, "Emily's playing a game at the arcade."

"Okay . . ." I said, knowing there had to be more. Emily is a student at RIT—Rochester Institute of Technology. She's studying technical engineering and is in a work co-op program at Rasmussem, which, long story short, means she's slave labor for them this semester, though I'm guessing Mr. Lawyer Kroll would try to qualify that statement. Rasmussem is the company that developed total immersion, the next step beyond virtual reality. When you play their games, sensations are fed directly into your brain: you can feel the warmth of the sun if it's daytime in the world you're playing in, just as you can feel cold and soaked to the bone if it's raining; you can taste the food and smell the flowers; and if you're riding a horse, after a while your butt goes to sleep. The difference between playing a Rasmussem game and a regular old virtual reality game is like the difference between watching an IMAX movie and one of those old black and white silent films.

I thought, *Of course Emily is playing games at the arcade.* No doubt most—if not all—of the people who work at Rasmussem are there because they love games. Well, maybe excepting the lawyers. But if the company wasn't going to pay their interns salaries, they couldn't be surprised at an unauthorized game or two. I assumed Emily was playing while she was supposed to be working, which apparently I didn't take as seriously as the legal department did. Was she getting fired? Was she getting expelled?

But surely that wasn't enough to account for Mom's distress, or for my getting called out of class.

Mom still seemed intent on kneading all my fingers into mush. She said, "They can't get it to stop."

Confused, I said, "The games last a half-hour. While you're playing, you feel like it's hours, but it's only thirty minutes." I figured my mother wasn't sure whether to believe me. She's not a gamer—hard as that is to conceive of these days. She's not into technology and can barely get her cell phone to cooperate. I said, "When the time runs out, the game just stops."

"Yes," Ms. Rasmussem-Engineer-Lady agreed. "Normally."

Okay, well, granted, something was not normal or we wouldn't all be here.

She continued, "Emily hooked herself into the game she was developing, and . . . she did something. She bypassed safety protocols. But the half-hour is up. The half-hour was up more than four hours ago."

"Can't you just . . ."—of course I *have* played Rasmussem's games, but Emily is the tech-type in the family—". . . unhook her?" I finished lamely, thinking of the wires they stick to your head when you lie down on a total immersion couch. Duh. Like the people who could think up total immersion weren't smart enough to think of that?

"We did," Ms. Bennett said, without sounding impatient or condescending at my obviousness. "She didn't revive."

Mom said, "I asked them to just pull the plug on the whole thing, but they won't." Pulling the plug is Mom's cure-it technique for *all* of our computer's ills.

Ms. Bennett said—and I could tell she'd said it before—"It doesn't work like that."

"There should be safeguards," Mom said.

"There are," Mr. Kroll told her. "Your older daughter, intentionally, with forethought, for her own reasons, disabled them. Leaving behind a note clearly showing her culpability."

From his briefcase, he pulled out a piece of paper in a clear plastic bag hand-labeled EVIDENCE.

Evidence? Like from courts and trials and cop shows? What sort of trouble was Emily in?

The note was in my sister's neat rounded penmanship. It said:

Not anybody's fault.
This is MY choice.

While the word *evidence* had set off all sorts of alarm bells in my head, now I think my body temperature dropped ten degrees.

Emily had *chosen* to go into a game and not come out? *Why?*

Mr. Kroll was still talking to my mother. "There may well be loss to company revenues because of her actions, beyond the time of the techs who have been trying to help her, beyond the time taken by Ms. Bennett and myself to explain things to you at your home, and now here again at your younger daughter's school because you wanted to consult with her." His expression clearly showed what he thought of a woman who would seek her fourteen-year-old's opinion.

"Be that as it may . . ." Principal Overstreet said.

We all looked at her, but she didn't really have anything to say; I guess she just didn't like our bickering.

Ms. Bennett stepped into the breach, too elegant to put up with bickering, either. "Be that as it may, we can tell, approximately, where in the Rasmussem-created scenario she is. I myself went in and tried to talk her out. She refused to listen to me."

This was so weird, so . . . *more* than weird. I couldn't even tell what I should be thinking.

I saw Ms. Bennett looking at me, waiting for me to realize she was looking at me. She said, "We're hoping she'll listen to you."

Me? Somehow this was coming down to *me?*

I had caught that part where Ms. Oh-So-Well-Dressed Bennett had said she'd *gone in* to talk to Emily.

"I think it's insane," Mom said. "First one of my daughters gets stuck in their crazy game; then they want my other daughter to just step right in after her."

"Mrs. Pizzelli," Ms. Bennett said, "I've already explained: there's no danger. I told you that I went into the game and was perfectly capable of coming back out again. Emily could come out, too. She's simply choosing not to. We're hoping Grace can get her to see reason."

Liking a game is one thing. Playing into the wee hours of the morning even though it's a school day is one thing. Shouting "Just a minute" when your mother hollers at you to get off the computer *now* because she's called you for dinner twice already—all of that is one thing.

Emily wouldn't come out?

"If," Mom said, "*if* someone from the family needs to do this, it should be me."

Ms. Bennett shook her head. "You're not a gamer. You'd be overwhelmed. Without experience, you wouldn't know where to begin, how to get around, what's important and what's only background. We'd lose valuable time. The programs are meant to last from thirty to sixty minutes. The equipment is rated safe for eight times that exposure. But it's not meant for sustained immersion."

Everything she said made sense, too much sense.

There was no way I could hope Mom would insist on being the one to go—not when I could see so clearly it would be better for Emily to have me there.

In the movies, the good guys always fight each other for the opportunity to do the dangerous stuff. The Rasmussem people were saying this *wasn't* dangerous. And *still* the responsibility was enough to freeze me solid.

Mrs. Overstreet, as a principal in charge of her students' safety, said to me, "Grace, you don't have to do this if you don't want to."

For the first time in my life, I wanted to hug her.

"No," Ms. Bennett agreed. "Of course she doesn't *have to.* But there's no reason she shouldn't. It's not like we're asking her to donate a kidney or something."

Suddenly we were into donating body parts? *Would* I donate a kidney? I wondered. Much as I loved Emily, I wasn't sure I could.

"Oh, I wish your father would pick up the damn phone," Mom said, "and tell me what we should do."

Somehow, that cleared my head. *We SHOULD,* I thought, *be able to make up our minds on our own.*

"No danger of me getting stuck in there?" I asked.

"Absolutely none," Ms. Engineer and Mr. Lawyer said in unison.

"Then," I had to admit, "I guess I don't see any reason why not."

My mother sniffled but didn't try to talk me out of it.

Mr. Kroll smiled his non-smile smile and opened his briefcase again. "Fine. We just have one or two papers for you to sign . . ."

Vivian Vande Velde has written many acclaimed books for teen and middle grade readers, including two other books about virtual reality games created by the Rasmussem Corporation, *Heir Apparent* and *Deadly Pink*, as well as the Edgar Award–winning *Never Trust a Dead Man*. She lives in Rochester, New York.

www.vivianvandevelde.com